THE BRIDE

THE BRIDE
Bapsi Sidhwa

St. Martin's Press
New York

Library of Congress Cataloging in Publication Data

Sidhwa, Bapsi.
    The bride.

    I. Title.
PR9540.9.S53B7   1983   823   83-9752
ISBN 0-312-09537-6

First published in 1983 in Great Britain by Jonathan Cape Ltd.

First U.S. Edition

10 9 8 7 6 5 4 3 2 1

For my children,
Mohur, Koko, Parizad

THE BRIDE

THE BRIDE

Chapter 1

Qasim was ten when his father, squatting by a raucous little mountain stream, told him:

'Son, you're to be married!'

The pronouncement had little effect on Qasim, but a moment later, when his father placed a heavy muzzle-loader in his arms, Qasim flushed with pleasure.

'Mine?' he asked, wishing to run behind a rock and seclude himself with the precious gift.

His father nodded. 'Sit with me awhile,' he urged, grinning at the boy's impatience.

'You know of the bad feeling between me and Resham Khan? It is because of a loan I made him last year. He hasn't paid me yet.'

The boy spat knowingly. Looking up from his ancient gun he met his father's gaze with theatrical intensity.

'I will kill him with this gun,' he announced, his hazel eyes flashing.

Chiselled into precocity by a harsh life in the mountains, Qasim had known no childhood. From infancy, responsibility was forced upon him and at ten he was a man, conscious of the rigorous code of honour by which his tribe lived.

His father laughed. Then, seeing the hurt in the boy's solemn face, he said: 'Haven't we settled enough scores? Anyway this will not lead to a feud. Resham Khan has promised us his daughter!'

The sturdy, middle-aged tribesman knew just how generous the offer was. Any girl – and he had made sure that this one was able-bodied – was worth more than the loan due. His three older sons were already married and now it was

Qasim's turn. The boy was still a little young, but the offer was too good to pass up.

To begin with, he had thought of marrying the girl himself. He had only one wife; but in a twinge of paternal conscience, he decided to bestow the girl on Qasim. It was his first duty.

He ruffled the boy's sun-bleached, matted hair. 'My young bridegroom,' he said playfully, 'you'll be fetching home a lovely girl. How d'you like that!'

Qasim was delighted. Not only did he have a gun; he was to be married. As a prospective groom he was immediately festooned with embroidered waistcoats, turbans, and new clothes. Chickens and goats were slaughtered. The women bustled about, and he was the glorious centre of all their activity and attention. The envy of every unmarried fellow his age, he was the recipient of man-to-man ribaldry and advice. Above all, there was the prospect of a playmate he knew he would have the sanction to tease, to order about, and to bully!

A week later the marriage party danced and drummed its way over tortuous mountain paths to finalise the contract and bring home the bride.

❖

Afshan sat amidst the huddle of women. Her head bowed beneath a voluminous red veil, she wept softly as befitted a bride. Her heavy silver bangles, necklaces and earrings tinkled at the slightest movement. She also wore an intricately carved silver nose-pin. Thrice she was asked if she would accept Qasim, the son of Arbab, as her husband and thrice an old aunt murmured 'yes' on her behalf. Then the mountains reverberated with joyful huzzas, gunfire and festivity.

It was almost midnight when the sleepy bridegroom was told, 'Now, son, you are to meet your bride. Smarten yourself up: don't you want to impress her with all your finery?'

8

The crest of Qasim's turban was perked up, his eyes lined anew with antimony, and the gathers on his trousers puffed out about his legs.

The drowsy boy was propelled into the bridal chamber amidst a clamour of catcalls. He heard the bolt shot from outside and was on his own, suddenly terrified. For a while he stood backed up against the door, his eyes fumbling over the dimly-lit room: then they focused on the stooped and veiled form of his bride. She sat on a brightly-coloured quilt spread on a string bed, with her back to him.

Afshan knew her husband was locked in the room with her, and her body trembled with anticipation. Overwhelmed by modesty, she bowed her head still further. The edge of her veil almost touched her toes.

It had been drilled and drilled into Qasim that he was to walk up to his bride and lift the veil off her face. The docile, huddled form of the girl gave his frozen heart courage and he padded towards her in a nervous trance. Reaching down, he lifted the edge of the veil and threw it back.

He stood rooted in panic. Before him was the modestly slumped form of a young woman instead of the girl playmate he had expected. He had been instructed to tilt up her chin and look into her face, but he dared not.

His bride had shut her eyes in confusion. When in all that time there was no flicker of movement, she peered through slit lashes and saw the sandalled feet of her husband, and then the shalwar-clad legs. Her heart constricted with dismay: she was married to a boy! Hastily she looked up. She stared in amazement at the childish, frightened face and the slanting, cringing eyes watching her as if she were about to smack him.

Was this a joke? She glanced beyond him, fervently hoping to see the man who had pushed his small brother forward to tease her. But there was no one.

'Are *you* my husband?' she asked incredulously.

Qasim nodded with woebegone gravity.

The girl didn't know whether to laugh or cry. She had been told that her groom was very young, but she had thought that he would be, like herself, at least fifteen. She began to laugh, while tears of disappointment slid down her cheeks. She laughed uncontrollably and Qasim, stung to the quick, rushed for the door. He threw himself against the bolted door and, rattling it savagely, shouted, 'Open! Open! I want to get out.' A distant sound of tired chatter crept in through the door. Flushed with anger and embarrassment Qasim sidled to a corner of the room. Sobbing angrily, he at last fell asleep.

Years later, Afshan recalled their marriage night to her husband when he asked her, 'But how did you feel? What had you expected?'

'I used to wander by streams,' she said, 'or sit on some high place dreaming of my future husband. Gusts of wind enveloped me and I'd imagine the impatient caresses of my lover. My body was young and full of longing. I'd squeeze my breasts to ease their ache . . .' she paused mischievously. 'Instead, I very nearly suckled my husband!'

That first night Afshan had lifted the sleeping boy to her bed. Brushing his tear-streaked cheeks with her full red mouth, she had tucked his legs between her thighs and fallen asleep.

Afshan accepted her lot cheerfully. She helped her mother-in-law, chaffed the maize, tended and milked the two goats and frolicked her way through her chores. Occasionally, when his mother scolded her, Qasim felt wretched. He loved her vivacious, girlish ways and was totally won by her affection. He teased her and played pranks. When he was particularly unkind or obdurate, his wife and his mother combined to give him a thrashing. Then Qasim would shout, 'I am your husband. How dare you!' and he would hate her.

One afternoon, some years after their marriage, Afshan was washing herself at the stream when Qasim strolled up and sat on a rock watching her. He was fourteen years old and gangling tall. A fine down lined his lip and cheeks. For some time now he had been persistently aware of his manhood. The wet black shirt clung to Afshan's body, the front strings open. Unselfconsciously she poured the icy water over herself. Qasim had often filled the containers while she washed and she looked on him as a younger brother. Dousing her face, she suddenly blinked and opened her eyes. Qasim was staring at the white undulation where her shirt parted. Her breasts and the taut nipples were clearly visible through the wet cloth.

'What are you looking at?' she asked severely. Before she could shield herself, Qasim had slipped off the stone and into the water. With a thrust of his young arm, he gripped her breast. 'Let me . . . Let me,' he begged in his cracked young voice. Afshan smacked his arm off. Aghast, she stared at his sheepish face. Again he tried to hold her and again she slapped him hard. Qasim cowered, shielding his face, while Afshan berated him, '. . . you shameless dog, you jackal, you! I'll teach you to be brazen.' She wept with embarrassment, lashing out and hitting him wherever she could. Qasim scrambled from the rushing stream. He stumbled. Afshan fell on him with a stick, screaming abuse.

Attracted by the rumpus, a stranger from the next village came upon the scene. His tribal sense of chivalry was outraged by the assault on the girl. He dragged the boy to his feet and with heavy blows started punishing him. He might have maimed him, had not Qasim, red with fury, cried, 'But she is my wife. Let go, she is my wife!' The man, tightening his hold on the boy, looked at Afshan. 'Is he your husband?' he asked incredulously.

Breathless with exertion and frightened, she panted, 'Yes, yes, let go, don't touch him.'

The man released Qasim. He stared at Afshan's wet body, at the colour that flushed her cheeks and at her suddenly darkening eyes. His expression changed. A wary indecisive-

11

ness crept into his features. He snickered, leering at her. Afshan covered herself quickly.

Edging sideways, drawn by the momentum of his new interest, the stranger sidled towards Afshan. Qasim's fear exploded into loathing at the stranger's lewd glance. Picking up a large rock he flung it at him straight, and then another. The man bent over and squatted in pain. His teeth glistened ferociously between cracked lips. But before he could get back his wind, Qasim, holding Afshan's arm, was skittering away through the winding gullies.

❖

After this, their relations changed. Qasim still teased Afshan, but with an awkward gentleness. She in turn seemed unduly severe and shy.

At sixteen Qasim became a father.

By cultivating the steppes, granting clearance to occasional smugglers from Afghanistan, and rearing a meagre string of cattle, Qasim and his family managed to survive. Survival being the sole aim of life in those uncompromising mountains, they asked for no more.

By the time he was thirty-four, Qasim and Afshan had lost three children, two to typhoid and one in a fall off a ledge. It did not matter really, because two sons and a daughter survived – a fair enough average. Then a fugitive from Soviet Kirgiz visited. He left the next day, and within a month they heard that he had died of smallpox.

A few days later Qasim returned to find Afshan weeping by their hut.

'What is it?'

She forced herself to be calm, lest 'Mata' the dreaded Goddess, so easily enraged, do even more harm.

'Zaitoon is not eating, "Mata" has honoured her with a visit.'

Qasim's throat contracted. He loved his daughter, a child with wide, tawny eyes, and limbs of quicksilver.

Brushing away tears with the edge of her tattered shawl, Afshan led him into a darkened corner of the room. Listlessly, the small five-year-old Zaitoon lay on the floor on a straw mattress. Her bright-eyed face and her small naked body were disfigured by a scabby eruption of pus-filled sores.

They did everything within their power. The dank, dung-plastered cubicle was darkened further, for the 'Mata' could not stand light. Herbs and leaves, procured with great difficulty, and reputed to have a cooling effect, were strewn near the girl's burning body. Zaitoon's needs were ministered to with great obedience, for the Spirit in her body was ruthlessly demanding.

The disease spread to her mouth and throat and to her intestines. The child thrashed about in agonised frenzy.

Neighbours slipped like shadows across the door, leaving behind some small gift of food or apparel in token of their awe. A holy man of their tribe hurried from afar at the summons of the 'Mata'. He placed amulets by the child and sprinkled her with holy water. But the girl, her eyes blinded by sores, grew worse. Finally, mercifully, she died.

The two boys were stricken also, and then Afshan, worn to a splinter, contracted the illness.

Within a month, Qasim, who had survived an attack of smallpox as a child, was the only one left of his family.

He was inconsolable. His face swollen with tears, and his throat hoarse with wailing, he flailed his chest with his huge fists, but death, swift, premature and grotesquely unfair, had to be accepted.

A year later a clansman who worked in the plains persuaded Qasim to travel down to Jullundur. He secured him a position as watchman at an English bank.

13

Chapter 2

Three years passed, and in the chaotic summer of 1947 there was serious political unrest in the North Indian plains. Savage rioting erupted and many minority groups felt insecure. One by one the hill-country tribesmen fled Jullundur. For a time Qasim, loath to return to his life in the mountains where he would be under pressure to re-marry, stayed on. He did not want to expose himself again to the bonds of love.

Hysteria mounted when the fertile, hot lands of the Punjab were suddenly ripped into two territories – Hindu and Muslim, India and Pakistan. Until the last moment no one was sure how the land would be divided. Lahore, which everyone expected to go to India because so many wealthy Hindus lived in it, went instead to Pakistan. Jullundur, a Sikh stronghold, was allocated to India. Now that it was decided they would leave, the British were in a hurry to wind up. Furniture, artifacts and merchandise had to be shipped, antiques, curios and jewellery acquired and transported. Preoccupied with misgiving and the arrangements attendant on relocating themselves in their native land, by the agony of separation from regiments, Imperial trappings and servants, the rulers of the Empire were entirely too busy to bother overmuch with how India was divided. It was only one of the thousand and one chores they faced.

The earth is not easy to carve up. India required a deft and sensitive surgeon, but the British, steeped in domestic pre-occupation, hastily and carelessly butchered it. They were not deliberately mischievous – only cruelly negligent! A million Indians died. The earth sealed its clumsy new boundaries in blood as town by town, farm by farm, the border

14

was defined. Trains carrying refugees sped through the darkness of night – Hindus going one way and Muslims the other. They left at odd hours to try to dodge mobs bent on their destruction. Yet trains were ambushed and looted and their fleeing occupants slaughtered.

❖❖

Near Lahore, men – mostly Sikhs – squat on either side of the rail-tracks, waiting. Their white singlets reflect the moon palely. These Sikhs are lean and towering, with muscles like flat mango seeds and heads tópped by scraggy buns of hair, loose tendrils mingling with their coarse beards. They are silent, listening, glancing at the luminous dials of wrist-watches.

They have raised a barricade of logs across the tracks, and the steel rails swerve slightly where the lines disappear in blackness. On either side, ploughed stretches of earth spread black wings to the horizon.

At first the men, bunched in loose groups, welcome the diversion when a voice rises:

'I saw them myself – huge cauldrons of boiling oil and babies tossed into them!'

Then losing interest in what they have heard so often, their faces turn away. By now these tales arouse only an embarrassed resentment. They are meant to stir their nobler passions, but the thought of loot undermines that resolve.

An old Sikh stands up. He wears a loose white muslin shirt, which makes him look bigger in the moonlight. They know him to be the sole survivor of a large family in the Montgomery district. They whisper, 'It is Moola Singh, cousin of Bishan Singh'.

Seething with hatred, his hurt still raw, Moola Singh resents their apathy. From the depths of his anguish, his voice betraying tears, he shrieks: 'Vengeance, my brothers, vengeance!'

15

He swallows hard. 'I thought we would stay by our land, by our stock, by our Mussalman neighbours. No one can touch us, I thought. The riots will pass us by. But a mob attacked our village – Oh, the screams of the women, I can hear them still . . . I had a twenty-year-old brother, tall and strong as a mountain, a match for any five of them. This is what they did: they tied one of his legs to one jeep, the other to another jeep – and then they drove the jeeps apart . . .'

Moola Singh stands quite still. The men look away despite the dark. Their indignation flares into rage.

'God give our arms strength,' one of them shouts, and in a sudden movement, knives glimmer. Their cry, 'Bole so Nihal, Sat siri Akal,' swells into the ferocious chant: 'Vengeance! Vengeance! Vengeance!' The old Sikh sinks to his knees.

Chapter 3

Sikander cut his way frantically through the ripe wheat as he ran towards the mud walls of his hut. His wife Zohra, standing in the courtyard, watched him. In the heat-hazed dawn neat squares of rippling wheat stretched towards the horizon and – riding on sudden swells of the breeze – came the distant chants of 'Hari Hari Mahadev!' 'Bole so Nihal. Sat siri Akal!' and an occasional, piercing, 'Ya Alieeee!' An ugly bloated ebb and flow of noise engulfed everything. The corn, the earth, the air and the sky seemed full of threat.

The child saw her father's brown legs flash towards them through the green stalks. Something in his movement checked Munni's usual delighted greeting. She clung to her mother's sari.

Sikander, panting, reached the open yard. He shouted, 'A train is leaving at four o'clock from Ludhiana. We must make it.'

Zohra turned her face away, sick with fright and the realisation of loss. The moment she had vaguely dreaded hit her like a physical blow.

The angry chants, fragmented by the distance, urged them into action.

'Hurry, for God's sake,' panted Sikander.

Zohra dragged out their tin trunks and bed-rolls. Listlessly she wrapped odds and ends into clumsy cloth bundles. The calf and two goats were tethered, ready for departure.

Sikander ran round to the back and, trotting abreast of the horse, brought their two-wheeled rehra to the spread of luggage. 'We can't take all this!' he cried. 'A trunk apiece, that's all. Hide the jewellery somewhere on your body.

17

Come on, hurry up.' He bustled Zohra out of her stunned apathy. Munni was lifted into the cart. Sikander hauled in the calf and goats while Zohra fetched the sleeping baby boy from inside. They drove through the fields on to a dirt road.

❖

The train at Ludhiana station already swarmed with Muslims who had boarded it at earlier stops. Panic-stricken families were abandoning their animals and possessions in an attempt to get on. Zohra glanced back at their mound of luggage now scattered and indistinguishable among the mounting litter of tin trunks and bundles. Their goats had already run off. She pressed closer to Sikander, roughly yanking Munni by the hand. The baby, secure on her hip, looked about him with interest.

Carrying the calf, protecting it with his arms, Sikander forced a way for his family. Inches from the train they were suddenly pushed back by a swell in the crowd. Sikander dropped the calf. Lunging desperately, he at last got a grip on an open window. Quickly he clambered on to the roof of a compartment. Zohra held up the baby. Someone took him and passed him to his father. Lifting Munni, arms outstretched, Zohra too was hoisted up by friendly hands.

'Abba, the calf! There it is!' cried Munni, pointing it out. It tottered below them on spindly, unsteady legs, its face raised, mute and trusting.

'Get the calf, Abba. Don't leave it, she's a baby, she'll die!'

'Shush,' her mother scolded. 'We haven't room for ourselves and you want to take that beast!'

'Abba, don't leave the calf . . . I want my calf,' Munni wailed, and Zohra, overwrought and on the verge of tears herself, raged, 'Shut up, or I'll slap you.'

'Don't be angry with the child,' said Sikander, holding his daughter close.

A few paces from them, jammed between two men, a boy

sat cradling a new-born calf. Munni dug her face into her father's shirt. She wept inconsolably.

❖

The train sped through the throng awaiting it at Jullundur and stopped instead at a siding a few furlongs past the station. It was a pre-arranged halt and the small, clandestine group awaiting it squeezed in as best they could. Qasim, a holstered pistol slung across his chest, a rifle swinging down his back, walked rapidly towards the engine, scanning the compartments. He tried one, but was churned out by the pressure of brown bodies. Afraid that the train might leave without him, he began to run. Just as it pulled away, he hauled himself on to the roof of the carriage nearest the engine.

Sitting on the roof Qasim could see the refugees who had been by-passed at the station closing in like a tide. Men and women carrying children surged forward with their cattle. The train picked up speed. There was an angry roar from the scrambling mass, and some, leaving their families, rushed forward.

But the train, with an indifferent hiss, drew away into the growing darkness.

❖

An old man with a wispy beard sits next to Qasim. Their legs dangle over the roof and from time to time the old man, afraid of losing his balance, grips Qasim's thigh. He chirps like a bird, philosophising, sermonising, relating the histories of various members of his family in his impeccable Aligarh Urdu. Qasim, who has picked up only a broken, make-do Urdu in his three years in the plains, is at a loss before the onslaught of such poetic fluency. Yet he nods his head. He gathers that the old man is from Central India and

19

is eager to settle in Pakistan with his wife, four sons and their families, all of whom are scattered about the train.

Smoke from the engine spews into their faces, and except for their irritated red eyes, they are black with soot. Brushing away sparks and tears, patches of Qasim's skin show unexpectedly white. Tall and bristling with weapons, he is unmistakably a mountain tribal. His narrow eyes, intent on the landscape, combine wariness with the determination of a bird of prey.

❖

It is nearly four years since Qasim left his mountain village. From the remote Himalayan reaches of Kohistan, he had travelled straight to Jullundur where his cousin worked as a messenger in a British firm. His cousin found him a job as watchman in the National and Grindlays Bank. The work suited Qasim perfectly. He stood all day, resplendent in a khaki uniform and crisp turban, guarding the bank entrance. The double-barrelled gun that he stood beside him and the bullet-crammed bandolier swathing his chest gladdened his heart and gratified his pride, for a gun is part of a tribal's attire. It shows his readiness to face his enemy and protect his family's honour.

Touchy and bewildered to begin with, Qasim nevertheless had been fascinated by Jullundur, a busy city in the North Indian plains. Each common object he saw was to him a miracle. Torches, safety-pins, electric lights, cinemas and cars whirled magically before his senses. The language posed a problem. Although he spoke Hindko, a distorted mixture of Punjabi and Pushto, Qasim was able to follow only very little of the zestful Punjabi spoken in Jullundur. Urdu and Hindustani were entirely beyond him.

In the evenings, with his Kohistani friends, Qasim perched atop the backrests of park benches, seeking with his mind's eye the heights and valleys of the land he had left.

20

Like prime-hooded hawks, the tribesmen squatted on the thin edges of roofs and walls, and their eyes sank into the women's brisk buttocks and bare midriffs. Qasim developed a taste for spicy curries and vegetables, a far cry from his daily mountain diet of flat maize bread soaked in water.

The difference was greatest in the really basic values. The men of the plains appeared strangely effeminate. Women roamed the streets in brazen proximity. These people were soft, their lives easy. Where he came from, men – as in the Stone Age – walked thirty days over the lonely, almost trackless mountains to secure salt for their tribes.

❖

The old man has not spoken for some time. Nervously he glances at Qasim's pistol when the holster stirs between them. He is certain the jerks will trigger a shot and shatter his thigh. At last he pats Qasim gingerly on the back.

'Do you think you could move this thing to the other shoulder, Khan Sahib?'

Qasim obligingly shifts the holster strap.

The old man gives a thin smile. Holding on to the roof-edge with one hand, he combs his scant beard.

'Say, why do you carry this dangerous weapon?' he asks in fatherly tones.

'To kill my enemies.'

In the dark, Qasim feels the man's shoulder twitch and move away. Enjoying the situation, he boasts: 'I killed a baboo just before getting here.'

'Why . . . what had he done?'

'I settled a score with him before leaving.'

Qasim pats his gun.

'But why?' persists the old man.

'He was a bloody Hindu bastard!' says Qasim with a finality that checks the old man's curiosity back into his throat.

❖

It was a fact. Qasim had killed a man before leaving.

His enmity with Girdharilal, a puckish, supercilious little clerk, had started a few months after he became watchman at the bank. Besides his clerical work, Girdharilal was responsible for cleanliness in the bank building, right down to the toilets.

Qasim performed his ablutions before reporting for work, but sometimes he was compelled to use the public place reserved for lesser employees. It was of sophisticated Indian style: a clock-shaped china basin embedded in the floor to squat over, with a rusty chain dangling from the ceiling to manipulate the flush. A tap was at hand and a mug stood under it ready for use.

On his rare visits, Qasim left the contraption clogged with stones and scraps of smooth-surfaced glass. Colleagues visiting the lavatory later would rush out in consternation. Girdharilal had the mess cleared out a couple of times and everyone wondered who had caused the mischief. Happily oblivious, Qasim understood none of their talk.

But Girdharilal had his suspicions. One day he followed Qasim and discovered him to be the culprit. He accosted him directly, asking, 'Did you throw the stones in there?'

Qasim, who did not follow the quick-spoken, alien words, merely smiled. A bunch of peons and clerks gathered around them. They explained the charge to Qasim. Admitting the facts, still smiling, he looked from one astonished face to the next, wondering what really was the matter. But there was no mistaking Girdharilal's truculence. He spluttered and gesticulated insultingly. He poked him in the ribs, and the smile left Qasim's face.

He realised he was being ridiculed. And then Girdharilal used a particularly vile obscenity. 'You filthy son of a Muslim mountain hog!' he cried. Qasim's face darkened. Lifting the slightly-built man he pressed him against a wall, and with his hands around the clerk's neck, he started to choke him. Death was the price for daring such an insult to his tribe, his blood, his religion.

Frantic cries rang out of 'Murder! murder! The Pathan will kill him!' and the two were wrenched apart.

Girdharilal, faint with shock, trembled while Qasim hurled abuse and threats of vengeance at him in his hill dialect. Girdharilal did not catch a single word, but he could not miss the meaning.

A senior officer appeared. The situation was explained to him, and Qasim was ordered to apologise. He refused, and his clansman was sent for. After a roaring argument, the clansman finally persuaded Qasim to say the necessary words. He uttered them with the grace of a hungry tiger kept from his victim by chains. An uneasy peace ensued. Qasim learnt from his cousin that killing, no matter what the provocation, was not acceptable by the laws of this land. He would be caught and hanged. These were the plains, with no friendly mountains to afford him sanctuary.

∴

Time passed. Tales of communal atrocities fanned skirmishes, unrest and panic. India was to be partitioned, and that summer the anger and fear in people's minds exploded. Towns were automatically divided into communal sections. Muslim, Hindu, Sikh, each rushed headlong for the locality representing his faith, to seek the dubious safety of strength in numbers. Isolated homes were ransacked and burnt. The sky glowed at night from the fires. It was as though the earth had become the sun, spreading its rays upward. Dismembered bodies of men, women, and even children, lay strewn on roads. Leaving everything behind, people ran from their villages into the towns.

Qasim had not been to work for a month. Riots were in full swing in Jullundur.

One night, defying the curfew, Qasim stealthily made his way to Girdharilal's quarters on the first floor of a squalid tenement.

He stood on the landing, letting his eyes get accustomed to the dark. Then, pressing a shoulder against the cheap wood, he quietly tried to force the doors. They were chained to each other from inside.

'Who's there?' a woman's frightened voice called.

Qasim paused. Regaining his composure, he knocked politely.

'I want to speak with Girdharilal. It is urgent,' he said, disguising his accent.

Girdharilal cleared his throat noisily. Any intruder would know there was a man in the house. Qasim heard him shuffle into his slippers. Next, the chain was being slackened enough for him to peep through the crack.

'Who is it?'

Qasim examined the slit of light, bright at the top, but dark where the clerk's face and naked torso blocked it. The crack looked paler where the light filtered through the white loin-cloth between his legs.

'Who is it? Speak up,' asked Girdharilal, peering into the dark, unable to see who it was.

Slipping the muzzle of his pistol between the door panels, Qasim felt it touch soft flesh. He pulled the trigger.

As he raced away, the clerk's wretched moan and a woman's scream rang in his ears. He wondered that Girdharilal had had time to moan. His hand twitched, and the naked gun still seemed to jump as crazily as it had when he fired it. Even as he fled, lights all over the building were coming on.

The next day Qasim heard of the train and rushed to board it.

❖

The train glides through the moon-hazed night, with a solid mass of humanity clinging to it like flies to dung.

From time to time a figure loses its hold, or is forced off and drifts away like discarded rubbish. A cry, then silence.

Compartments and lavatories are jammed with stifled brown bodies; some carry the dead weight of children asleep on swaying shoulders. Women hold on to flush chains, they lean on children cramped into wash basins. The train speeds on.

Zohra sits on the train roof within the protective crook of Sikander's outstretched arm. He holds on to a projecting water-spout to secure his family against the sway and jerk of the train. The girl sleeps cramped between his legs, her head bobbing on his chest. Zohra holds the baby snugly between her thighs and breasts. The baby presses against a sachet of gold and silver ornaments hanging from her neck. The metal bruises her flesh and the young mother makes little squirming shifts.

Sikander feels a dampness along his thighs. Glancing over his shoulder he sees a black wetness snaking its path down the slope of the roof. In desperation, men and women urinate where they sit. He feels the pressure in his own bladder demanding relief.

'God, let me hold out until Lahore,' he prays.

❖

Whistles screaming their strident warning, the train speeds through Amritsar. Past the station it slows, resuming its cautious, jerky passage. They are nearing the border with Pakistan. Already the anticipation of safety lulls the passengers, and tensions lessen. Here and there a head slumps down in sleep.

❖

25

Zohra has been praying silently. Now that the danger has abated, she dares to think out loud.

'What about the five hundred rupees we lent to Meera Bai for her daughter's wedding?'

An emaciated old woman crouching next to her peers inquisitively into her face.

Sikander looks fixedly into the darkness. He doesn't answer. Zohra senses his tension, and bitterness shoots through to her. They have abandoned their land, their everything, and she thinks to remind him of money lent to a Hindu woman they will never see again. Abashed, she lays her head against his arm, mutely begging forgiveness.

Chapter 4

Qasim has no conception of the city the train is rolling towards. Swaying with the motion of the train, his life in transition, his future uncertain, he absently scans the shadowy flat landscape.

Another forty-five minutes and they will cross the border. The engine is taking a bend. Momentarily the smoke in front drifts to one side and Qasim has a glimpse of the tracks ahead.

It is enough. His wary mountain instincts warn him. In a flash he turns to the old man shouting, 'Jump!' Terrified by the tribal's erratic behaviour, the old man leans back, but Qasim slides off the roof.

Rolling neatly down the gritty embankment, he scuttles towards the deep shade of a clump of trees. Night engulfs him.

As the centre carriage moves past him he sees the train buck. Only now does the engine-driver realise there is something farther down the track. A roar rises from the mass of jolted refugees. The train's single headlight flashes on. It spotlights the barricade of logs and some unaligned rails. White singlets flicker in and out of the glare. The train brakes heavily and the engine crashes into the logs. People are flung from their scant hold on footboards, roofs and buffers. Women and children pour from the crammed compartments.

Now the mob runs towards the train with lighted flares. Qasim sees the men clearly. They are Sikh. Tall, crazed men wave swords. A cry: 'Bole so Nihal', and the answering roar, 'Sat siri Akal!' Torches unevenly light the scene and Qasim watches the massacre as in a cinema. An eerie clamour rises. Sounds of firing explode above agonised shrieks.

A man moves into Qasim's range. He is shouting, 'Run, Zohra! Run into the dark.' Qasim can just hear him above the clamour. He is a young, broad-shouldered man, and the peasant lungi wrapped around his legs causes him to stumble.

⁂

Sikander pushed Zohra and the children off the train and yelled, 'Run. Hide in the dark.' He watched from on top. Zohra was pushing her way through the swirling bodies. She was almost beyond the range of his vision when he saw an arm clutch at her. The sea of faces swayed beneath him. Pin-pointing her position he leapt, clasping his knife. He half slid, half fell down the embankment and sprang up. A Sikh, hair streaming, lashed a bloody sword. Another slowly waved a child stuck at the end of his spear like a banner. Crazed with fury Sikander plunged his knife into the Sikh's ribs. He stumbled over soft flesh and the mud slushy and slippery with blood. 'Zohra! Munni!' he screamed, barely conscious of his own futile voice.

Forcing his way forward, he is suddenly without his lungi and his long, surprisingly scrawny legs trample the live body of a child. He is moving towards a young woman. The flap of her burkha is over her head. A Sikh, sweat gleaming on his naked torso, is holding one breast. She is screaming. Butting a passage with his head, Sikander pushes past the woman and stabs her tormentor. Again and again he plunges his knife into the man's back. Frantically waving her arms, the woman is swept away.

'Run into the dark, Zohra! Run!' he screams. A white singlet flashes before him. Sikander crumples to the ground, astonished by the blood gushing from his stomach. A woman tramples over him. He tries to ward off the suffocating

28

forest of legs with his arms. More and more legs trample him, until mercifully he feels no pain.

❖

Qasim sees figures flee the glare like disintegrating wisps of smoke. He sits still, in the undergrowth, biding his time. Although he is horrified by the slaughter he feels no compulsion to sacrifice his own life. These are people from the plains – not his people.

The carnage is subsiding. Already they are herding and dragging the young women away. The dying and the dead are being looted of their bloodied ornaments and weapons. An eerie silence settles on the stench of blood.

❖

Qasim, as far as he knew, was alone. He moved swiftly, in shadows, aware that he had to cross the border before daylight.

He had barely started when suddenly a short form hurtled out of the dark at him. He stopped, his heart pounding. That same instant he realised it was a child, a little girl.

Clinging to his legs, she sobbed, 'Abba, Abba, my Abba!' For a moment Qasim lost his wits. The child was the size of his own little Zaitoon lost so long ago. Her sobs sounded an eerie, forlorn echo from his past. Then, brutally untangling her stubborn grasp, he plunged ahead.

The child stumbled after him, screaming with terror.

Fearing the danger from that noise, Qasim waited for the child to catch up. He slid his hand beneath his vest and triggered a switch. A long thin blade jumped open in his hand. His fingers were groping for the nape of her neck when the girl pressed herself to him for protection.

Qasim gasped. Was it a trick of the light? Quietly, with one hand, he closed the knife. She looked up and in the

29

mould of her tear-stained features, he caught an uncanny flash of resemblance to his daughter thrashing in the agony of her last frenzy.

Kneeling before her, he sheltered the small face in his hands.

The girl stared at him. 'You aren't my Abba,' she said in accusing surprise.

Qasim drew her to him. 'What is your name?'

'Munni.'

'Just Munni? Aren't all little girls called Munni?'

'Just Munni.'

'You must have another name . . . Do you know your father's name?'

'My father's name was Sikander.'

Her use of the past tense startled him. It showed a courage and a forbearance that met the exacting standard of his own proud tribe.

'I had a little girl once. Her name was Zaitoon. You are so like her . . .'

She leaned against him, trembling, and he, close to his heart, felt her wondrously warm and fragile. A great tenderness swept over him, and recognizing how that fateful night had thrown them together, he said, 'Munni, you are like the smooth, dark olive, the zaitoon, that grows near our hills . . . The name suits you . . . I shall call you Zaitoon.'

A simple man from a primitive, warring tribe, his impulses were as direct and concentrated as pinpoints of heat. No subtle concessions to reason or consequence tempered his fierce capacity to love or hate, to lavish loyalty or pity. Each emotion arose spontaneously and without complication, and was reinforced by racial tradition, tribal honour and superstition. Generations had carried it that way in his volatile Kohistani blood.

Cradling the girl in his arms, he hurried towards Lahore.

30

Chapter 5

A dingy, heat-hazed dawn crept down on the landscape. Shadows along the horizon turned out to be clusters of squat mud huts and Qasim could make out the faint stir of awakening rural activity. He had been on the run for two hours and was beginning to feel the weight of the child. Every little while he swept his thumb across his forehead to prevent the sweat from running into his eyes. His clothes were soaked with perspiration and his trousers stiff and black with dust. The girl had not said a word. Sensing his strain, she shifted her weight to ease him.

The sun cleared the horizon, and Qasim made out the glimmer of a canal winding to one side. The bridge spanning it, a slender sleeping funnel, lay straight ahead. Already the asphalt reflected a white heat that dazzled his eyes. They were on the outskirts of Lahore and Qasim wanted to plunge into the heart of the city, into the thicket of Muslim safety.

The uneasy city was awakening furtively, like a sick man pondering each movement lest pain recur. The slaughter of the past weeks, the exodus, and the conflagrations were almost over. Looted houses stood vacant, their gaping doors and windows glaring balefully. Men, freshly dead, their bodies pale and velvety, still lay in alleys and in open drains.

Qasim walked along a path bordering the Grand Trunk Road, and the fine talcum earth, in little puffs, rose up around his knees. He did not see the dust-covered gunny sack until he almost stumbled over it. Casually prodding it with his foot he was appalled to see a body half spill out. The youth, flat-stomached, broad-shouldered, honey-hued, lay incongruously asleep in the dust. Stemmed in its prime the body did not look vacuous – like the discarded shells of the old and sick – it still emanated vigour. His legs were in the sack and just above the lungi tied low on his hips was a wide-V-shaped gash, clean as if hacked out of wood. Qasim knew the youth's life blood had spilled from that innocuous-looking wound. By the amulet around his neck, by the trim of his hair and moustache, Qasim could tell that the man was of his own faith. Hindus and Sikhs had fled the area and he wondered what passion had caused a Mussalman to kill this handsome Muslim youth. Death, cheapened by the butchering of over a million people, became casual and humdrum. It was easy to kill. Taking advantage of this attitude to settle old scores, to grab someone's property or business or woman, Hindu killed Hindu – Sikh, Sikh – and Mussalman Muslim.

'Is he sick?' the girl asked.

'No, dead.'

A man, his erect head balancing a huge bundle of fire-wood, walked some distance ahead. Quickening his stride, Qasim caught up with him and lightly held his arm. The man swung around, his straight neck still balancing the wood.

'What do you want?' he rasped. His chest heaved with panic.

'Am I in Lahore, brother?' Qasim asked. He felt a lessening in the man's quivering tension.

'Yes, you are.'

'We are from Jullundur. Our train was attacked. Allah saved us and we have run all the way to Lahore.' Qasim's grip on the man's arm slackened. 'What do I do now?'

The man relaxed completely and noticed the child for the first time. He pointed.

'Carry on straight. Then ask someone the way to the refugee camp at Badami Bagh. You will find food and shelter there.'

❖

The girl, perched on Qasim's shoulder, gazed excitedly at all the people grinding together like wheat kernels in a mill. Refugees sprawled on and spilled over the vast, welcoming, hospitable acres of Badami Bagh. Qasim waded into the flood of brown sweating bodies, swimming in heat and dust.

'Will we find my mother and father here?' the child asked in sudden hope at the sight of so many. A thickly turbaned head over a broad back, a tall man crouched over a hookah just that way, a village printed sari, a brown arm aglow with bangles; they all were her fathers and mothers. Riding high, she peered eagerly this way and that, expecting the loved faces to emerge at any moment. 'No', she said, shaking her head with disappointment every time she discovered instead a masquerading stranger. But her attention was easily trapped by yet another similarity and hope welled up once again.

The crowd was thickest under the trees. Qasim bullied his way through and sat down against the trunk of a shady mango. Tired out, he cradled the girl against his chest. Tugging at his shirt she cried, 'Don't you want to look for Abba?'

Qasim caught her face between his palms and looked long into her restless eyes: 'I think your people are dead . . . you saw what happened last night . . . I am your father, your new father. You are my little Zaitoon bibi . . . aren't you?'

The girl gravely regarded the strange, fair-skinned face and slanting eyes.

'You want to be my father?' she asked solemnly.

'Yes,' he said, pulling her face to his cheeks.

She twisted her neck to learn each new facet of his features.

'We won't find my Abba?' she asked.

Qasim shook his head.

When she fell asleep, Qasim looked at his commitment

speculatively. The resemblance was less than the night before, but it was there. He stroked the child's hair and shut his eyes.

Qasim and Zaitoon slept exhausted under the tree all day. When the sun dipped the heat was still blistering, and it was oppressively humid.

As evening approached a faint breeze at last joggled the scorching mass of air, and moments later they were in the midst of a dust-storm.

Wave upon wave of fine, sooty dust struck with the force of slashing water – mouthfuls, earfuls, nosefuls of dust. Dust was ground between teeth, breathed into lungs, gulped into stomachs. Throats choked. Stooped figures huddled against the mighty wind. Qasim crouched, protecting the tiny Zaitoon with all he had of arms and clothes. The child clung close. Qasim held the flap of his shirt against her mouth. 'Breathe through this,' he shouted, spluttering.

The wind roared like an aeroplane taking off.

'O, Pathan! Get the child away from the tree!' someone shouted close to his ear.

Pushed hard by a savage gust so that he almost fell, Qasim scuttled away, hugging Zaitoon. The gigantic branches of the mango fought and slashed at the phosphorescent dust. An instant later, wrenched from its roots, the whole tree heaved and crashed slowly to the ground.

Debris hurtled through the air. Bits of wood, empty cans scavenged by the refugees, aluminium utensils, struck Qasim with the force of bullets. String-beds, their frail wooden frames askew, thrashed along, limping like grotesque animals. Flashes of lightning lit the scene as all across the city mattresses, beds, and mosquito nets took off from roof-tops. Signboards, tree branches, windows and odd bits of furniture were flung about. Thunder grew insistent, exploding louder and quicker. The wind worked up into a heightened frenzy. Qasim closed his eyes, blocked his ears and every nerve screamed, 'Allah! Allah! Allah!'

34

A huge drop of rain at last plopped on his back, then another. The wind slackened with the moisture. It began to pour. The rain cleared the air, washing the dust off their hands, hair and clothes, and soaking the parched earth. Cool, clean and sweet, it sucked away the heat. The air grew luminous. The suddenly newly bright-green, rich-brown city was bathed in soft, evening light.

A man walked up to Qasim. Dripping gloriously, arms akimbo, he grinned, 'Well, Pathan, I certainly saved you from that tree!'

He was about thirty. A black cord, stringing a silver amulet, hung from his neck. He was shorter than Qasim but magnificently built.

Qasim touched his forehead in gratitude. Must be a wrestler, he thought, noting the cropped hair and the smooth, well-oiled face.

'You a pehelwan?' he asked, diffidently.

The man nodded.

'Ah! I thought so.'

'Nikka. They call me Nikka Pehelwan. Come, let's have a look at the tree,' he said in Punjabi, his even teeth gleaming in a vigorous smile.

He strutted ahead jauntily and Qasim followed.

The rain exhilarated the camp. Irritated, bitter tempers gave way to camaraderie. Men and women teased each other, laughed and romped around like children. Naked children wallowed in foamy cushions of mud, splattering the slush, dancing and shouting.

'Put me down. Put me down,' cried Zaitoon fretfully, but Qasim, enthralled by the confident stride of his new-found friend, did not hear her. The wrestler reminded him of a velvet-brown pedigree pony that is reined in to keep its neck arched and high.

They reached the fallen tree and Nikka tried to lift a branch. Each of his gestures combined grace with a hint of arrogance.

'This would have flattened you like a chappati,' he said impassively.

Zaitoon beat Qasim on the chest. 'Abba-a-a, put me down, Abba-a-a-a.'

'Hush, child,' he said absently. For a flash, his heart constricted. Was her 'Abba-a' directed at the stranger? No, she was looking at him. He was flooded with a sense of relief and tenderness.

Zaitoon smiled happily at the affection shining in his face. 'Put me down. I want to play.'

'All right,' he said, lowering her.

'Is she your daughter?' the Pehelwan asked.

Qasim grew tense. 'You heard her.'

'Where is your wife?'

'Dead.'

'Was she also Pathan?' Nikka inquired. 'The girl is dark.'

Qasim glared at the wrestler. 'Look,' he snarled, with a sudden hold on the man's wet, muslin shirt, 'nothing about my wife concerns you . . . And I am not a Pathan. I am a Kohistani.'

'Calm down. I was only asking. What's the harm in that?'

Qasim loosened his grip.

'You don't ask a hill-man anything about his womenfolk, understand? I would have slit your throat for less had you not saved me and my child from that tree.'

'Lay off, friend, I meant no harm,' the man flashed a warm smile. 'I'm not a hill-man. I don't know your ways.'

Qasim's anger subsided as quickly as it had begun. 'Let's sit down.' He offered a placatory gesture, clearing away a few twigs. Then he asked, 'Where do you come from?'

'Pannapur, near Amritsar,' Nikka paused, and Qasim waited attentively.

Then Nikka said, 'Do you know what those swine did in my village? They herded the Muslims into a camp for protection . . . Protection, mind you . . . because of some fool rumour – Allah grant it be true – that a trainload of Hindus

36

and Sikhs had been slaughtered near Wagha. Once inside
the camp, a Sikh police inspector – the dog's penis – picked
up a machine-gun and went 'tha-tha-tha-tha!' He killed
them all. By Allah's grace, we had already left.'

They brooded awhile. Qasim was the first to look up.

'You had no land?' he inquired hesitantly.

'No, only a small paan and betel-nut shack.'

'Any family?'

Nikka probed the simple, inquisitive face, and a wide grin
stretched his mouth.

'I have a wife. Does it offend you to hear me tell of my
own womenfolk?'

Qasim glanced at him sheepishly.

'She's barren.'

Nikka detailed the probable causes of her barrenness,
mentioning her ailments, her temperament, her age, and
Qasim blushed up to his pale eyelashes.

'Women are strange. I know she cries her eyes out thinking I will get myself another wife. Why should I? It's Allah's
will. I'm content.'

He flashed Qasim an irrepressibly mischievous grin.

'Hah! I forgot to mention my other profession! You must
have heard of the Shiv shrine at Benares?'

Qasim nodded.

Nikka affected the mien of a Brahmin priest and chanted:
'Hey Bhagwan – Harey Ram, Harey Ram . . . ' He sighed,
rocking cross-legged on the wet tree trunk. He rolled his
eyes sanctimoniously to the clouds. 'Every year I was summoned to Benares for the Holy Spring Puja. Childless women
flock to the temple to invoke Shiva's pity and assistance;
plump young things married to dotards. There is much
chanting of mantras, burning of incense, distribution of
sanctified sweets and drink; until the women get stupefied –
quite stupefied. You can do with them what you like. The
Brahmins have a good time. But you know those lentil-
fattened Hindus, they don't have much seed. I was paid

handsomely but, I tell you, I had to work hard at being Shiv – a circumcised Shiva! Hai, Hai . . . I wonder if I will ever get there again.' He pulled a long, droll face.

Qasim guffawed. He fell against Nikka in helpless mirth and clung to him laughing. He was secretly incredulous of the wrestler's boast, but here was a man after his own heart. This was one up for the lusty meat-eaters. Identifying with Muslim virility, Qasim's pride soared. His acceptance in these new surroundings was, as it were, assured by the wrestler's ribald Punjabi humour. He now told him how he had travelled from Jullundur. He told him about the girl.

Nikka at once sensed his anxiety.

'As far as I'm concerned, you're her father. There is no need to tell me or anyone all this. You've done a noble thing, leave it to Allah's will,' he said, endearing himself to Qasim.

❖

It was growing dark. Throughout the camp chappatis and potato curry were being distributed at various hurricane-lit centres. Nikka arranged for Zaitoon to be left in the care of his wife Miriam, and the two men pushed their way through the throng to obtain their rations. When they returned, Nikka invited Qasim to eat with them. They sat on the ground in a rough circle. Miriam shaded her candid, heavy features with her chaddar, and Qasim did not glance her way even once. When she told her husband, 'Ask your friend if he would like to have this chappati,' Qasim, his eyes riveted to the ground, replied, 'Thank you, sister. I have had my fill.'

Nikka was reassured by the tribal's polite ways and seemly behaviour.

❖

Next day, as they sat idly in the shade of a crumbling wall,

38

Nikka asked, 'Didn't you do any money-lending in Jullundur?'

This reference to a hill-man's proverbial occupation in the plains irked Qasim. He looked at the Pehelwan sharply, but no insult had been intended and he admitted, 'Yes, some.'

'Care to do business with me? I have no money, but I know the guts of the paan and betel-nut business inside out. Two hundred rupees would be ample for a start.'

Qasim's eyes suddenly were as wary as those of a threatened cat, and Nikka hastily added: 'Brother, you can trust me. I have a wife – where can I run? I won't let you down. Anyway, think about it.'

Massaging the back of his neck, Qasim pondered. At last he looked up. 'Neither I, nor my forefathers, have ever done business. But I could lend you the money – on interest.'

'Of course!'

'You said two hundred rupees? At the end of the month you pay me four hundred.'

Nikka glared at him incredulously. 'You can't mean that! Surely no one ever borrowed from you on those terms?'

'They have,' Qasim retorted.

'See here,' said Nikka, dismissing Qasim's proposal with a shrug, 'I will accumulate the interest at ten per cent and give you the whole lump sum when I can.'

Qasim sniggered. 'Look at him! Look at him,' he said to the world at large. 'Do you think I am a child – a dimwit? I haven't bitten upon the years so long for nothing. You can't fool me . . .'

'Oh, Khan Sahib, I've not been the leading strong man of my village for nothing either. I have also bitten upon the years! Talk reasonably, man.'

Nikka stood up and Qasim caught him by the arm.

'How can we come to terms without talking?' he said as if he were placating a child.

They came to a series of decisions. Qasim would lend Nikka two hundred rupees. Twice that amount was to be returned to him at the end of six months. Nikka would, in compensation for these easy terms, provide them with food.

'My wife will keep an eye on your girl,' concluded Nikka magnanimously.

At the end of six months, the terms were to be freshly negotiated. Both retired with the drawn expressions of men having conceded too easily. But their hearts were jubilant.

That evening they walked some distance to a secluded spot between a grove of sheesham saplings. Qasim, delving deep under his shirt into the private folds of his trousers, pulled out a soiled cloth pouch. Turning slightly away from Nikka, he withdrew two limp hundred rupee notes.

'Here's the money,' he said. 'Mind, don't try any tricks.'

Nikka folded the notes and knotted them into the edge of his lungi. Then drawing his singlet down, he said, 'Can't say, but you'll get to know me better.'

They walked back to the camp.

❖

Zaitoon had not mentioned her parents for a week. She had fretted awhile but, blessed with the short memory of a five-year-old, appeared to be caught up in the excitement of her new life at the camp.

By eleven o'clock all the refugees crawled beneath whatever shade they could find or improvise. The sun struck with white-hot fury. The streets of Lahore lay deserted and the shops were closed.

One afternoon, while Qasim sheltered beneath a banyan tree, a girl, about thirteen years old, ran past. Zaitoon, her head pillowed on Qasim's lap, was asleep.

Giggling with mischief and defiance, the girl had run only a little further when a querulous voice shrieked, 'There she goes! Off to play just when I need her. Come back, Zohra! Zohra, I said come back at once!'

The girl stopped and turned.

40

Zaitoon stirred in her sleep and Qasim, who had been watching idly, smiled at the sulking adolescent.

There was the mother's voice again, 'Wait till I get my hands on her! Zohra, where are you? Come back at once. Zohra! Zohra!'

Suddenly Zaitoon sat up. 'Ma?' she cried, and before Qasim knew what had happened, she was racing towards the voice she had heard.

She flitted through the heat-drugged camp screaming, 'Ma? Ma? Where are you?' and the burly tribal, floundering behind her, bellowed, 'Zaitoon. Munni, wait . . . where are you going? Wait!'

Qasim caught up with her and carried her back screaming and kicking. He was appalled at the coincidence.

When the girl quietened down he asked her: 'You told me your father's name was Sikander . . . You haven't told me your mother's name yet?'

'Zohra,' she answered.

'Run, Zohra, run.' A tall peasant moves across the gory tangle. Light from waving torches licks his ravaged, blood-stained face . . .

Oh, the vulnerability of scrawny, stumbling legs – the futile plea, 'Run, Zohra,' lost in the dark.

Qasim wanted to say, 'I saw your father on the last day of his life. He was a brave man,' but he felt she was too small. He vowed to tell her all when she was older.

❖

Despite Nikka's reassurances, Qasim was cautious. He watched him carefully. Each morning, when Nikka slipped out of the camp, taking his mug up some deserted alley or into the pampas grass edging an irrigation ditch, Qasim followed with a fistful of toilet-stones. Both disappeared in the reeds, but Qasim was sure to keep the shadow of Nikka's black hair in sight. At night, he slept as near to Nikka as possible, springing awake at the slightest rustle. He accom-

41

panied Nikka in his search for accommodation and helped carry back the merchandise purchased for the business venture: paan-leaves, tobacco biris, betel-nuts, cheap sweets and cigarettes. Nikka laboured hard, vending his wares around the camp on a tin tray that hung from his neck, and Qasim was surprised by the quick turnover.

One afternoon Nikka asked, 'Still afraid I might vanish with your money?'

'No, no! What nonsense you talk. You are my brother.' But he continued his guardianship.

Many hawkers worked the camp, peddling a variety of goods, and among them were a couple of other paan-biri wallas.

Nikka learnt of their presence and was offended. He kept an alert lookout, and early one sultry evening, he spied a hawker with merchandise similar to his own. He nudged Qasim and they steered a passage towards the unfortunate man.

Leaving his tray in Qasim's charge, Nikka sauntered forward. He planted himself squarely before the surprised hawker and, raising his voice, spun off a facile string of practised Punjabi expletives.

'You incestuous lover of your mother, lover of your sister, son of a whore, imbecile owl, dog, how dare you peddle this stuff here!'

Stepping forward, he slashed the clumsy tray from the man's arms.

The pedlar set up a cry. 'Why, you crazy bastard, what right have you to dump my merchandise?' A throng of onlookers gathered. 'Here I stand,' he whined, 'minding my own business, and this bully scatters my goods! I am a poor refugee. What right has he to harass me, I ask you . . . I ask you?'

He stooped to pick up his belongings.

Nikka glowered at him.

Qasim, holding the tray, edged closer.

Three men at the inner ring of the surrounding crowd helped the pedlar gather his strewn goods.

'Look, you fool,' Nikka shouted ominously, 'I sell paan and biri in this camp. No one but I shall do so, understand?' He thumped his massive chest with both arms, arching his strong neck ever more like a stallion. 'Go peddle your goods elsewhere. Peddle condoms.'

Emboldened by the throng of sympathisers, the man screamed, 'You think you're the only man in Lahore? Who do you think you are anyway! Don't you glare at me like that! I shall sell my stuff where I wish!'

'I'll show you who I am!' said Nikka, and cutting swiftly through the crowd, he once again struck the tray to the ground.

The man wrapped himself round Nikka's waist, and they fell rolling in the mud.

Nikka forced the pedlar flat upon his back. With one knee pinning his chest, he twisted the man's arm brutally.

Two young men tried to hold on to Nikka. 'Let go, Pehelwan,' they cried, 'let go of the poor man.'

The hawker sobbed pitifully, tears parting the dust on his cheeks. At last he screamed, 'Hai, maaf kar – forgive me brother. Leave me, for God's sake.'

More men fell upon Nikka, trying to wrench him away. Abruptly he let go of his prey and wiggled his powerful, oil-moistened body free of its oppressors. He stood facing them in the alert stance of a wrestler. The young men were moving in cautiously. 'Come on, you cowardly suckling heifers. Come, all you effeminate cry-babies all . . .', he egged them on.

A thick-set youth, wearing only a baggy shalwar, flung himself at Nikka's knees and the others closed in quickly.

Nikka grappled with them expertly. Bloody and hurt, he still punished them. The throng grudgingly acknowledged his skill. Hitting hard, slipping free, hanging on to an arm, twisting a knee, he held his own.

43

Qasim placed Nikka's tray on the ground and drew his pistol from its holster. Casually he blew specks of dust off it. A man stared in amazement.

The fight was getting vicious. Mean, sweat-filmed eyes and pain-parted teeth flashed through the haze of dust they kicked up as now one face, now another, bobbed up in the tangle.

Qasim watched. Suddenly his attention was riveted to the stooped glistening back of one of the fighters. Nikka held down the man's head as in a vice and the youth danced and twisted on his thick legs trying to loosen the hold. Qasim saw his arm swivel to his back and his hand grope in the gathers of his shalwar. At once he fired into the sky.

The shot cracked, stunning the onlookers for an instant. There was panic. The wrestlers straightened, aghast and bewildered.

Qasim held the gun aloft and shouted, 'Stop the fight. This swine was reaching for a knife!' He stalked through to the wrestlers and contemptuously pushed back the thick-set youth. 'Nikka Pehelwan has proved himself. Everyone disperse. The fight is over. Move on, come on, move!'

'Your friend is a strong man,' someone said and Qasim glowed with pride.

The crowd broke up reluctantly, leaving a knot of about ten admirers. They brushed the dust from Nikka's hair and clothes and handed him his slippers. He walked away erect and silent, followed by this group, the undisputed strong man of the camp and the only paan-biri vendor around.

❖

A month later in the seedy neighbourhood of Qila Gujjar Singh, Qasim and Nikka secured adjacent rooms on the second floor of a narrow three-storeyed building. Constricted balconies, floored by sagging planks, ran the full breadth of the façade one above the other. The rent was twenty rupees a month.

Nikka wasted no time in establishing his trade. He set up a wooden platform that projected right out on to the busy pavement. It was nailed to the building at one end and supported by stumps and bricks. Here he sat all day, cross-legged, shaded by a canvas canopy, near-buried under his wares. Trade was brisk, and Qasim hung around, offering occasional help.

They had been in business a week, when immediately after the Friday prayers, a massive customer sauntered up to Nikka's new stall.

Here comes trouble, Nikka guessed. He had been expecting a confrontation of sorts: a test to establish his trading rights. Glad of the opportunity, he turned to the stranger.

'Packet of Scissors,' the man said, demanding one of the cheaper brands of cigarettes. He opened the packet, removed the silver folder, and sniffed at the cigarettes. Throwing back the packet, he sneered, 'Stale!'

Nikka studied the white scars criss-crossing the man's black, closely cropped head. He bided his time.

'A paan,' the man next ordered, 'with crushed tobacco.'

Nikka withdrew a glossy leaf from a sheaf of betel-leaves wrapped in wet cloth and began coating it with a red and white paste.

The man was fingering a careful arrangement of biri bundles and cigarettes with clumsy irreverence. A tower of cigarette packets fell over.

Nikka swore, '... lay your leathery hands off my merchandise.'

The man folded his arms with an offensive smirk that appeared to suggest, 'Just you wait, you innocent.'

Nikka handed him the paan saying, 'Six paisa.'

The man popped the paan into his mouth, chewed, slurped and declared, 'Also stale! Not enough tobacco either!' As he turned to go, he said, 'Better learn your trade

45

first. I don't see how I can allow a sloppy cheat like you to settle in my locality.'

'My money!' shouted Nikka, half rising and gathering his lungi up above his knees.

Ignoring the demand, chewing on his paan, the man stepped away.

Nikka leapt down to the pavement and his hand pounced on his huge customer's back.

The man swung round. 'What do you want, shopkeeper?' he sneered.

'My money!' said Nikka, holding out his palm.

'Are you deaf? I told you, the betel-leaf is stale.'

He knocked Nikka's hand aside.

Nikka slapped him full in the face. 'Spit out my paan first,' he said, striking him on the back of his neck so that the red, syrupy mixture shot out of the man's startled mouth.

The man clawed back in humiliated anger, and the two pehelwans grappled.

The crowd cheered the taller pehelwan, the acknowledged leader among the local roughs. Two policemen stood by watching the fight with professional detachment.

Keeping a wary eye on the shop, stretching on tiptoe, Qasim looked over the heads of the spectators. The stranger was a good wrestler, and the crowd fell silent when they saw Nikka get the better of him. He pinioned him to the pavement with his knees, and he twisted his face, crushing it into the gravel. The man cried out in pain.

Nikka stood up slowly. He looked around cool-eyed and arrogant. Dusting his torn clothes, and wiping blood from his palms, he jumped calmly on to his platform and settled down to business. He sat all evening as he was, victorious and blood-plastered.

News of the fight, of the strength of the new biri-walla in their midst and of the ignominious defeat of the extortionist, spread like a fire in dry leaves. Qasim felt a new admiration for his friend.

Nikka, born with the instincts and destiny of a leader, knew just how to entrench himself. Three days later, the stall prominently displayed two intimidating photographs of his person. Clad only in his wrestling briefs, exhibiting the might of his muscle-bound body, Nikka posed before two stiff rows of diminishing cypresses, behind which hung a lavender Taj Mahal. In the other photograph, Nikka's image scowled handsomely at customers from between a pair of snarling stuffed tigers. Beneath them, inscribed in Urdu, were the captions, NIKKA PEHELWAN and TIGER NIKKA.

❖

Qasim, with nothing to do, wandered along the crowded bazaars of Lahore. Perched on his shoulders, captivated by the intriguing odours of fish frying in the Shalmi, of barbecuing liver and kebab, smiling at the colourful pageant thronging the streets and pouring out of cinemas, Zaitoon relished all his interests. They were blissful, absorbed by the shop windows, their noses glued to sweetmeat and fancy-goods casements.

Often they sat on the spidery mud-caked grass of the parks, watching boys at a kabbadi match. The boys would crouch in rows facing each other. One of them, brown, his limbs shining with oil, would dart into the clearing slapping his naked thigh, calling 'kabbadi kabbadi kabbadi kabbadi,' until holding his breath, he would touch a boy of the opposing team and swerve and dodge back to his line. If caught, the two would wrestle, trying to pin each other down on their backs.

They visited Shahdara, Emperor Jehangir's tomb, its marble minarets rising in delicate towers set like a jewel in the jade of the gardens. They lay in the cool, fountain-hazed Shalimar Gardens, the summer sanctuary of Emperor Shahjehan, and strolled down Anarkali, the crowded bazaar named after the beautiful dancing girl who was bricked in alive by the Emperor Akbar because Prince Salim was determined to marry her.

Qasim perched a frightened Zaitoon on the tall, proud snout of the Zam-Zam cannon, known because of Kipling as 'Kim's gun.' They sat on the sands of the shallow Ravi, gazing at its gentle brown eddies . . . Lahore – the ancient whore, the handmaiden of dimly remembered Hindu kings, the courtesan of Moghul emperors – bedecked and bejewelled, savaged by marauding Sikh hordes – healed by the caressing hands of her British lovers. A little shoddy, as Qasim saw her; like an attractive but aging concubine, ready to bestow surprising delights on those who cared to court her – proudly displaying Royal gifts . . .

'Don't you want to find some work?' Nikka inquired once, but Qasim, with typical tribal disdain, saw no need for it. 'I get my keep from you for so little. And don't forget, at the end of six months, I'll be receiving four hundred rupees from you. We shall see later.'

Nikka didn't mind, especially since Qasim was often at hand for odd jobs. Besides, a burly tribal – a bandolier across his chest – added to the shop's prestige. Once he borrowed Qasim's pistol and holster and garlanded them round his photographs.

When Qasim accompanied Nikka to a fair he was surprised how easily the wrestler picked off an array of balloons strung up to test marksmanship, and with a gun that Qasim suspected had been doctored to miss.

At the end of six months Nikka returned Qasim his two hundred rupees with an additional two hundred in interest. The new terms they arrived at compelled Qasim to find work. He was to give Nikka forty rupees a month for his and Zaitoon's keep. Zaitoon would be looked after by Miriam while he was at work. Good jobs were hard to find. Qasim sheepishly asked Nikka to take him on as a partner in his business. Nikka brushed him off with a casual, 'Too late,

48

friend. Too bad you missed the bird when it sang at your window.'

Qasim worked at odd jobs as a construction labourer and coolie.

Chapter 6

Lahore was getting cooler. A soft breeze from the foot-hills of the Himalayas gently nudged the merciless summer away. Disturbances subsided. October, November and then December, with its icy cold, checked the tempers. Hordes of refugees still poured in, seeking jobs. The nation was new. The recently-born bureaucracy and government struggled towards a semblance of order. Bogged down by puritanical fetish, in the clutches of unscrupulous opportunists – the newly rich and the power drunk – the nation fought for its balance. Ideologies vied with reason, and everyone had his own concept of Independence. When a tongawalla, reprimanded by a policeman, shouted, 'We are independent now – I'll drive where I please!' bystanders sympathised. Fifty million people relaxed, breathing freedom. Slackening their self-discipline, they left their litter about, creating terrible problems of public health and safety. Many felt cheated because some of the same old laws, customs, taboos and social distinctions still prevailed.

Unused muscle, tentatively flexed, grew strong, and then stronger. Dictatorial tyrants sprang up – feudal lords over huge areas of Pakistan.

Memory of the British Raj receded – shrinking into the dim past inhabited by ghosts of mighty Moghul Emperors, of Hindu, Sikh and Rajput kings.

The marble canopy that had delicately domed Queen Victoria's majesty for decades looked naked and bereft without her enormous, dour statue. Prince Albert, astride his yellowing marble horse, was whisked away one night from the Mall; as were the busts of Viceroys and Lords from various parks. No one minded. Portraits of British gentlemen bristling with self-esteem and dark with age vanished from club halls and official buildings, to surface years later on junk stalls.

Jinnah's austere face decorated office walls and the Jinnah-cap replaced the sola-topee. Chevrolets and Cadillacs gradually edged out Bentleys and Morrises and, the seductively swaggering American Agency for International Development (A.I.D.), the last sedate vestiges of the British East India Company.

Jinnah died within a year of creating the new State. He was an old man but his death was untimely. The Father of the Nation was replaced by step-fathers. The constitution was tampered with, changed and narrowed. Iqbal's dynamic vision of Muslim brotherhood reaching beyond the confines of nationality – a mystic-poet's vision – became the property of petty bureaucrats and even more petty religious fanatics.

Despite the unsettled times Nikka's business prospered. He and Miriam shifted to three rooms on the ground floor of a tenement. He acquired for his home a cheap sofa set and a radio for the shop. The new living quarters were painted parrot-green, gratifying the tastes of his friends and acquaintances.

Miriam, reflecting her husband's rising status and respectability, took to observing strict purdah. She seldom ventured out without her veil.

Qasim and Zaitoon remained in their solitary room on the second floor.

Nikka's prowess in wrestling and his enormous strength became legendary. Qila Gujjar Singh pitted its pehelwan against wrestlers of other localities and gloated over Nikka's unfailing victories. Nikka's generosity and his capacity for arbitration also were widely acclaimed.

One of the political factions sniffed him out – embraced

51

and flattered him – and he became a miniscule part of a huge political package.

Policemen became courteous. All appreciated his ability to intercede for friends, and some shady characters from the political underworld aired their grievances to him.

Qasim was wafted upward on the swell of Nikka's success. Nikka procured him a job as night-watchman at a steelware warehouse. His leisure hours he spent loitering around Nikka's shop.

As for Zaitoon, Qasim laughed at her prattle. He was continually touched by the affection she lavished on him.

Zaitoon had the short memory of a happy child. Recollections of the horrendous night, of her parents, of tilled earth and lazily dipping wheat fields soon dimmed into oblivion. She played with the little urchins of her street, and came to look on Miriam and Nikka as part of her family. Though Qasim rarely saw Miriam, Zaitoon was constantly in and out of her rooms.

Their own room was dingy, and except for a single misshapen door, it had no ventilation. Qasim and Zaitoon slept on straw mats spread on the bare, brick floor. The chief piece of furnishing was a shiny new tin trunk in one corner which Qasim hoped to fill with clothes. Later, when he could afford it, he bought two charpoys and they carried these to the roof and slept beneath the stars during the summer.

He saw to it that Zaitoon attended school for a full five years. Awed by her recital of the mysterious Urdu alphabet and by her struggle on the *takhti*, a wooden slate coated daily with mud-paste, he tried to learn from her. When she began writing in a book he gave up. Miriam, scandalised by such a foolish waste of the girl's time, at last told Nikka, 'Now that she's learned to read the Holy Quran, what will she do with more reading and writing – boil and drink it? She's not going to become a baboo or an officer! No, Allah willing, she'll get married and have children.'

Another time she sighed, 'Poor child . . . had she a mother she'd be learning to cook and sew . . . does Bhai Qasim think he's rearing a boy? He ought to give some thought to her marriage . . . who'd want an educated . . .'

'But she's only a baby,' protested Nikka.

'A baby? She's ten! I can already see her body shaping. The Pathan doesn't realise she is in the hot plains of the Punjab: everything ripens early here . . . she'll be safe only at her mother-in-law's . . . A girl is never too young to marry . . .'

❖

Qasim glimpsed Zaitoon walk past the store. It was too early for school to be over.

'I'm here, Zaitoon,' he called.

He stepped out and noticed her drawn face. 'What is it?'

'I have such a belly-ache.'

Zaitoon doubled over and Qasim carefully picked her up.

'Did you eat raw mango?' He knew she loved the sour mangoes smothered in salt and red-pepper sold outside the school.

'No.'

Her forehead felt damp and cold and he buttoned up her cardigan. 'I'd better take you to Aunt Miriam's.'

He knocked on a curtained window. Miriam opened the door and saw them through the bamboo blind screening the entrance.

'Zaitoon has a bad stomach-ache,' he explained.

'Come in, brother.'

Miriam held the screen apart and, stooping, Qasim edged past. He laid Zaitoon on the sofa. Miriam darted into another room and hastily having covered herself with a shawl, sat by Zaitoon.

'I'll take care of her, Bhai: she'll be all right.'

'Let me know if you think I should take her to the hakeem for some herbal medicine – or if you need anything.'

'Don't worry: it's probably something she ate.'

Qasim nodded his silent thanks. Miriam turned away, and with respectfully averted eyes he left.

Miriam rubbed Zaitoon's stomach with mustard oil and gave her an aspirin. She heated a brick and, wrapping it in a towel, coaxed the child to lie on it. Stroking her hair, she recited a verse from the Holy Quran known to ease pain. Exhausted, Zaitoon fell asleep. When she awoke it was evening and her pain had gone.

Next day she went to school.

The pain recurred; low in her belly and sometimes in her back. Qasim took her to the hakeem on his street and when that did not help, to the Parsi doctor near the station.

Miriam told Nikka, 'Tell Bhai Qasim not to bother with hakeems and doctors; they won't do her any good . . . She'll probably start menstruating in a few months!'

Qasim stopped taking Zaitoon to doctors and she went to Miriam instead. Miriam ministered to her and soothed her with tales about the valour of Hazrat Ali, the wisdom of Hazrat Omer, and the brutal tragedy of Hazrats Imam Hasan and Husain at Karbala.

She also told her that any day now she might find blood on her shalwar. She was to tell no one and come straight to her. 'We all bleed. It's to do with having babies and being a woman . . . of course you won't have babies — not till you're married — but you're growing up . . .' Zaitoon was too distracted by her garbled talk to understand anything.

❖

Zaitoon was eleven. They were playing during the morning break when a classmate excitedly pointing, said, 'Your shalwar is red. Are you hurt?'

Zaitoon raised her shirt and looked down. She sat in the dirt, wondering.

'Are you hurt?' her friend asked again.

Zaitoon shook her head, mystified.

'You'd better see Nurse.'

A clutch of sympathetic girls accompanied her to the sick room.

Nurse took her aside. She placed a wad of cotton between her legs and tied it in place with a strip of cloth. She told Zaitoon to wash her shalwar and go home. Zaitoon walked to Qila Gujjar Singh holding her legs apart, a little astonished that she felt no pain.

She went straight to Miriam.

'I told you it would happen, didn't I?'

Zaitoon gaped blankly. She wondered, considering the blood, if she should cry. Taking her cue from Miriam's calm face she decided not to. Miriam looked happy, almost triumphant – as if Zaitoon had accomplished a feat.

Slowly it dawned on Zaitoon that Miriam had told her something about bleeding and not to tell anyone. She looked bewildered and crestfallen. Miriam held her close and kissed her.

She asked questions and to some of them Miriam gave evasive answers. 'You'll bleed every month,' she said, and, 'Don't be silly child, boys don't menstruate; only women!' and, 'How do I know how babies come – do I have a baby? Allah alone knows! But enough; you'll understand everything when the time comes . . .'

She gave her strips of cloth, frayed with washing, and taught her the discipline of washing them for re-use.

'You are now a woman. Don't play with boys – and don't allow any man to touch you. This is why I wear a burkha . . .'

She decided it was time she had a chat with Qasim. She insisted Zaitoon stop going to school and he agreed.

From her Zaitoon learned to cook, sew, shop and keep her room tidy: and Miriam, who spent half her day visiting neighbours, took Zaitoon with her. Entering their dwellings was like stepping into gigantic wombs; the fecund, fetid world of mothers and babies.

The untidy row of buildings that crowded together along their street contained a claustrophobic warren of screened quarters. Rooms with windows open to the street were allotted to the men: the dim maze of inner rooms to the women – a domain given over to procreation, female odours and the interminable care of children. Smells of urine, stale food and cooking hung in the unventilated air, churning slowly, room to room, permeating wood, brick and mortar. Generations of babies had wet mattresses, sofas and rugs, spilled milk sherbets and food, and wiped hands on ragged curtains; and, just in case the smells should fade, armies of new-born infants went on arriving to ensure the odours were perpetuated.

Redolent of an easy-going hospitality, the benign squalor in the women's quarters inexorably drew Zaitoon, as it did all its inmates, into the mindless, velvet vortex of the womb.

Zaitoon loved best going to the Mullah's. His tall, malodorous hive, adjacent to the mosque, sheltered a large joint family and his two wives. His second wife was his elder brother's widow. Rather than leave them to the hazards of widowed and orphaned destitution, he had married her and adopted her three girls. The two wives got along no worse than the other brothers' and cousin-brothers' wives. The female sphere was enlivened by an undercurrent of intrigue and one-upmanship and the effort expended in the struggle was no less there than it was in the corridors of power and politics. Men, although favoured, were not specially welcome. Proud husbands, fathers and brothers, they were the providers. Zealous guardians of family honour and virtue, they sat, when in their homes, like pampered patriarchs, slightly aloof and ill at ease, withdrawing discreetly whenever the household was visited by unrelated women, which was often. As soon as Miriam, in her burkha, appeared before a screened door a signal passed and the few men who had strayed in left. If in going they happened to see her, they saluted, 'Salaam-alaikum, sister' and continued their unobtrusive passage. Once in a while Miriam might, to show her trust in and friendship for the family, address a few remarks, and the men invariably returned the courtesy by inquiring after Zaitoon's and her health.

While Miriam settled crosslegged on a charpoy, sometimes taking over a friend's knitting or embroidery as they gossiped, sometimes helping a girl cut her kurta or shalwar, Zaitoon played with the children. She ran to hide with the others and yelled and laughed when caught. Often she helped the little girls feed and wash their younger brothers and sisters. On summer evenings they spilled into the comparative cool of the alleys, little girls burdened with even younger children on their hips, the babies' necks wobbling dangerously as their carriers played hop-scotch or crouched over a game of bone knuckles. In the winter they rushed up the steep, spiral steps winding to earth-packed roof tops, the boys to fly kites and the girls to play at house-keeping with their dolls and miniature earthenware pots and ladles. In spring when the sky was dotted with paper kites, the young men and boys allowed the girls to hold the *manja*, kite string made abrasive with finely crushed glass. The girls, afraid of cutting their hands, handled the strings carefully and at the first hint of battle gingerly handed the *manja* back. Experts tackled attacking kites. The air was shrill with their thrilled 'aiii-boooows' when their kite managed to set another's adrift; and the 'Ooooos' when their own lost the battle were happy nevertheless. There was always a mad scramble to catch the strings of drifting, defeated kites and the triumph of hauling them in was shared by all. Nikka, too, loved flying kites and there were many good-natured fights between him and the experts on the Mullah's roof.

❖

In the Mullah's house the men wore beards. It was an austere household and even the little girls covered their heads at the warning click from the microphone which preceded the Mullah's call to prayer. The men gathered in the mosque and the women who had performed *wazoo*, that is, had washed themselves as specified in the Quran, spread their mats wherever they could. They knelt, facing Makkah, to pray, undisturbed by the children crawling, squalling, running and quarrelling around them. The rest of the women covered their heads and prayed silently for the duration of the call, carrying on with whatever they were doing, stirring the pot in the kitchen or breast-feeding the babies.

Once Zaitoon overheard a woman saying that a ten-year-old was pregnant. 'How can that be?' she asked incredulously. 'She's not married: it's impossible!'

'It has happened, strange as it might be.' Someone confirmed it, and Zaitoon believed it was a miracle. For a while after that she yearned for the miracle to strike her as well.

Besides the Mullah's, Miriam and Zaitoon regularly visited the butcher's, electrician's, haberdasher's, and hakeem's families. All of them were as well off if not better off than Miriam, considering the quantities of lamb cooked in their kitchens, and the presence of servants.

Chapter 7

One warm Friday morning towards the end of spring, just after prayers, Nikka was offered his first important political commission.

A grave, imposingly attired man, whom Nikka recognised, walked purposefully to his stall. He ordered one of Nikka's celebrated paans and discreetly indicated that he wished to speak to him alone.

Leaving the shop to Qasim, Nikka took the man home. Miriam, who spied the important-looking visitor through a curtain, cloistered herself in the kitchen.

Nikka seated his guest on the sofa. He locked all the doors.

'What is it, Chaudhry Sahib?' he inquired solicitously.

Chaudhry Sahib, his eyes demurely averted, sighed, 'Our illustrious benefactor needs help.' He spoke with a faraway look, as if talking to himself. 'Such a great man, such a prince. One would think he has no worries, no cares . . . a king among men – the flower of our nation!' Chaudhry Sahib's dingy cheeks sagged in melancholy folds beneath his squirrel-tail moustache. Nikka leaned forward full of concern. 'Can I help in any way?' he asked. Chaudhry Sahib was reputed to be one of the most trusted associates of the Mighty One.

'Our inspired leader has deadly enemies,' he complained. 'One particularly venomous snake has to be dealt with. Somehow he will have to be liquidated. Can you manage it?' He shot the question direct and swift. Removing his tall, gold-domed turban he carefully placed it beside him on the sofa.

As if in a dream Nikka studied the elaborate folds of the fine, starched muslin. Caught unawares, he felt as if a goat had butted him in the stomach.

Before he could recover, the man, suddenly hard and overpowering, said, 'You will be given protection, my friend. Our benefactor is a man of his word, loyal to his followers, a king. Not everyone gets a chance to oblige him. Of course, he knows nothing about this strategy, you understand?' Chaudhry Sahib made a suave gesture. 'Naturally, you will incur all sorts of expenses. I am in a position to reimburse you up to five thousand rupees.'

He waited, and at last, meeting his steely glance with numbed candour, Nikka said, 'I am greatly honoured, Chaudhry Sahib, that you should take me into your confidence. But, to be frank, I don't want to become a fugitive all my life, grovelling for protection. I'm a married man. I have built my business, my reputation, my prestige. I am the most respected man in Qila Gujjar Singh . . .'

'That is why I have come to you and none other!' interposed Chaudhry Sahib, springing to his feet with an agility surprising in so heavy a man. 'Only a man of your calibre can be trusted in this matter. As to your being a fugitive, rest assured. I give you my word as a Mussalman and the word of our Leader . . . my word is his word . . . You will live where you wish, and maintain your status and respect. Not a soul will dare touch one hair on your head. In fact, you will be favoured. If it is more money you wish, maybe I . . .'

'No, no Sir,' said Nikka hastily. 'That is not the point at all. Let me think on the matter. Could I see you tomorrow?'

'Yes, think by all means!' Chaudhry Sahib picked up his turban and lowered it on to his head with practised precision. 'If I were younger, I wouldn't bother you. By the way, we will give you a gun – and any information you need. We know the man's habits. That should help. You will have to study him yourself, of course. He is a wily landlord. Anyway, think it over. We will discuss details after you decide.'

60

That evening Nikka took Qasim into his confidence.

'What do you think?' he asked.

'Why, kill the man of course! What is there to think about? Haven't you killed before?'

To Qasim's amazement Nikka said, 'No, I haven't. I broke a man's neck once and he died. But that was in a wrestling bout, a professional accident. Why should I kill a man who has done me no harm?'

'Because you will receive five thousand rupees!' retorted Qasim. 'Why, there is nothing to it. I will help you, if you like. You know they won't let you down.'

Nikka's scruples dwindled. Eventually he was given a photograph of the victim, a thin, tall, predatory-looking man dressed in a heavy silken lungi and achkan-coat; bespectacled and balding.

The man lived in Lalamusa but visited Lahore frequently. Here he stayed at his brother's bungalow on Lawrence Road, the exclusive domain of the rich. There was no point in gunning him down at Lalamusa where he wielded influence. It would be almost impossible to escape his followers and bodyguards. The villages around Lalamusa were loyal to him, whereas at Lahore his support was limited. All Nikka had to do was kill him and get away undetected. Chaudhry Sahib had promised that Nikka would not be pursued or traced. 'That,' he said confidently, 'is my responsibility. If need be, we will provide a scapegoat.'

The man was expected in Lahore in two days.

Nikka scouted around. He discovered that their quarry was nervous about just the sort of event that was being plotted. Obviously, outside his domain he had numerous enemies and took every precaution. He arrived and departed in a convoy of three identical black Chevrolets with green-curtained windows. Nikka kept his eyes peeled for the predatory-looking bespectacled man, but each time the cars disgorged confusingly similar personages, swarthy men in extravagant floor-sweeping lungis, lordly achkan-coats and tall turbans. It was days before Nikka learnt to identify his charge.

Disguised alternately as a fruit vendor or a gardener tending the patch of municipal shrubbery in front of the bungalow, he kept his quarry under surveillance.

'He must be scared out of his piss,' Nikka thought when he saw him once change places with the driver and open doors for his laughing henchmen.

Past the gates, the cars curved away in screeching, dust-raising haste.

Qasim had requested leave for a week. One morning he strolled by the bungalow studying it carefully. The whitewashed house gleamed like a mottled bird through the foliage of peepul and eucalyptus trees. A vacant lot on the right of the bungalow held a petrol pump. The spot occasionally served as an open-air car-repair garage. On the other side, standing behind driveways carpeted with luxurious layers of red earth, was a row of palatial bungalows.

Qasim didn't repeat this reconnaissance. Nikka told him, 'You're too obviously a Pathan. Better stay away.'

In the early stages of their friendship Qasim had tried to explain why he disliked being called a Pathan; he was Kohistani. But Nikka said, 'Friend, all you hill people are Pathan to us.'

❖

On the fourth evening of their target's visit, Qasim, deprived of action and tense with private misgiving, decided to console himself with a trip to the brothel streets of Hira Mandi. He enjoyed the narrow lanes streaming with men, and the tall, rickety buildings leaning towards each other. He could stroll in these lanes for hours, his senses throbbing . . . the heady smell of perfume, the tinkle of payals on dancers' ankles, the chhum-chhum of feminine feet dancing behind closed doors excited him. He watched the gaudily dressed,

62

heavily made-up girls lolling on carpets, leaning on bolsters, chatting with each other and with their musicians. Doors flung wide open showed harmoniums and tables waiting to entertain.

The girls smiled their invitations boldly. Qasim knew he had only to step up with money and the doors would close about him, shutting off the street, intriguing passers-by with the sound of music and the tinkle of ankle-bells. He would be inside relishing their charms and dances.

Occasional seekh-kabab and sweetmeat stores brought a pleasing touch of reality to the incandescent mirage of the area. The men jostled each other, eyes peering behind arching doorways as they looked at the girls leaning from balconies. And from the structures cocooning the girls pulsated the melody of verses sung to the pleading, sweet, high pitch of a shehnai – and with the merry twirl of belled feet throbbing upon carpets.

The pungent whiff of urine from back-alleys blends with the spicy smells of Hira Mandi – of glossy green leaves, rose petals, and ochre marigolds. Silver braid hems blue dancing-skirts; tight satin folds of the chooridar pyjama reveal rounded calves; girls shimmer in silk, georgette, and tinsel-glittering satin. Qasim, like a sperm swimming, aglow with virility up to the tips of the hair on his knuckles, feels engulfed in this female street.

❖

A string of black, parked cars suddenly blocked Qasim's way. The pedestrians swirled, compressed through the narrowed passage. The gleaming chrome and black shapes looked vaguely familiar . . . and instantly Qasim was alert. He sensed that the celebrity Nikka was after was right here.

He looked around. It was still a bit early for business and many open doors displayed their merchandise.

He sauntered up to a girl leaning invitingly on a railing by the first car. Her long, thin plait of hair, fattened by a garland of jasmine, swung forward when she rocked her head and tilted her eyes in rhythm to hummed verses. Noticing Qasim's interest, she smiled encouragingly.

'Look at those big cars!' he said, eyeing them with exaggerated admiration. 'Where are the owners?'

The girl tossed her head, indicating the untidy tangle of arched windows and balconies overhead.

'With the grand Maharani Sahiba I suppose.'

Qasim laughed, feigning a careless, lewd interest.

'Come inside,' she invited him.

'Maharani Sahiba must be quite something,' he said, moving so close he almost touched her. 'What's her real name?'

'Shahnaz. But she's too grand for the likes of you,' she teased him good-naturedly.

Another girl and two musicians were looking at him with curiosity. The girl inside smiled. She was prettier.

'Why don't you come in?'

'I will . . . very soon,' said Qasim. He spread his arms helplessly, 'I'll be back on pay day.'

'Don't forget. You'll like us. She dances,' she said, pointing her thumb at the girl inside, 'I sing.'

'I will definitely come,' mumbled Qasim apologetically, but the girl was already looking past him.

❖

He scouted the congested place for an access to Shahnaz's upstairs apartment. He had no plan, but the shock of the target's presence galvanised him. Discovering what appeared to be an entrance, he groped his way along a narrow passage into the dank guts of the building.

In a labyrinth of dingy tunnels, he kept looking for stairs. Stale air, poisoned by the stench of ammonia, frying onions, mustard oil and sweat suffocated him. He stumbled over a

64

child defecating, and the discordant sound of music filtering through the walls was pierced by a distant wail. He groped for balance and his hands along the wall slid into grime. He looked into squalid rooms, nauseated by the reek of poverty and decay; the syphilitic reverse side of the tinsel. Qasim grew frantic. He ran blindly through the red betel-juice-stained corridors, brushing at cobwebs that clung to his skin.

The thoroughfare issued into a slushy, unpaved gully. He had penetrated right through the building and the air he now breathed beneath the starry sky felt fresh as a pine-laden breeze.

An old man sat on a charpoy vacantly puffing a hookah. A little further up, in the middle of the lane, was a structure of bamboo poles enclosed by scraps of jute sacking. Light filtered through a circle of men peering at the centre. The grating, irregular chhum of payal-bells coming from it intrigued Qasim and he walked up to join the spectators. A man shifted, making room for him. The crude sack fence came up to Qasim's chest. A woman, bells tied to one twisted ankle, was hobbling around in the small enclosure. Her short, thick-waisted body jerked grotesquely. Now and again, a man standing with her in the enclosure shouted, 'Naach, pagli!' – dance, mad-woman – and jabbed her with a cane. At this she would raise her arms and twist her wrists in a grim caricature of dance movements. Her jaw hung slack in an expressionless face, and sick yellow eyeballs stared unseeing. Qasim was horrified. Would any of these men sleep with her, he wondered? This was nothing human. It was a sick excrescence. Did the pimp think that by exercising the excrescence he could stir sensuality? The woman continued her monotonous, mechanical spasms, one hip jerking higher, jaws dribbling spittle. There was laughter, and Qasim realised they were mocking her. A man, obscenely shaking his body, called to her as to a monkey. A couple of men laughed, enjoying the sport. 'Don't touch her,' the man from inside warned when an arm reached across the fence.

A spectator threw a coin into the enclosure. It lay half-hidden in the dust at her feet. Qasim threw an eight-anna bit and silently withdrew.

He wanted to hasten to the glittering side of the building, back to the tinsel-dusted girls and the pink, spicy haze.

Loath to re-enter the inner hallways he walked until he came to a passage between the building and the next block. It was a mere gash, a slice of dark open to the sky, a channel for the sewage drain that flowed through it.

Walking astride the drain to keep from touching the walls, Qasim was more than halfway across when a slit of light fell across the drain. It came from a dimly-lit entrance. Qasim glanced casually through the open door. He hesitated a moment and then stepped inside.

A dust-coated bulb barely lit the stone parapet fencing the steps. This side-entrance, he realised, led upstairs. Feeling his way through the gloom, Qasim carefully began to climb.

'Just where do you think you're going?'

'Upstairs,' replied Qasim freezing in surprise. Only then did he notice two men sprawled on the landing at the top. They wore white lungis and Qasim could just make out the deeper shadow of achkan-coats beneath their turbans. He was glad of the murky light that masked his face. Recovering his composure almost immediately, and acting the part of a harmless buffoon, he set up a plaintive wail, 'I want to see my Shahnaz.'

One of the guards stood up. 'My masters are in there,' he snarled. 'Now scram.'

Snatches of laughter and the shrill voice of a singing girl came from behind the closed doors. 'The bastard is having a good time,' thought Qasim.

'Why can't I go in? Your masters are not the only men around, you know,' he whined in the half-scared, half-defiant manner of a garrulous dimwit.

One of the men climbed down and, pushing Qasim

66

roughly, threatened, 'Will you go – or do I have to throw you out?'

Feigning terror, Qasim stumbled backwards. 'All right, all right . . . I'm going,' he mumbled. His heart thudded at his bold histrionics.

The man sniggered. 'Sneak up some other night, you love-sick lout. Our masters won't leave till two.'

A riotous burst of laughter came through the closed doors. Qasim wondered if the men inside were drunk.

'Are those whoring pigs drinking sharab?' he called insultingly.

There was an angry shuffle. Qasim stumbled down the steps and through the vestibule and safely reached the anonymous jostling main street that flowed between the dancing girls.

'Yes, the bastards drink alcohol!' he thought, his puritanical feelings on edge. 'What Muslims!'

Scandalised and humiliated, Qasim grew venomous.

'I'll get them tonight. Damn that Nikka. Why doesn't he do his job? I'll get them,' he vowed.

❖

Qasim walked rapidly to Lawrence Road. The luxurious, moonlit neighbourhood was hushed in sleep. The faint rustle of a breeze in the peepul and eucalyptus trees, the mellow midnight chimes of a clock, the protective thump of a watchman's lathi, all hummed a lullaby of the district's security.

Qasim slipped into the garage plot adjoining the bungalow and in a crouch he slid along the wall, startling Nikka by his sudden appearance.

'What is it?' Nikka gasped.

'Relax. The sparrow won't come to roost till two o'clock. He's at Hira Mandi!'

Qasim told of his encounter with their target's henchmen. Nikka was furious.

'You fool!' he hissed. 'You're sure to have my throat cut. What if they traced you?'

'I tell you it was too dark to see my own shadow. And what if they did see me? Why would they connect me with the assassination?'

'Well, thanks,' said Nikka, 'but do go away now.'

Qasim obstinately settled on his haunches, his back to the wall. 'I'm staying.'

Nikka knelt before him. 'Qasim, for God's sake, go! I can handle this better by myself.'

Qasim was hurt, but at last he nodded and withdrew.

⋰⋱

He awoke late the next morning. Zaitoon had left the room so quietly he did not know she had gone. He slipped a shirt over his shalwar and hurried down.

Nikka sat cross-legged and clear-eyed. Customers were collecting their stock of cigarettes and paan for the day. The transistor, perched on the cash-box to Nikka's right, was blaring out the news. Qasim tried to catch his friend's eye, but handing change to a customer Nikka gave no sign of either fatigue or relief.

Suddenly the radio announced, 'Sardar Ghulam Ali Hussain, landlord and politician, was assassinated this morning. The Governor has sent a message of condolence. The funeral will start from 217-A Lawrence Road at 11.00 a.m. The police . . .'

Nikka turned off the radio. Offering Qasim a small, green bundle he said, 'Here, have a paan.'

Qasim popped the paan into his mouth, smiled, touched his forehead in salutation, and sauntered on.

Chapter 8

Nikka and Qasim spent the next afternoon sprucing up. Sleekly oiled and extravagantly perfumed, they rode by taxi to Hira Mandi.

Qasim fidgeted uneasily. He peered at himself in the rear-view mirror of the taxi and didn't care for what he saw. 'I look what I am — an illiterate coolie!' he thought. Scrutinising his broad, large-nosed face, his uneasiness mounted to terror. Finally voicing his misgivings, he said, 'I don't think Shahnaz will care much for the likes of us. Let's go to some less fancy girls.'

Nikka roared with laughter. 'Good God, man! Are you afraid of a dancing girl? Don't worry, she'll think you are a grand fellow. This,' he said, thumping his bulging pockets, 'makes us as good as anyone. You just do as I do.'

Qasim fondled the crisp bundle of notes Nikka had shoved into his pockets.

'Don't you want to save any of it? And do I have to give all this to the girls?'

'Friend, that's chicken feed. I've got more than twice that much in my pockets. She's not one of your cheap floozies who flash their teeth from the balcony. Stop fretting.'

They paid the taxi at the entrance to the narrower Mandi lanes and walked towards the main street.

'Hold on to your money. It's not for pickpockets.' Nikka, at least, was alert. Walking leisurely, often he stopped to ogle, bandying coarse pleasantries with the air of a veteran. Qasim, by his side, peered at the girls with his customary, moony admiration. Again he was whisked away into a world of sensuality. A benign smile settled hypnotically on his features. Had he died at that moment, that smile would have stayed.

He had a twinge of conscience when they passed the girl he had promised to visit on pay day. She, rocking her jasmine-plaited hair over the balcony, didn't even see him. 'Next time,' he vowed to himself, relieved, and he looked back in the hope that she might show some sign of recognition or disappointment. But the plait of hair went on swinging, and she did not turn towards him.

A fat, sweat-drenched man greeted Nikka. 'Pehelwanjee, I've been waiting for you,' he cried. Embracing Nikka and Qasim in turn, he led them through a small doorway. They mounted the narrow steps, and Qasim whispered, 'Ah! The front entrance!'

Nikka, with a deft backward kick of his heel, warned Qasim to be discreet.

The man ushered them into an oblong, soft-carpeted room that glowed with a garish coat of pink oil paint. A middle-aged woman sat on the floor near some musical instruments, an open silver paan-box spread on her voluminous lap. Chewing on her paan she smiled up at them through red, catechu-stained teeth.

'Won't you sit down?' she invited them, pointing a fat, bangle-jingling arm towards the cushions.

Nikka and Qasim sank comfortably into the downy satin bolsters. It was a small room but it looked spacious. Besides the carpets, pink drapes, and musical instruments, there was no clutter. The woman – she called herself Shahnaz's mother – put the betel-nut box aside and, leaning heavily on the harmonium, levered herself upright. 'Can I get my lords some fresh paan? Yes? Excuse me a moment,' she smiled, and left.

'She's the Madam,' Nikka whispered, nudging Qasim. 'Must've been quite something in her youth! She still retains the gracious manners of a trained courtesan, doesn't she?'

70

Qasim, who knew even less about courtesans than he did about kings, nodded sheepishly. Nikka informed him:

'To entertain, a courtesan knows how to elicit laughter. "That is our destiny," a nautch-girl once told me. "We automatically smile in the presence of men. We are taught to from childhood. I'd never allow myself to be moody before a man." '

The Madam waddled up and sat beside them. As if in league with Nikka, to prove the truth of his pronouncements, she channelled the conversation along flippant, laughter-laden lines. Ordering tea, calling for silver trays heavy with dried fruit, almonds and sweets, she put them completely at ease.

All at once she cupped her ears, intent on listening.

'It's them,' she announced, fluttering her lids. The gesture hardly became her age, yet she carried it off with assurance. 'I think we can begin now. The other guests have arrived.'

Nikka sat up. 'I thought we were to be the only ones.'

'It's just an old American: poor fellow. He is so besotted by my Shahnaz! Poor old fool . . .' she added, to appease Nikka.

'I'll reveal a secret,' she confided, leaning forward. 'Shahnaz is like a peacock. The more admirers, the better she dances!'

Two men entered through the curtains and the Madam greeted them effusively. Leading the stringy, middle-aged American by the arm, she made a place for him amidst the cushions. There was no hiding her pride. The foreigner was her prize catch. He was accompanied by a dapper Pakistani.

The newcomers settled with an air of familiarity that excluded Nikka and Qasim. They whispered occasionally in monosyllables but for the greater part maintained a disdainful silence. Nikka squirmed on the cushions. He felt slighted. After a few loud remarks addressed to the uncomprehending Qasim, he subsided into a scowling silence.

The Madam bustled about trying to ease the strain. Each

71

guest was given some Scotch, and a fragrant, elaborately carved hookah was passed around. Two musicians appeared from the recesses. The drummer, a plump, effeminate man – a rim of long hair fringing his bald head – tapped the edge of his drums with a tiny mallet. The harmonium player, a younger man with smallpox marks, played a few careless notes on his instrument and sat back.

'Let me see if Shahnaz is ready. She shouldn't keep such distinguished guests waiting.' Smiling apologetically, the Madam vanished.

The tabalchi snuggled his pair of drums closer and slapped the vibrant skin until his palms found a clear, resonant beat. The harmonium player nodded his long-haired head in approval.

Qasim sipped his Scotch and reclined luxuriously in the pink-and-golden haze. The Scotch smoothed the edge of his anticipation and he grew oblivious to Nikka's fidgeting.

The American and his companion kept talking in English and Nikka's resentment of their presence deepened at the alien tongue. Opening his mouth cavernously, he yawned with a yowl reminiscent of jackals baying in the wilderness. Aware of the attention focused on him, he thumped Qasim drowsily and demanded, 'When does our dancing bulbul appear? I am getting fed up with these American crows cawing in my ears.'

Glancing at the strangers, he caught a satisfying flare of their resentment.

Measured, bell-tinkling steps drew near. Parting the curtains, the girl continued with the same balanced tread until she stood before the guests. She knelt, bowing her head and smiling between salaaming fingers. Her eyes, now bold, now shy – black irises shifting in languorous slits – welcomed each in turn. She stood up and walked tall towards the musicians. A thick, black plait of hair bounced on her buttocks. Folding her legs to one side, she settled by the players. She consulted them and began with a popular film song.

Shahnaz's voice was low-pitched and throaty, her expression earnest yet volatile. The whites of her elongated eyes appeared to be blue-white between heavy, black lashes. The nose, slender and smooth, flared delicately. The left nostril supported a gold nose-ring that nestled daintily on curling lips. Every now and again, she would cup her palms in an outstretched, beseeching gesture in character with the words of the song and touch the tips of her ear-lobes in a charming avowal of virtue.

Oh, let me stay in purdah – don't lift my veil.
If my purdah is removed . . . my mystery is betrayed.
    Allah . . . forbid! Allah . . . forbid!
My veil has ten thousand eyes.
– Yet you cannot see into mine.
But if you raise my veil even a bit –
Beware! you'll burn.
So . . . let me stay in purdah – don't lift my veil.
    Allah – meri Toba! Allah – meri Toba!
Oh God – who can have made me? –
Whoever it is – even he doesn't know me . . .
Man worships me – Angels have bowed their heads . . .
If my purdah is removed – my mystery is betrayed.
    Allah forbid! – Allaaaah – forbid!
    Allah forbid! – Allaaaah – forbid!

Next she sang a few romantic ghazals by Iqbal and Faiz.
The traditional rhythm of the famous verses pulsated in hypnotic monotony to the tempo of the tablas. The tabalchi's head rocked in rhythm, his oily fringe flaring to the beat. The musicians watched the singer incessantly. At the climax of a particularly well-worded stanza, they looked at each other in wonder. 'Ahha – Ahha' they groaned, rolling their eyes in appreciation. The sensual rhythm, the wistful delicacy of the girl, the swaying musicians, all wove a spell. Infected by the atmosphere the guests, too, moaned

'Ahha, Ahha, great! great!' in the age-old manner of ecstatic orientals.

The suave Pakistani held out a ten rupee note as a more tangible sign of his appreciation. The girl stood up and without discontinuing her song, collected the money. The American held a note between his teeth and kissed Shahnaz's fingers as she plucked it. Qasim stuck a note on his turban and blushed unbearably when Nikka shouted, 'Tweak his hair! Pinch his cheeks!'

One, five, and ten rupee notes peeped out of hip pockets and shirt fronts. Nikka held a ten rupee note between his crossed thighs and Shahnaz knelt prettily amongst the men, until she could sing no more. Sitting there, laughing, teasing, she charmed more and more money off them. The chiffon chaddar with its silver border framing her face slipped from her head and lay back. The Madam joined the circle. Their conversation in subtle, expressive Urdu, was rich with nuance; intimate as moist tongues mingling. Laughter, Scotch and the hookah caused an inane merriment in which all animosity, all cares, were forgotten.

After a while, adjusting her bells, Shahnaz began to dance. The tablas lashed the air with a savage, resounding beat, commanding the dancer's precise movements.

'Tha, tha, taka-tha! Ta dhin, dhin, na! Taka tha! tha! tha!' The girl's sinuous arms obeyed the beat, her fingers now fanning out in imitation of the fronds of a palm, now undulating like ripples on water. The bells round her ankles jingled to the stamp of her feet, dictating the sedate movement of her neck and eyes. 'Tak-a-tha, Tak-a-tha'. Slowly she faces away beating one toe on the carpet. The plait of hair sways severely – side to side. Tablas explode faster. Faster the rhythm of the harmonium: and twirling on flying toes, she slips with relish into the less classic, more becoming dance of the dancing girls – lips smiling, eyes roguish, silver toe-rings twinkling on hennaed feet. A shimmer of payals swirls beneath the long tight sweep of golden churidar

74

pyjamas – and under the flaring skirt, the shape of each thigh flashing. The uplifting of silk-cupped breasts, the blue-black electricity of plaited hair, the sparkle of silver fringes and silver ornaments on a writhing, sinuous body, all induce a mystic gyration. She dances on the money beneath her feet and through the money being pitched feverishly at her. In a blur she sees the Pehelwan hold up a note. 'Why doesn't he throw it?' she wonders, until she notices its value. Salaaming, smiling, she withdraws with it, dancing.

Nikka held up another hundred rupee note and then tossed a wad of ten rupee notes at the retreating dancer. At that, Qasim surfaced from his lascivious stupor. He scrutinised Nikka's profile in alarm.

The girl spun closer. Kneeling, she touched the money to her forehead. She resumed her dance, her lissome body suggestive, her eyes luminous slits flashing under heavy lashes.

Qasim pressed against Nikka. 'Enough! Stop it now,' he hissed. 'What the hell are you doing?'

'I know what I'm doing! Something special for my simple Pathan friend.'

Nikka was up and before Qasim could restrain him, he staggered across the small room. His lumbering presence shattered the scintillating atmosphere and the air grew tense. The man who had received them in the street materialised from nowhere and stood at the entrance, looking in. His sweat-drenched shirt outlined the menace of his muscles. Qasim blanched. He missed the reassuring pressure of his pistol against his thigh and wished he hadn't left it behind. He knew these people were not to be trifled with. Nikka would be no match for these Mandi pimps.

They thought the Pehelwan, intoxicated with Scotch, was about to rough up the girl. Shahnaz, her face pale, backed cautiously, but Nikka veered from his course. He moved towards the Madam.

Instantly she stopped chewing on her paan. Her puffy

features congealed into a haughty mask. She appeared to be bracing herself for the stock remark: 'Shahnaz is a dancing girl, not a prostitute. We are a respectable house!'

She tilted a defiant ear when Nikka sat down by her.

Qasim prayed that his friend would accept the inevitable rejection amiably.

Nikka whispered something, and as though in answer to Qasim's prayer a smile softened the Madam's features. She laid an affectionate arm on the pehelwan's shoulder and leaned closer. Nikka crushed some money into her enveloping palms. She nodded, as if giving in with great reluctance – indulging a difficult favour. Nikka strode across the room and settled amidst the cushions with a grand mysterious smile.

'What's up?' whispered Qasim.

'You'll see. Just sit back and watch.'

The American wiped his forehead with a damp handkerchief. 'I thought those bastards were going to louse up the show.' His voice was limp with relief. He sucked in a long draught of Scotch and his unperturbed companion nodded agreement.

Shahnaz and the Madam joined the circle, and their laughter, lacing the room with merriment, instantly restored a sense of delicate abandon. The American often caught Shahnaz's flitting hands, kissing her fingers, his eyes tremulous and pleading.

Despite the levity, the presence of the dancing girl, the Madam, and the nature of the establishment, a certain over-gallant, flowery decorum was maintained.

❖

Nikka rubbed his palms together and looked around with the air of a Moghul conqueror about to relish the spoils of his victory. The musicians were ready and once again the measured chhum of the dancer's tread approached. She continued through the curtains as before and bowed before the four men, salaaming Nikka for almost a full minute. The tabalchi set up a slow sharp beat. His fingers flew across the taller drum vibrating the background for the hollow, almost metallic 'tha! tha! tak-a-tha!' of the wider, shorter tabla. The dancer flexed her knees in the classic pose of the Kathakali dance, thighs sloped sideways. She lifted her bent knees, stamping the floor in a heavy, rocking tread. The thick band of bells round her ankles struck in time to the staid whip of the tabla. She turned, thighs wide, and then, facing the men, danced to a quickening tempo; now straightening, now spreading her thighs open. Her arms rippled and swayed, controlling the fanning, tapering fingers.

Keeping to the stylised classic movements, she removed her chiffon chaddar and flung it floating to the floor. Next she removed the black velvet waistcoat that edged the swell of her breasts.

At last the nature of Nikka's mission to the Madam dawned on Qasim. The American and his companion cast inquiring glances. 'How far will she go?' Nikka, his eyes fixed on the girl, encouraged, 'Ahha, Ahha, Great! Great!' and the men surmised she would go pretty far.

Leaning forward, Qasim gawked at each movement, astonishment wreathing his face. Four pairs of protruding eyes locked on the girl's body.

❖❖

The dancer's movements still follow the classic beat, but they grow more sinuous. Clothes lie scattered at her small, bejewelled feet. The body barely reveals its ribs, its spine — it is draped in colour. Her flushed skin glows like molten, pliant copper, flaming in the pink haze that highlights the voluptuous flow of long dark thighs and the soft swell of perfect breasts lightly swaying. Shadows accentuate the incurving areas, the opulent hollows. While the feet move, her arms rise above her head stretching the body in all its marvellous perfection. No melody. Only the staccato resonance of the drums and the echoing chhum of bells on her ankles. Bending, a soft breast touching one knee, she removes one payal, then the other. Now she is free of the tyrannical bells. Her feet twinkle, she sways unrestrained, while the black reptilian plait of her hair flays her body. She curves her back until the plait rests on the floor. She is bent back like a bow, her nipples smooth and firm as carved mahogany, gazing at the ceiling.

It is past midnight and Nikka and Qasim have spent over six hours with the dancer. Qasim's lids feel unnaturally heavy. His head throbs, racked alternately by waves of blinding desire and the need of sleep. He notices the other men reclining heavily on the cushions, resting their heads against the wall. Their puffy faces are battling a deep drowsiness. 'The bastards,' he thinks. 'They have doctored our last drink!'

Shahnaz is swaying, undoing slowly her thick plait of hair. Her fingers run down to the tip of each strand, keeping apart the lengthening coils. All undone, the hair falls in three skeins covering one entire side of her body. A deft untangling flick of her head and the heavy silken hair cascades down behind her. The final nudity. Wild, serene, natural as a forest tree at sunset.

Shahnaz stands still. Raising her arms she sways against the long jet mane of hair, throwing her head this way and that until hair froths around her like thick, inky dust.

When her dance resumes it becomes erotic, her movements sensual and brazen. She teases wantonly, secure in the knowledge of her inaccessibility.

Poor Nikka and Qasim. Never having possessed riches, they know not the savour of so rich a toy. Theirs is a world of villages and mountains; of brash wrestlers, privations and primary appetites.

The evening's entertainment merely titillated the American

78

and his companion, but in Nikka and Qasim it unleashed a primordial frenzy, a ferocious tangle of desires. 'God! These bastards put something in our drinks . . . These bastards,' Nikka squirmed, gurgling the words.

They might easily have fallen on the girl, tearing, ripping, and dismembering her to satisfy their anguish.

As it was, Shahnaz backed to the centre of the room. She jerked her head forward and her hair splashed on to the floor when she knelt in a final curtsey. She remained bowed. Then, touching her dainty fingers to her forehead, she salaamed several times and – gathering her payals and her scattered clothing – she disappeared through the curtains.

The musicians quietly slipped cloth covers over their instruments and stepped into their moccasins. The rosy haze in the room brightened into a yellow glare. Nikka groped for Qasim. He meant to say, 'Come on, the show is over,' but he uttered only inarticulate croaks.

His head lolling back, Qasim stared with glazed eyes.

'Let's get home,' thought Nikka, struggling monumentally to sit up.

The Madam loomed over them with a pile of blankets. 'I think you'd better stay the night.'

The American and his friend lay slumped, their heads at uncomfortable angles on the cushions. Qasim's mouth hung open in sleep. Nikka closed his heavy lids, gratefully surrendering to the Madam's care. The musicians helped her straighten the limbs of her charges. They covered them with blankets.

At about five o'clock the next morning the groggy men were propelled into two taxis. The fat pimp saw them off, his singlet wet with perspiration even at that hour. The cars wound their way, one behind the other, through the tawdry, now deserted alleys of the sleeping Mandi.

That day, Miriam, who took everything in her stride, quietly assumed charge of Zaitoon.

The girl, stricken by terror, flung herself at Miriam

screaming, 'Oh, my Abba doesn't awaken. He is dead!'

Miriam burst into laughter. Hugging the child to her bosom, she soothed her. She took Zaitoon to the room where Nikka lay sprawled on a charpoy. 'See?' she chuckled, prodding her inert husband. 'See how he sleeps? They are both tired. Soon your father will awaken, dangle you on his lap, and tickle you like this . . .' Laughing, she tickled Zaitoon, and all fears were forgotten.

❖

Qasim and Nikka slept through the day. In the evening, over the tea steaming from his saucer, Qasim asked, 'Tell me, how much did you spend in all?'

'About two thousand . . .'

'Two thousand rupees!' exclaimed Qasim incredulously.

'Well, at least now we know how the rich blow their loot!' Qasim nodded solemnly.

Chapter 9

Nikka came to look forward to assignments that required his particular skills. Patronised by the powerful political group that sought his services, he began to enjoy certain liberties. He was no longer an ordinary citizen.

From the recesses of the underworld right through to the patrolling policemen, everyone knew that Nikka wielded influence. His promises, his opinions, carried weight. Word of his ability to help extended to Qasim. For a fee he interceded with Nikka specially on behalf of tribal petitioners.

❖

The following summer, the Leader summoned Nikka into his august presence. 'Tell him to bring along the Pathan as well.'

The interview was discreet. Qasim and Nikka were led through a thickly carpeted corridor, opulent with the gleam of copper and carved mahogany, into a luxurious room. A tall, dark man with sleekly oiled moustaches sat behind a desk. They knew he held most of the power in the land. His blood-shot, heavy-lidded eyes appeared to measure them in the subdued light. He extended his hand. Qasim and Nikka padded nervously through the air-conditioned space scented by tuber-roses and expensive cigars. Stiff with awe, Qasim stood, studying the pattern in the Persian carpet.

With an ease born of generations of gracious living, the leader motioned them to a corner of the study darkened by black leather upholstery. Qasim, who had never sat on anything so soft, sank, he thought, into a cloud.

Nikka stammered ingratiatingly, 'Yes, my lord, yes, my lord,' to everything the man said, and Qasim, who had never seen him so obsequious, blushed for the two of them.

After what seemed an eternity (but was not more than five minutes in fact) the mighty one supplied the cue for their departure. With a humility that won their hearts, he touched his fingers to his forehead and said, 'We are deeply indebted to your loyalty and services. Our cause is just, and you are worthy. God be with you.' Fixing Nikka with grateful eyes, he said, 'I wanted to thank you myself.'

Nikka flushed.

'My lord, it is my privilege and honour to serve you always.'

An arm across each of their shoulders, the mighty one led them to the door. 'My car will take you home. God be with you.' He embraced each in turn, 'And don't forget. My house and my heart are always open to my friends.'

Flattered, they walked to the waiting car. Nikka was a rooster trying to smooth his puffed feathers. He looked with disdain at the shoddy crowds streaming past the tinted glass of the air-conditioned Cadillac. 'I wish the whole of Qila Gujjar Singh were gathered to see us arrive in this,' he whispered.

The chassis swayed in its deep suspension springs. It wafted them over the potholes with the airy ripple of a yacht. By the time they reached Qila Gujjar Singh, Nikka felt he was tottering on a cushion eleven feet high.

❖

Soon followed the fall from grace.

In his new self-importance, Nikka turned insufferably arrogant. To quote a Punjabi proverb, he would not let a fly alight on his nose.

He became a bully. He described graphically to those he

82

wanted to intimidate what he would do to their balls and the chastity of their women. He bought a shop next to his for much less than the going price and expanded his business to include a provision store. He sat solidly on his charpoy outside and lorded it over the alley.

'O, ay, you one-eyed jinx, if I see you bring your solitary eye into our district again, I'll thrash you,' Nikka threatened once, and sure enough, when he noticed the half-blind man a month later, he chased and thrashed him.

He forced the milkman to take a circuitous route because the jangle of cans suddenly jarred his delicate senses.

He was feared and even the police could not control him. Their reports, though, reached the man in the scented, luxurious room. At first he regarded his protégé's antics with indulgence. 'Leave him alone – the man means no harm.' But the complaints grew urgent, and Nikka's high-handed conduct ceased to please. The weary black brows atop the blood-shot eyes puckered. 'If that's the case, let's put him right. To be sure, he has his uses, but rough him up a little. Show him his place . . .'

∴

His masseur gossiping next to him, Nikka sat upon his sagging charpoy, blocking the pavement. He was in a foul mood. Somehow he sensed trouble. The evening traffic rushed by in a tangle of cycles, tongas, bullock-carts and trucks, squashing the dung on the wide road. Nikka glared at the traffic, his shifting eyes intent on mischief.

In one leap, suddenly he stood plumb in the path of a galloping horse and cart. Trucks came to a screeching stop, tongas reined in, cyclists wobbled to one side, and men on the pavement shifted to the edge. The cart driver yelled, rising and trying to draw his stampeding animal to a halt.

Mouth foaming, head high, the horse towered above Nikka who firmly seized the bridle. The animal's

83

momentum staggered him, but not letting go, he slipped to one side. With a palm over the scraping wooden wheel and wrenching at the bit, he stopped the beast.

The cart driver glared at Nikka in disbelief;

'What's wrong with you, you crazy fool! You want to die?'

Nikka held the reins just above the horse's heaving neck.

'Come on. Get down,' he commanded.

'Why?'

'Because I'll castrate you for driving recklessly in our district.' Nikka was fiendishly calm.

The driver glanced around into a swarm of inquisitive faces. He raised his whip and struck the horse and Nikka in a panic to charge through. The crowd pushed apart slightly. Cursing furiously, Nikka pulled the man from the cart and struck him.

There was a surprised rustle. Shouts of 'Police! Police!' rose hysterically.

Qasim, on his way to work, looked over the heads in amazement. Policemen came running with sticks. Something was amiss. They never interfered in Nikka's brawls. He shouted, 'Watch out, Nikkayooooo! The police are here!'

Nikka, busy with his work, heard Qasim dimly. 'So what?' he thought. The battered man was crying piteously. And then, Nikka was wrenched away.

Whirling in a hot rage, he looked in disbelief at the handcuffs clamped on his wrists. The swelling crowd pressed forward.

'Why, what's this? A joke?' asked Nikka.

'You're under arrest for assault,' said a policeman he had never seen before. The man pulled him along by a chain while another pushed him into a few bewildered steps forward.

Stung into a sudden realisation of his position by this indignity, Nikka roared, 'You pimps. You bloody swine.

Don't you know who I am? I am Nikka Pehelwan! Nikka Pehelwan of Qila Gujjar Singh! How dare you . . .'

Ignoring the outburst, the policemen dragged him off the road.

'Where is the S.S.P. Sahib, you bastards, where is my friend?' he screeched, trying to intimidate the policemen by his acquaintance with the Senior Superintendent of Police.

An Inspector, distinguished by a trim, belted coat, stepped forward.

'Come on, Nikka, don't throw a tantrum. No one's going to help you. At least keep your dignity.'

Nikka glared at him. 'Why you unfaithful dog! Don't you know whose protection I command? Ask the S.S.P. Sahib . . . he'll tell you.'

'We're arresting you on the Superintendent's orders. Now shut up!'

'The pig's penis! I'll have him hanged – all of you,' Nikka roared, slashing about blindly with his manacles.

Screaming threats, delighting the children and the crowd with his colourful invective, he was thrust into a van with wire mesh at the windows and was driven away.

❖

Towards the end of his four-month prison sentence, he requested an audience with the Senior Superintendent of Police. Impressed by reports of Nikka's exemplary behaviour and considering it politic, the officer acceded to the pehelwan's wish.

The prison square bustled in preparation for the Superintendent's arrival. Nikka, lined up with the prisoners, stood at the far end of the square. Two whistles shrilled, and a bell drove the prison officials into a further frenzy of pushing the prisoners into line.

The Superintendent strode into the square. Smiling complacently, he walked in a cloud of dust caused by the boots of five prison officials chaperoning him.

He strode pompously, hands and baton behind his back. Scrutinising the prisoners, shooting random queries, he finally stood before Nikka.

'I understand you wished to see me. Well, what is it, you badmash?'

Nikka studied the Superintendent, his eyes inscrutable.

'My lord, I am a lowly man. I have a request only your grace has power to bestow . . . '

'Yes?'

'I'm afraid, Sir, that you may misunderstand me . . . ' Nikka shuffled his feet. A swift glance up and he was satisfied by the impression he had made.

Flattered by the deferential behaviour of this notoriously arrogant bully, the Superintendent's tone became kinder.

'Go on, man, let's hear what you have to say.'

'My nights in prison, as you know, Sir, are lonely . . .' Nikka appeared to hesitate. 'But I'm afraid you may take me amiss . . . '

The Superintendent, scenting mischief, rasped, 'You are wasting my time, pehelwan!' He turned to walk away.

'Just a moment, my lord,' Nikka's voice, of a sudden bold, boomed through the square. 'Oh, share my lovelorn prison bed with me. My nights here are so lonely.'

Spontaneous guffaws exploded all over the square.

'Why, you bastard! You shameless swine . . .' The dignitary spluttered, his nostrils flaring. Crazed with fury, he struck Nikka with his baton, and straining mightily for dignity he snarled: 'Fifteen lashes! Give him fifteen lashes!'

Nikka was soundly thrashed and his tenure extended by two months. He bore the punishment with gloating fortitude.

The incident, inflated gloriously, made him an instant legend. It was related with gusto in sophisticated drawing-rooms, inside the suffocating tangle of the walled city, in

Rawalpindi and in Karachi – and when he completed his sentence, Qila Gujjar Singh welcomed back its hero with a warm heart and open arms.

Nikka emerged from prison, his equilibrium recovered. His stay there, he knew, had been a mild reprimand, to teach him his bounds. Soon, political commissions were again entrusted to him, and his influence was fully restored.

Chapter 10

Marriages were the high points in the life of the women. As she grew older Zaitoon became an eager participant in the activity centred around them.

Wedding preparations dragged on for months and the attendant ceremonies for days, and sometimes even weeks. The twilight interiors of the women's quarters flashed gold and silver braid, orange, turquoise and scarlet satins, as women cut cloth, sewed and embroidered to make the twenty, fifty or hundred sets of clothes for the bride's dower. Rose and jasmine itars were tested and indulgently daubed on children. The perfume mingled with the domestic smells. Servants, squatting on floors to feed children, appreciatively eyed the rich colours of fabrics and sets of gold jewellery. The squatting maids moved like indolent crabs, on their haunches, always smiling, happy to indulge the whims of a child if pressed, or the demands of their easy-going mistresses, whose legs or shoulders they were forever massaging.

A month before the wedding the dholaks arrived; sausage-shaped wooden drums with taut skins on either end. Young girls clustered about them, sitting cross-legged, singing ribald ditties, mocking the groom, insulting absent mothers-in-law and sisters-in-law, teasing the bride, and taking turns to beat out the rhythm with both hands. The singing went on late into the night. Towards evening the girls got up, singly or in groups, to dance. Zaitoon was in constant demand and obliged with energetic dances copied from Punjabi films. Jumping and gyrating, making eyes and winking, shaking her shoulders to set her adolescent breasts atremor, she flaunted her young body with guileless abandon. The older women gathered about her, delighted in her innocent exuberance. Her muslin kurta clinging to her, she collapsed at last amidst the girls, smiling at the whoop of laughing 'shabashes' – 'Well done!' – and applause. Miriam also laughed and, sharing her good humour and sensing her pride, Zaitoon's great black eyes lit up with happiness.

The absence of men permitted an atmosphere of abandon within the zenanna. Occasionally youths and even young men burst in, grinning mischievously. The dancing stopped and they were shooed out in good-natured outrage. Old men were sometimes invited to watch the girls' antics and participate in the fun.

As the ceremonies started the women of the neighbourhood converged on the wedding house. Inside the zenanna they removed their burkhas and revealed their finery; the older women displayed the generosity and worth of their husbands, and the unmarried girls the beauty of their forms and the cunning of their fingers in fashioning embroidery. They admired each others' jewellery, joined the girls in their singing, and sat about gossiping and consuming huge quantities of pillaus, spinach curries and sweetened rice flavoured with saffron.

After the wedding the burkhas, which hid a multitude of sins, allowed the women to revert to their usual sloppy style of dress. With no men to show off to or compete for, complacent about their husbands' sexual attentions, they visited one another in their house clothes; none too clean and perhaps torn under the arms. Young girls who did not observe purdah dressed tidily, covering themselves merely with their chaddars. Qasim, whose kinswomen perhaps were not even aware of such a garment, forbade Zaitoon the use of a burkha. She slipped in and out of her friends' homes as unobtrusively as she could, her head and torso wrapped in a shawl. Delighting in a simple deception, she would sometimes borrow Miriam's burkha and, sheathed from

89

head to toe in the tent-like cloak, would walk past him unrecognised.

Zaitoon's closest friend was the Mullah's step-daughter, Nusrat. Though Zaitoon's friendships had all the intensity young girls bring to friendship, there was always something that kept her the slightest bit apart: a dimension in her life that was not in theirs – of Qasim's far-away background and of his dreams.

Years slipped by. Qasim, nostalgic for the cool mountains, wove such fascination into reminiscences of his life among them that Zaitoon longed to see what she considered her native land. Her young, romantic imagination flowered into fantasies of a region where men were heroic, proud, and incorruptible, ruled by a code of honour that banned all injustice and evil. These men, tall and light-skinned, were gods – free to roam the mountains as their fancies led. Their women, beautiful as houris, and their bright, rosy-cheeked children, lived beside crystal torrents of melted snow.

Often she asked, 'Father, when can we visit home?'

'Soon, bibi, soon,' he murmured.

❖

At last even Nusrat got married. Zaitoon danced and sang until she was ready to drop. She sat with Nusrat, sharing her desolation at leaving her family, and teased her with speculations about the charms of the unseen groom.

For a whole week the bride sits, her body and hair greasy with oil massages, in old clothes; the better to bloom, bathed and perfumed, swathed in red silks, hair, throat and arms aglow with jewels, on the day of the marriage.

The day before the wedding, at the Henna ceremony, Zaitoon helped to hold the canopy of flowers over Nusrat's huddled, yellow-robed form. When the henna platters were ceremoniously placed before the bride Zaitoon drew intricate floral designs on the soles of Nusrat's feet and the palms

90

of her hands, fashioning rings round her toes and staining her fingertips with the orange-red paste.

At the brief Nikah ceremony, the actual wedding, the Maulvi asked Nusrat if she would accept the groom; and the groom was asked separately. They first saw each other in a mirror. The weeping bride, supported by weeping women, at last climbed into the tonga to be driven to the station. Zaitoon sobbed her heart out. All that night she wept.

She was sixteen years old.

❖❖

Zaitoon gazed down from the tenement balcony. She was curious. Sitting on the charpoy, Qasim was talking to a stranger, a fine-looking tribal. Nikka sat by listening. He frowned, apparently keeping his opinion to himself until the stranger had left.

Qasim had several Kohistani friends, who, like himself, lived in Lahore; but this man was distinctive, somehow more authentic. Voluminous gathers, like a dancer's skirt, circled his baggy pantaloons. His turban, too, was different. Its careless swirls partially covered hair that fell to the tips of his ears in a straight red bob. His black velvet, gold-threaded waistcoat slid back to reveal a double row of cartridges. As Zaitoon watched, his expansive, robust gestures conjured up the world of the wilderness, of tall, jubilant men pirouetting on the balls of their feet, heads thrown back, hypnotised by the guns turning in their strong arms – the mountain world of Qasim's memories, of Zaitoon's fantasies.

Every little while, the two tribals clasped each other close, their hennaed beards mingling in an uproarious exchange of pleasantries. Nikka, who sat scowling to one side, shifted his sullen bulk when they fell against him.

'Bring the pehelwan along. He shall be our guest,' declared the stranger, affably resting his palm on Nikka's shoulder. 'What do you say, pehelwan? Will you honour us with your presence?'

Nikka gave him a non-commital look. Slowly he turned away.

'Of course he will. I'll see to it,' interposed Qasim quickly.

Reverting to their tribal dialect, they ignored the taciturn pehelwan.

Finally, Zaitoon saw them get up from the charpoy for a parting embrace. Qasim, conspicuous as a mountain-man anywhere in Lahore, looked curiously unlike one when facing the stranger. At least so Zaitoon thought as she hurried in to warm his tea. He would be coming up any minute and she would soon find out who the visitor had been. Twenty minutes went by, and she leaned over the balcony to see what was delaying him.

The stranger had gone. Nikka was talking to Qasim and Qasim, looking at the pavement, kept trying to force the toe of his shoe into it. They seemed to be arguing, and Qasim looked hard and cold as he did only in rare moments of obstinacy. Zaitoon had seldom seen the two friends in such solemn disagreement. She grew uneasy.

Then a strange thing happened. Nikka beckoned towards the house and Miriam, with only a chaddar over her head instead of the burkha, came out and sat down with the men, out on the busy pavement. This was without precedent. Miriam sat stooped, shading her face from Qasim with her chaddar as she listened to Nikka. Zaitoon saw the chaddar slip off her hair and lie unheeded on her shoulders. She appeared agitated and glanced frequently at Qasim. Then turning to him, she addressed him as boldly as she might a woman in the privacy of her own rooms.

Qasim, not lifting his studied gaze from the pavement, spoke but little. Miriam, her agitation mounting, talked faster, gesticulating, and pushing back strands of grey hair that fell forward into her eyes. People passing by looked at her inquisitively.

Miriam brushed her cheeks with her fingers and Zaitoon guessed she was weeping. Should she go down? She des-

92

perately wanted to discover what this was all about, but a young girl added to the scene might attract too much curiosity. She fidgeted, but stayed upstairs, waiting.

❖

It was almost six years since Nikka's release from prison. As he listened to his wife expostulate with Qasim, he showed a weariness, a reluctance to impose his will as forcefully as of old.

Miriam blew her nose into her shawl. She wiped the damp left on her fingers on the strings of the charpoy. She had no control over the tears that slipped down her face.

'Sister, I gave him my word,' Qasim spoke gently.

'Your word! Your word! Your word! What has your word to do with the child's life? What? Tell me!'

Qasim did not reply.

Miriam glanced up and noticed Zaitoon's intent face at the balustrade.

'Brother Qasim,' she coaxed, 'how can a girl, brought up in Lahore, educated – how can she be happy in the mountains? Tribal ways are different, you don't know how changed you are . . .' And as rancour settled on Qasim's compressed lips, she continued in a rising passion, 'They are savages. Brutish, uncouth, and ignorant! She will be miserable among them. Don't you see?'

Qasim stiffened. A beggar, his limbs grotesquely awry, manipulated his platform to Qasim's feet. He grimaced defiantly. 'Paisa,' he demanded in a hoarse inhuman whisper. 'Babooji from the hills, paisa.' Attuned to the whims of alms-givers, he sensed the futility of his plea and wheeled himself away before he was kicked.

Qasim tried to control his fury. 'Sister, you forget I am from those hills. It's my people you're talking of.'

'But you've been with us so long, you're changed. Why, most of them are bandits, they don't know how to treat women! I tell you, she'll be a slave, you watch, and she'll have no one to turn to. No one!'

Qasim flushed. He glared at Nikka while directing his icy remarks at Miriam.

'How dare you,' he said. 'You've never been there! You don't understand a thing. I have given my word! I know Zaitoon will be happy. The matter should end.'

'I know she won't! Oh dear, how I love her. She's like my daughter . . . I've reared her . . .'

'But she is *my* daughter!' Qasim cut in with biting finality.

Miriam flushed into hysteria.

'Is it because that Pathan offered you five hundred rupees — some measly maize and a few goats? Is that why you are selling her like a greedy merchant? I will give you that, and more,' she said with contempt. 'Nikka will! How much more do you want? We will buy her!'

Qasim now looked at her directly, his face white with anger, his eyes malevolent.

Miriam felt the chill impact of his fury and an anguished stab of futility broke her voice. She continued in a crazed whisper. 'Why not marry her to my husband here? Yes, I'll welcome her, look after her. We have no children and she'll be my daughter. She'll bear Nikka daughters and sons.' Nikka vainly tried to cut in. 'Look!' she said, 'I have grey hair. I'm getting old. She will comfort our old age.'

The men were struck silent.

'Miriam, Miriam, you don't know what you are saying! You are overwrought,' Nikka soothed her.

Qasim was in an angry sweat, ashamed and touched.

'Sister Miriam, it is not for the goats and maize, please believe me. It is my word – the word of a Kohistani!'

Nikka was dazed by the trend the conversation had taken.

'It's the suddenness of the news that is upsetting us so much. I'm sure it's not as bad as we imagine. After all, Zaitoon is Qasim's daughter, and he will do his best by her . . . look, bibi, why don't you ask the girl yourself

94

. . . see what she has to say? That is, if Bhai Qasim agrees . . .?'

Qasim remained silent. Heedless of the impatient honk of a truck, a horse-cart rumbled by. The warning jangle of tonga bells, shrill cries of tea-stall urchins taking orders, all the clamour of the dense place, combined to spin a cocoon of privacy around the charpoi.

'Come bibi, let's go in,' Nikka said finally.

Qasim watched them go indoors. After a while, deep in thought, he got up and went into his own room.

❖

Setting his hookah by the bed, Zaitoon handed Qasim his cup of tea. Lowering her lids, tipping her head back, she eyed him with melting consideration. All the screen heroines she admired practised this trick, and Zaitoon frequently peered at the world tipsily through her thick lashes. Once, mimicking her, Qasim had teased, 'What's the idea of this . . .? You look like a freshly slaughtered goat.'

Recalling the remark, she widened her eyes artlessly, and began to massage his legs. 'Stretch out, Abba, you look tired.'

Qasim lay down and the girl expertly kneaded his legs.

'Abba,' she asked at length, 'is something troubling you?'

Qasim didn't answer.

'Why was Aunt Miriam crying? She sat outside without her burkha . . .'

Qasim studied her lithe body as it rocked to and fro. The pressure of her supple fingers felt curiously dainty and child-like.

'Bibi, we talked of your marriage.'

Zaitoon felt her body tremble. She froze, digging painfully into Qasim's legs.

'Sit down, child,' he said, 'What do you think of it?'

95

Zaitoon pulled her chaddar forward over her face. Her voice was barely audible. 'Anything you say, Abba.'

She waited. The hookah gurgled soothingly whenever Qasim drew on it.

'You saw the stranger I was talking to?'

She nodded.

'That was Misri Khan, my cousin. I've promised you in marriage to his son Sakhi.'

Zaitoon sat still. A blind excitement surged through her.

'I think you'll be happy,' he said at last. 'We will set off for the hills before the month is over. I'll ask for leave from the warehouse.'

Zaitoon sat, unable to move.

Qasim's eyes wandered about the room assessing their luggage.

Beneath a cotton rug stiff with years of grease and dust was the tin trunk. It served as a shelf for an assortment of cans containing condiments and tobacco, bottles of oil, tonics and aphrodisiacs. He noticed a china bowl filled with dark-red henna paste and his eyes lit up. Zaitoon had ground the henna leaves on a stone mortar that morning. Qasim was nearing fifty and he dyed his beard not to disguise the grey, but to accentuate it. White hair, a sign of wisdom and age, entitled him to respect. His head, hidden by his turban, he kept clean-shaven because of the great heat in the plains.

Qasim's glance lingered on the only decoration along the flaky walls: his pistol and his rifle. They hung by their holsters from rusty nails, and above the pistol, on a crude rack, wrapped in a square of frayed red silk, the Holy Quran.

'Bibi, read me some verses.'

Zaitoon's prowess with the holy scriptures never failed to awe Qasim, and he followed the sombre movement of her lips with pride.

Their bodies rocked to the lilting Arabic cadences.

96

Miriam held Zaitoon's arm in the bustle at the station. Neighbourhood women who had come to see Zaitoon off moved in a black, burkha-clad bunch behind them. Carrying bundles, Qasim and Nikka walked ahead. In front of them, leading the way with the tin trunk on his head, stalked the coolie.

'Buch key! Take care!' the coolie warned, and the people parted to make way.

Zaitoon's eyes flashed at the excitement of travel. Families, gathered with their luggage, waited like untidy mounds of rubbish. Bangled arms reached out of burkhas when mothers chased after straying children.

An old man was awaiting the Khyber Mail train. Garlands of roses and crisp paper money encircled his shoulders, and pressing about him in a clamorous throng were his children, grandchildren, relatives and neighbours. Disentangling his beard, the old man beamed at them. Impatient to start, he had arrived at the station four hours before his train was due.

'Bring us water and a talisman from the Holy City,' shrilled the older women from behind their veils.

'Bring us wrist-watches, and cameras,' shrieked the young.

Coolies trotted past, trunk upon trunk of luggage towering on their heads. Enormous hold-alls swayed from their arms, 'Buch key! Take care!' they cautioned.

Then, at some esoteric signal, the coolies squatted in a red row along the platform. Within seconds the engine steamed in.

Qasim and Nikka pushed their way into a crowded compartment. The women remained on the platform while the men arranged the luggage.

Miriam had tried her best to dissuade Zaitoon from going. 'You are ours. We'll marry you to a decent Punjabi who will understand your ways. Tell your father you don't want to marry a tribal. We'll help you.'

But Zaitoon, swung high on Qasim's reminiscences, beckoned by visions of the glorious home of her father's forefathers and of the lover her fancies envisaged, merely lowered her head and said shyly, 'I cannot cross my father.'

Then Miriam, knowing Zaitoon's mind was made up, stroked her head and said 'Bismillah' – 'God bless you'. She gave her a gold necklace embedded with coloured glass, a dozen gold bangles and her red wedding outfit.

Miriam stroked Zaitoon's arm as if she were a blind woman leading a loved one. She could feel the girl quiver with excitement. 'Are you happy, child?' she asked. 'Yes,' said Zaitoon, and at once felt embarrassed. 'God give you a long life, keep you always happy and smiling.' Miriam caressed her head. She, too, had married at sixteen. 'Bless you,' she said, and Zaitoon, suddenly tearful, hugged her close.

They clung together weeping, the girl lost in the folds of Miriam's burkha. Zaitoon did not need to say, 'Thank you for everything,' or, 'I'll miss you.' She sobbed, whimpering, 'I'm leaving my mother . . .'

❖

A whistle shrieked. Qasim and Nikka embraced hurriedly.

'Come on, Zaitoon,' Qasim urged, and Nikka gently pulled the girl away from his wife. Qasim saluted Miriam.

Nikka blessed the girl. 'God be with you, child,' he said tenderly. 'Remember you are our child as well. If you're not happy, come straight back to us. God be with you.'

Ever so slowly the train began to move.

Chapter 11

The three-tonner wound along the dirt road with an easy, powerful drone. It was going to Dubair with the routine supply of vegetables and stores that included the Major's beer.

'See that?' The driver glanced at Ashiq Hussain but the young mechanic slumped by his side, his army cap over his face, was fast asleep.

The road rose and swerved sharply round a projecting cliff and the driver saw a fallen bulldozer, strewn on the rocks far below. A week ago, it had plunged two thousand feet down the river canyon. Two men had died.

Instinctively, the driver steered another arm's length clear of the edge of the gorge. They were in the region described by the ancient Chinese pilgrim Fa-Hsien as the Black Mountains.

❖

A shot rent the still air and the bang of a bursting tyre echoed through the mountains. The three-tonner lurched crazily. Its heavy back wheels skidded and wrenched it in a wide arc across the road.

'Damn! Some bloody fool fired at us!' the driver said to the dazed mechanic.

The truck had its nose to the sliced mountain wall, its back wheels barely clearing the treacherous edge. Both men ducked and knelt crouching on the floor-board. Ashiq Hussain loosened the safety catch on his gun. He bobbed up swiftly but saw nothing.

'Stay low, you idiot,' cautioned the driver.

❖

'Oh God! Why did you do that, Abba?' gasped Zaitoon, her voice faint with shock.

'Hush . . . keep your head down,' Qasim whispered. The gun shook in his hand. Crouching low, he held her down.

❖

After years of longing, Qasim was returning to his people at last; to the house of his ancestors and the beloved land of his youth. The vigorous air and the sight of the stark mountains elated him. They stirred in him a long dormant pride. His mood was expansive as they trudged along the road. A bedding-roll and the tin trunk were strapped to his back, and Zaitoon carried an assortment of bags and bundles. Qasim talked incessantly.

'Bibi, you will like my village. Across the river, beyond those mountains, we are a free and manly lot.'

He searched the girl's face wistfully. Zaitoon, ecstatic with the wonder and beauty of all she saw, paid him flattering attention.

'You'll see how different it is from the plains. We are not bound hand and foot by government clerks and police. We live by our own rules – calling our own destiny! We are free as the air you breathe!'

The spirit of his forebears stirred in Qasim. Already he had forgotten the plains and the humiliations he had endured there. These raw, wild ranges were his element.

Setting their burden down, the two rested in a rocky niche just beneath the road. Qasim had heard of the new road, yet to see it hewn into the cliffs and wind like a tape-worm through the mountain-fast sanctuary of his youth, galled him. They were creeping up, these people from the plains:

100

penetrating remote valleys. Their intrusion hurt his sacred memories, and rekindled the Kohistani hatred of all outsiders.

The moment the roar of the passing truck had been close enough to compete with the noise of the river, Qasim had fired.

Now he crouched, shaking.

Suddenly, the edge of the road bounced dust. A spray of bullets ripped through it.

'We'll be killed! Hai . . .' whimpered Zaitoon, her face to the earth. The boulders sheltering them appeared to her fragile, as transparent as glass.

They waited in silence for what seemed an interminable moment.

In the truck Ashiq Hussain and the driver also waited, mute and tense. Cautiously the driver peered at the deserted road. Then cupping his hands round his mouth, he shouted.

'Attention! There are five of us in this truck. Each jawan has a machine gun. Give yourselves up or we will blast you . . . all of you. Our aeroplanes will bombard your villages. You know the agreement the Major Sahib has with your Khans. You know the vengeance of the army!'

He paused, gathering his breath, licking his dry lips.

'I will count ten. If you don't come forward by the time I finish, we'll start firing. You can't hide from our machine guns. I guarantee your safety if you come out.'

Certain of an organised raid, the driver relied on his bluff. It was their only chance. He counted 'One! Two! Three . . .'

And a voice piped up hysterically, 'It's a mistake . . . forgive us. It's a mistake.'

The men watched in amazement as a girl clambered out from behind the rocks. Instead of the traditional black dress of tribal women she wore a flowery print. The shawl, which had slipped off her head, showed a thick, black mass of plaited hair. The jawans here had not seen any civilians from the plains, let alone a young girl.

A man, obviously of the hills, stood up behind the rocks at the rim of the road. The fingers of both soldiers tightened on their triggers.

Sensing their suspicion, the girl flew towards them, shouting, 'He is my father. It's a mistake. Please forgive us.'

The driver remained suspicious: 'Are there any others?'

'No, only us. There is no one else.'

Zaitoon reached the truck and looked up at the men in their seats. She was terrified. Qasim's sheepish gaze was supplicating. He walked up, the muzzle of his gun pointing at the ground.

'It's all my fault,' the girl cried.

The men were dark and, like herself, from the plains. She spoke to them in Punjabi, 'Brother, please believe me: I begged my father to allow me to shoot his gun . . . and you happened to pass by. I did not see you, I swear.'

The men were helpless in view of this apparition from the Punjab. The young mechanic looked at Zaitoon with soft, apologetic eyes.

Qasim held his peace. Each time he went to speak, Zaitoon's voice rose and prevented him.

The two men dismounted. The driver resignedly kicked the shattered wheel.

'It's over now. You might as well help me change it. Allah knows how I'll explain this.'

The men fell to work. Ashiq Hussain kept his eyes politely averted from the girl's face. When he stole a side-long glance, he caught her watching him. Her eyes were bold and large, contrasting roguishly with the dewy softness of her features. The skin of her full lips was cracked with cold. She kept flicking the pink tip of her tongue between them. Ashiq's lowered eyes stayed a moment on her small feet, encased in childish, buttoned shoes. No wonder she had seemed to fly when she ran. He imagined her bare feet, narrow, high-arched and daintily plump. The man whom she had called father had the flaky, light complexion of a

102

hill-man. He wondered at their relationship. The girl's taut brown skin was obviously of the Punjab, as was his own.

'What brings you here, Barey Mian?' he inquired while Qasim helped him pump up the jack.

'We are returning to our home in the hills. I haven't been here in fifteen years.'

'Then this is the first you have seen of our road?'

'Yes.'

'It will make it much easier for you to get to your village.'

Respecting Qasim's age, Ashiq spoke courteously. Besides, he wished to impress the girl.

'Sit back, I can easily fix it,' he said.

The driver, having lit a cigarette, strolled behind a bend.

'Where are you heading?' asked Qasim.

'To our camp at Dubair. It's two hours' drive. We have a bridge there, if you wish to cross the river.'

Qasim nodded. 'So I was told; we shall be crossing there.'

'We have just completed another bridge, at Pattan.'

'Yet another bridge?'

'Yes,' the mechanic boasted proudly, 'the army works fast.'

He looked up, hoping to impress the girl, but Zaitoon had crossed the road. She was gazing down the gorge at the Indus.

Unlike the sluggish, muddy Ravi that sprawled through Lahore, the river here was a seething, turquoise snake, voluminous and deep; and for the hundredth time she thought of Miriam and Nikka. She would persuade them to visit her and share her delight in the mountains and the river. A dreamy smile played on her face.

Having put on the spare wheel, Ashiq wiped the grease from his hands.

'Have you far to go?' he asked Qasim.

'A long way yet.'

'We could take you up as far as Dubair. It will be nearing dark when we get there. You might want to spend the night at the camp.'

Qasim accepted the offer gratefully. 'Son, that would suit us. We can continue tomorrow. The girl is tired.'

'That's settled then. We'll have to ask the Major's permission of course, but he won't object.'

Qasim and Zaitoon gathered their belongings and put them into the truck.

Chapter 12

Carol sat on the mangy patch of lawn in front of the Officer's Mess. Her hair was damp from washing and the tepid sun petted her gently through the settled January cold.

Major Mushtaq raised his voice to be heard above the gush of water that hurtled and exploded down the boulders to his right.

'I think Farukh said you're from California?'

'Yes, San Jose. We moved from Indianapolis when I was a little girl.'

'You're still a little girl,' the Major said smiling.

'Not so little: I'm twenty-five.'

'What does your father do for a living?'

Carol had become quite used to having questions fired at her. To begin with she had bristled, finding the questions indiscreet and much too personal, but amiably she had realised that American mores of privacy could not be applied to the friendly, chatty horde of Pakistani relatives she had acquired.

'My father's in insurance,' she replied.

Clearly not satisfied by the brief answer, Mushtaq's questioning eyes invited her to continue. She smiled resignedly. 'Father went through college on the G.I. Bill, after the Second World War. He's the standard American success story, I guess. House in a good suburb. Two-car garage . . . He still talks about the rough time he had in the 1930s though. But after the deprivations of his own childhood, he delighted in plying my brother and me with gadgets. He would have gone without to make us happy,' said Carol fondly.

'What were you doing before you married Farukh?'

'I'd started at Berkeley. I meant to major in psychology. Then I got sidetracked – I met Farukh! And now here I am, exploring the Himalayas. I'm so glad Farukh took you up on your offer of a vacation here.'

Carol laughed, her green eyes conveying their excitement at the sight of the mountains and the stream hurtling by in its urgency to connect with the Indus.

❖

At Berkeley Carol had discovered that she did not have the required dedication for sustained study. The pressure of school assignments could not stand up to the livelier pressure of parties and jazz, and of drives in fast cars.

In the area of sex, however, she had moved timorously. Her conventional upbringing, though modified by Californian liberality and the relaxed morals of an affluent neighbourhood, did not permit her to go all the way – except once. She necked passionately. She even tried marijuana. This was just before Rock rolled its way into the history of American music and Elvis Presley into teenage hearts.

The study assignments became intolerable.

On impulse, Pam and Carol went off for a week of skiing in Nevada. Later they drifted into San Francisco and, liking it, decided to stay. They took jobs at Capwell's (Carol did not tell the Major this. Having experienced a bewildering snobbishness towards working girls since her arrival in Pakistan, she had learnt to keep that information to herself.)

At the cosmetics counter at Capwell's Farukh had diffidently handed her a list of creams, lotions, lipsticks and perfumes to be purchased for his sisters, cousins, aunts and mother; and a list of after-shaves and deodorants for his male relatives and friends. Carol's lithe golden arms had reached for the items in a graceful flurry. The bill had mounted to a giddy five hundred dollars. Farukh was handsome, and in a slender, fastidious way, arrogantly male.

106

Immediately she knew he was taken with her fair, good looks. She had agreed to have dinner with him the following evening at the Brown Derby.

Farukh showed her photographs of his family taken in the lawns surrounding his marble-faced bungalow, of nieces and nephews splashing in their swimming pools. Over the next few weeks he gave her expensive perfumes, bits of jewellery and finally a mink coat. His manner, courtly to the point of slavishness, alternated with an assertive possessiveness that made her feel cherished.

'Oh, how I love that man!' she said to Pam.

She gave up her job. 'I don't like to see you waiting on all kinds of men,' Farukh had said.

He also made it plain he did not want her to go out with anyone but himself. There had been a row when she had gone to a movie with Pam. She had been terribly hurt, but had later decided it was a sign of his deep and unique love.

There had also been a row when she had told her parents she was determined to marry Farukh. They were sure her husband would convert her to Islam and force her to live in a harem. Carol considered herself an agnostic, and Farukh put no pressure on her to adopt his religion. Eventually her family was reconciled to the marriage, and the young couple had left for Lahore.

❖

Lahore seemed to love Carol. Pakistani men bent over her gallantly, pressing drinks and lighting cigarettes. Beautiful women, graceful in soft flowing garments, chatted with her in exquisite English. There was a party every single evening. She felt like someone in *Gone with the Wind*.

Farukh's sisters took Carol on shopping trips into the mysterious narrow alleys of the Old City, where two people cannot walk abreast. She stared at artisans making gold and silver jewellery, embroidering wonderful gaudy colours on silks, beating copper and brass and fashioning it into enormous jars straight out of Ali Baba, into samovars and round-bottomed cooking utensils and pots and pans. She stood before shops the size of piano packing cases, spellbound by the swirl of colour and texture, until Farukh's sisters, laughing at her delight, affectionately pulled her away.

The older women initiated her into managing servants. Carol could not bring herself to practise the harsh measures they prescribed. They told her that she was spoiling them: that they would take advantage. She didn't mind the slight liberties they took. She was courteous and kind and the servants appreciated her generosity and restraint.

'I love Lahore,' she wrote to Pam. 'It's beautiful and ramshackled, ancient and intensely human. I'm a sucker for the bullock carts and the dainty donkey carts. They get all snarled up with the Mercedes, bicycles, tractors, trucks and nasty buzzing three-wheeled rickshaws. The traffic is wild!

'Some things are hard to get used to,' she went on, 'like the sanitary napkins strewn outside houses in the fanciest suburb. And sometimes I still think if I can't get away by myself I'm going to scream, but nobody understands that! You can't plan anything and have it come out the way you expect. Things happen, and you roll with them. But the most wonderful thing here is I don't feel programmed! The people are kind and hospitable. I'm having a ball.'

After the parties, though, increasingly Carol had scenes with Farukh.

'Why are you sulking? Please tell me . . . I thought we were having such fun. How do I know what's bugging you if you don't tell me?'

'I'm so ashamed of you! Displaying your honky-tonk pedigree! You laugh too loudly. You touch men . . .'

'But they're your friends . . . And what do you mean, touch men! I only . . .'

'Don't you know if you *only* look a man in the eye it means he can have you?'

'That's ridiculous! I don't believe it.'

'Don't you? You looked at me, and you got laid.'

'Jesus, Farukh! I'm married to you, remember?'

She did not mention Farukh's jealous quarrels in her letters.

❖

A conscript walked by, saluting Carol and her husband's friend, the Major.

'I've sent for some beer. It'll be here by the afternoon, with the weekly provisions,' he said.

'Ummm . . . I'd love it. Oh! What was that?' A prolonged crash echoed through the mountains. 'Shooting?'

'No, a tree felled perhaps.'

'It frightened me. I've heard the tribals can be trigger-happy.'

Carol's pink nails nervously plucked at her blue sweater.

'Trigger-happy? Yes, I suppose so.'

The Major frowned. Eerie and violent, the atmosphere had already affected her. She had arrived with Farukh only yesterday, and the Major wondered why her thoughts should fasten on death at such slight provocation. Did she realise that life here meant little? A man killed was a candle snuffed out, a tree felled, no more. Lately he had been finding his work in the desolate mountains a burden. After almost two years, he was looking forward to a transfer. His wife had refused to stay in the remote camp. She occasionally visited him from Peshawar where she was living with her parents.

'It's so good to have you and Farukh with me in this wilderness,' the Major repeated for the third time that morning.

'It's nice of you to have us,' Carol replied. 'Setting up the second foundry really took it out of Farukh. There were delays in obtaining sanctions. When it got going the furnace blew up! Dr Zaffar said Farukh must get away . . . and you know how much he loves the mountains!'

She stretched her legs and arms and threw back her head. Her sweater rode up to reveal a slip of firm white stomach. Mushtaq turned a little. Smug behind his dark glasses, he gazed obliquely at the tidy fork between her trousers. A glass of orange juice and a childish-looking box of smeared water colours lay open on a small table beside her. Carol shut the paint box absently.

'I went down the gorge earlier and tried to paint the river. It's such a lovely colour, but I can't get it right. I thought I'd go down again this afternoon.'

Languidly, she moved her long, trousered legs further apart and looked at the snow-capped mountains beyond the immediate range. She knew the direction of the Major's eyes and was warmed by an exultant female confidence. He must be around thirty-six, she thought, and in comparison to Farukh so easy-going and self-assured.

Farukh's absent person, his nervous, suspicious face, suddenly became hateful. The hell with Farukh, she thought, and his whining explosions of jealousy. Always in the mad mornings, noons and nights, put-puttering through the crackle of the 'phone, between the lines of a letter, his insatiable suspicions, his morbid craving for what he called 'the truth'. 'Be honest with me. I can take it.'

'Then what happened?' Farukh would say.

'I told you, he tried to touch me.'

'Where?'

'You know where.'

'Like this?' his hand would crawl up, hurting her, 'like this?'

'Yes. Stop it! Yes. But I told you I hated it. I slapped him. He stopped.'

'You're lying. You enjoyed it. Every bit of it. Most likely you encouraged him. You welcomed him. You devoured him. You opened your arms wide thrusting out your pink tits!'

110

'My pink tits! There's nothing special about them!'

'Oh, you're changing the subject. Don't be smart with me! You widened your legs like this, and . . .'

'Stop it. You're insane!'

'Insane? I'm insane? If I am it's because I don't know what to believe. You are driving me mad.' Farukh pulled his long fine hair and little tufts of it came off in his fists. 'Be honest. You enjoyed it. Don't lie! I can take it. I can stand anything but deceit.'

He was upon her, shaking her, his pale brown face flushed with ugly red blotches, his eyes insanely wide.

'Okay, okay. If you say so, I enjoyed it.'

'If I say so? Who're you trying to fool?'

'Yes, yes. I enjoyed myself. I admit, I enjoyed myself.'

The eternal dissection of the slightest details, an interminably reopened wound.

'But I love you so much, you see, you understand? I love you so much. Come on now, be nice to me. I can't bear it. You're driving me mad.'

To hell with your madness. Your sadistic, possessive, screwed up love . . .

The scene occurred with monotonous regularity. Now lounging on the chair, facing the Major, her bitterness boiled up. God, I'll show Farukh. I'll give him something to be jealous about! And to think she had at first found his jealousy endearing! Of course, it had blossomed into full monstrous bloom only after they were married and in Lahore. She hated what it had done to her. It had corroded her innocence, stripped her, layer by layer, of civilised American niceties. She was frightened to see a part of herself change into a hideously vulgar person.

. . . And the atmosphere of repressed sexuality in Pakistan had not helped. Slowly Carol had begun to realise that even among her friends, where the wives did not wear burkhas or live in special, women's quarters, the general separation of the sexes bred an atmosphere of sensuality.

111

The people seemed to absorb it from the air they breathed. This sensuality charged every encounter, no matter how trivial. She was not immune. Her body was at times reduced to a craving mass of flesh . . . It was like being compelled to fast at a banquet . . .

'A penny for your thoughts?' Snapping his fingers beneath Carol's nose, Mushtaq smiled into her eyes.

Carol started, 'Oh nothing really . . . It's so peaceful here, it makes one dream.'

The Major removed his sun glasses. Carol had particularly noticed his eyes the night before in the glare of the hurricane lamp at coffee after dinner. Major Mushtaq, with the unit doctor and a few officers, had joined Carol and Farukh in the Mess sitting-room. After coffee they had played Scrabble. Carol had basked in a surfeit of attention. The Major's tawny eyes, flecked with black like a leopard's coat, glancing now at her, now at Farukh, had obliterated the presence of all others. He had maintained an uncanny balance, keeping Farukh off the brink of gloom and suspicion even though Carol's vivacity would normally have been enough to secure his jealous anger. Instead Farukh had himself been warm and relaxed in his friendship with the Major.

Later, alone in their room, Carol and Farukh, for once, had not quarrelled.

Now, looking into Mushtaq's raffish eyes, she felt lightheaded. He had this strange effect on her. She wanted to revel in the appreciativeness of his stare. But she knew better. Earthy and brazen, the men here expected subtlety from women. She had already responded too much.

Besides, they were too exposed to the curious stares of tribals filing across the steep track overlooking the lawn.

Carol's face hardened. Three tribesmen had stopped on the track looking down at her. They held the ragged ends of their turbans between their teeth and their eyes examined her insolently. Primly she crossed her legs.

112

Observing her discomfiture, Mushtaq lifted his head. At once the men turned away.

He laughed, 'They haven't seen the likes of you!'

Carol was furious. What did he mean? After all, she was not naked! The hell with them, she thought, removing a cigarette from her packet of Gold Leaf. At once Mushtaq leaned forward with his lighter. She drew a quick breath and exhaled.

'Maybe I should wear a burkha!' Her voice was sharp with annoyance.

'It's not as bad as all that . . .'

'It is,' she snapped. 'Haven't they ever seen a woman before?'

'Come now, I should have thought you'd like being noticed,' teased the Major. 'You know how it is with us – segregation of the sexes. Of course, you only know the sophisticated, those Pakistanis who have learnt to mix socially – but in these settlements a man may talk only with unmarriageable women – his mother, his sisters, aunts, and grandmothers – a tribesman's covetous look at the wrong clanswoman provokes a murderous feud. They instinctively lower their eyes, it's a mark of respect. But let them spy an outsider and they go berserk in an orgy of sight-seeing! Don't take it personally. Any woman, whether from the Punjab or from America, evokes the same attention.'

'I . . . I felt they were undressing me.'

'That's why I told you last evening not to go wandering off on your own.'

Carol looked away.

'Do you know,' he continued, 'this morning I had to post a picket to guard you while you painted the river?'

Unexpectedly she glowed with excitement. 'Did you really? I didn't see them. Where were they?'

This was it! A sense of being catered to and protected – servants and leisure. Unhurried sessions with the dress-maker and languid gin-and-tonics on well-groomed lawns.

These compensations made her stay despite Farukh's morbid jealousy. They prevented her from carrying out her repeated threats to divorce him – to go back home. Prolonged morning coffees and bridge, delicious sessions of gossip with the band of women who increasingly formed her social group – American, Australian, British, and other Europeans, married to Pakistanis, who otherwise had very little in common. Sunk into cushions of leisure they shared confidences and wept with homesickness on each other's shoulders. In moments of lonely alienation, turning hostile, they sneered at strange customs, at modernisation not yet achieved, at native in-laws, and dirt, and dust, and primitive plumbing.

Once purged of their resentments they regained the sporty sense of adventure and curiosity that had brought them to this remote land in the first place. Their compensations were the Majors! The bright blue sunlit days!

Carol suddenly thought of Pam, still promoting lipsticks and lotions behind her counter, while she braved the Himalayas and lived in mountains teeming with handsome cave dwellers, tall, sun-burnt ferocious men. She fashioned phrases for use in her letter to Pam. 'The darling of an isolated camp deep in the Himalayas' – 'venturing where no white woman had ever gone before' – 'protected by pickets!'

Pam would circulate her letter. Carol viewed her old friends with the condescension she had bestowed on her arrival in Lahore on fat, garishly made-up begums. Jammed together they slumped on sofas at 'dinner parties', their tender jelly-bellies giggling.

Chapter 13

The raucous stream hurtled headlong in a spray of foam into the main waters of the Indus. Half a furlong ahead, the purr of the river became a husky, pervading growl. From where she sat, Carol could see the bridge spanning the deep, secretive gorge of the Indus. Mushtaq's voice poured pleasantly into her ears. His eyes, barely glancing at her face, nibbled on the curves beneath her sweater.

'. . . this set off a string of counter-murders. Seven men dead in two days. The man who had actually molested the girl vanished across the river. But the girl's relatives are sure to get him one of these days.'

'Can't you stop this senseless killing?'

'Me?' The Major gave a wry smile. 'It's like this,' he explained. 'This side of the Indus, where we're sitting, is Swat Kohistan. There is a semblance of law and order here . . . at least a killer is fined! If he makes it across the river, we can't touch him.'

He turned in his chair and swept his arm towards the hills across the bridge.

'That part of Kohistan has no administration. It is inhabited by isolated pockets of feuding tribes, for centuries imprisoned by the Karakoram Range. They have their own notions of honour and revenge; a handful of maize stolen, a man's pride slighted, and the price is paid in bloody family feuds. Possibly they are better off . . . At least they know where they stand.'

Carol liked the way he talked, the flashes of earnestness that lit his face and his patient, didactic delivery.

'I'll tell you what happened just a month back. We had to

115

take the construction of the road through a village. It had been evacuated and in compensation the Khan was paid six thousand rupees. Now, that's a lot of money: you can't imagine how poor these people are. I thought they'd use the money to better their miserable lot. Do you know what they did?'

Carol shook her head. Her hair fell forward in a flattering, sun-yellow filigree.

'The Khan shot the male members of an entire clan. The next day, a load off his mind and his conscience at ease, he paid his fine to the Wali of Swat. Six thousand rupees, the fine for ten murders!'

'How dreadful!' cried Carol.

'Had he killed them on the other side of the Indus, he would not have had to pay anything at all.' A hint of admiration crept into his voice. 'The Kohistanis are quite untameable really. The British tried their darndest . . . They gave up after Sir Bindon Blood had fought and failed to subjugate them at the turn of the century.'

They remained silent for a while. The Major stood up.

'Well, young lady, it's been delightful sitting in the sun talking to you, but I think I should get back to work.'

'Oh, please don't go! What will I do all by myself?' begged Carol, eager to sustain the glow his eyes kindled in her. 'Can't you take the day off? Farukh won't be back until nightfall and I'll be lonely.'

Mushtaq decided to stay.

A few minutes later she extended her hands. 'Come,' she said, 'let's try the "other side of the river". Shall we?'

Mushtaq caught the proffered hands and drew her up. 'Anything you say, my dear. Wait just a minute. I will arrange for a picket.'

Striding over to a khaki-uniformed jawan by the gate, he issued instructions and walked back to Carol.

'Put a scarf over your head and we will be ready.'

This concession to modesty, he felt, would have to suffice.

116

Carol complied. She was too excited to make an issue of anything.

❖

Carol and the Major leaned over the bridge. Fifty feet below them, the river thundered in blue turbulence.

'Oh, how beautiful . . . how absolutely lovely!' cried Carol. 'How did you ever build it?'

'Well, that's our work.'

'What are those?' she asked, indicating a row of red-painted animal figures that perched, like benign deities, on slim concrete pillars fencing the bridge.

They had to shout though they stood so close that Mushtaq could smell her slight, inoffensive sweat.

'Chinese Lions. They are a gift from the People's Republic of China,' he went on. 'At one time they were believed to frighten off evil spirits – and bring good luck. I like to think of them as sentinels guarding our bridges.'

'They look more like bull-dogs, but they're cute!' said Carol.

'We have just completed another bridge at Pattan, twenty-five miles upstream.'

'Isn't that where Farukh has gone?'

'That's right. Why didn't you go?'

'I don't know. I'm glad I didn't,' she added impulsively.

Straddling the gorge over a distance of more than four hundred feet, the bridge dissolved abruptly on a shelf of sand. There a few indefinable tracks led into the cliffs.

They walked over to the sandy bank. It was desolate and Mushtaq looked about uneasily.

'We'd better not lose sight of the bridge,' he said. 'Of course, they are scared of the uniform, but you never can tell.'

'What can they do?'

'Take a pot shot at us just for sport.'

'Would they dare?'

'Why not? To avenge us our jawans would just as casually blast some of their villages, routing them out of their filthy caves. A lot of good that would do once we're dead!'

'Really!' cried Carol, thrilled by the threat of danger, yet convinced that no one would actually kill her. The thought of the possibility of rape vaguely entered the rim of her consciousness.

They stepped up a trail leading from the gorge. A few minutes later, enclosed by granite, they were miraculously isolated on a tiny island of sand.

'How warm it is. Feel it.' Carol let the pulverised crystals run through her fingers. She dropped down on all fours, and a slice of white waist gleamed invitingly. Mushtaq knelt beside her. He was unable to keep his eyes off her ebullient behind. His hand reached out to encircle her waist, and they collapsed on a heap of sand.

❖

Three clansmen had watched the Major and the American woman cross the bridge into their territory. Their shalwars trailing the grit like soft fox-fur, they effortlessly leapt over the boulders. They settled on a sunlit ledge high along the slope.

'It's the Major Sahib,' whispered Sakhi.

His eyes slit into dancing sapphires reflecting the deep cold sky. 'Hah! The show is about to begin,' he proclaimed, gleefully observing the man and the woman in their small domain of sand. His companions smirked contemptuously, gluing their eyes on the interlopers.

Mushtaq lay flat on his back, scanning the arid tumult of rock and cliff. Carol reclined by his side.

'I could fall asleep,' she said. 'Let me know if there's any danger.' She pillowed her head on his arm.

Turning slightly Mushtaq inhaled the shampooed fragrance

118

of her hair. A few strands touched his cheeks, and he closed his eyes.

Carol sighed, looking at the towering jungle of slate beyond them. She felt strangely unreal – adrift. 'What a jumble. As if God scratching through the earth, had smashed the mountains in a mad rage . . . He too must have His frustrations.'

Mushtaq's hand crept under her sweater, kneading her satiny skin. His voice was a husky gurgle, 'Ummm . . . When Atlas lifted the world, he held it here. His fingers forced the earth into chasms and the rising mountains; the Himalayas, the Hindu Kush and the Karakoram . . .'

❖

Their eyes met in quick, exultant triumph and, as if on cue, the three tribesmen broke into a tumult of laughter and catcalls that echoed boisterously.

The Major sat up and straightaway spotted the trio jeering on their sun-washed ledge.

They saw him glance up. High on the ledge, Sakhi pirouetted in a riotous stamping dance, his turban swirling and ballooning.

Mushtaq moved away from the woman. To all appearances, he was unconcerned. At this point it would not do to get up and run. His face set in a dusky scowl, he swore under his breath. Lifting some sand, he allowed it to run nonchalantly through his fingers. Embarrassed, Carol shifted away.

The little tableau on the ledge continued. Intermittently the tribals swung their arms in puppet-like, swirling movements, but the pebbles they hurled did not reach as far as the vulgar smacking noises they made with their lips.

Mushtaq stood up.

'We'd better get out of here.'

He glanced at the wall of granite surrounding them, wondering which path to take. And suddenly he froze.

Barely three feet from where he stood, peering through the recess of a dark fissure, gleamed a pale, unblinking face. The Major stood rooted to the spot, taken aback by cool hazel eyes that stared back, unsmiling.

God only knew how long the man had been there, immobile, as though hewn in stone.

Retrieving his wits, Mushtaq sprang forward in a menacing rush and the face dissolved.

Finding their way through the maze of rock, Carol and Mushtaq emerged in full view of the bridge.

At a short distance from the boulders ringing their retreat, slouched a scruffy tribal. The long muzzle of his flintlock rose jauntily above his frayed turban. Legs spread wide apart, he sprawled on a rock. His cold hazel eyes stared at them unabashed.

Walking past, the Major fixed the man with a glowering look and the tribal's face cracked into the dirty ridges of a smirk. There was no genuine mirth in the face, only mockery. The tribal's eyes shifted and skewered the woman in ruthless speculation. For the first time Carol knew the dizzy, humiliating slap of pure terror. The obscene stare stripped her of her identity. She was a cow, a female monkey, a gender opposed to that of the man – charmless, faceless, and exploitable.

Catcalls from the ledge heightened to a crescendo. Mushtaq turned away. An intruder in the tribal domain, he was nevertheless livid with humiliation and anger. Followed closely by Carol, he marched across the bridge.

In a frenzied bid to hold the attention of their quarry the men on the ledge leapt, shouted, whirled and laughed. Tears streaming down their cheeks, they moaned for breath and wiped their noses with the ends of their turbans.

Sakhi fell helplessly against his brother. His hands groped down Yunus Khan's sheepskin jacket. He lay at his feet writhing in mirth. The sun gilded his thick, dark-blond hair, bronzed his flushed skin, and, excited by the joyous vitality

120

of his laugh, the other two men fell beside him. Teasing him, they grabbed between his thighs. He kicked in self-defence and they lunged and tumbled one on top of another, grasping each other to their panting chests, thighs and arms entwined.

Swamped by the smell of uncured sheepskin and the sweat of unwashed bodies, Sakhi battled for air. He crawled through at last and hooting with laughter, the three clansmen got up and disappeared down a gully behind the ledge.

❖

Carol poured herself a gin and tonic.

'Hasn't the beer arrived?' she asked.

'No,' Mushtaq's tone was uncommonly abrupt. He stood just outside her door, looking in.

Carol glanced at him quickly and grew embarrassed.

'It's good to be back,' she said nervously.

Outside, the high whine of a truck labouring up the mountains grew more distant.

'Damn those tribals,' said Mushtaq more to himself than aloud.

Carol stood against the table looking into the glass which was trembling slightly in her hands. 'They made me feel so . . . so inhuman . . .'

'Hey, don't be upset,' said Mushtaq.

Hesitating a moment, and then closing the door behind him, he walked up to her. He folded his hands over hers and raised the glass to her mouth. Carol took a sip. His hands were warm and reassuring. Moving the glass towards himself, he lightly brushed his lips across her fingers. Carol felt her will drain from her body. Her feet flattened in her rubber sneakers and rooted her to the cement floor. Mushtaq detached the glass from her fingers and put it on the table. His khaki shirt blurred as he moved closer. His hand, pushing

121

back her hair, stroked her as in a blessing. He pressed her to him. She felt the rough wool of his trousers and the hard length of his body all along hers. She was at last feasting at the banquet.

Chapter 14

Army vehicles lined one side of the road and straight ahead rose the stone façade of the Officers' Mess. Jawans, clad in militia shalwars and shirts, were washing the vehicles and tinkering with machinery beneath gaping hoods. They glimpsed the girl as the truck lumbered by and paused to watch.

Zaitoon was disappointed in her first glimpse of Dubair. She had expected a settlement with at least a few shops and civilians. Through the windscreen she saw all there was to see of the camp – the stone Mess with its low compound wall, the row of trucks and a swarm of tents that settled on the rocky terrain like moths on wool.

Qasim helped Zaitoon from the truck. Once on the ground, the girl wrapped the shawl tighter round her shoulders, embarrassed by the avid curiosity of the men closing in from all sides.

'Come, Barey Mian, I will take you to the Major Sahib,' Ashiq volunteered politely.

Bowing her head, Zaitoon walked between the two men in a self-conscious shuffle. They approached the Mess in constrained silence and Zaitoon, for no reason except the curiosity she had aroused and the prospect of meeting strangers, was on the verge of tears.

Once again, Ashiq, the young mechanic, found himself musing about her relationship with the middle-aged tribal. He glanced at her shy, dusky profile, and wondered uneasily why she was here.

❖

Carol stretched her body languorously on the lumpy cotton mattress atop the string-bed. A paperback lay open on the quilt. She sat up the moment she heard Farukh's voice in the hallway.

The door latch clicked and as Farukh entered she composed her features and, pushing back the covers, half stood up.

'Hello. How was the trip?' she asked, trying to relax within his arms. Farukh beamed.

'Missed you, darling.'

His fingers stroked down her spine and his voice grew husky. Carol did not meet his eyes. When she did eventually risk looking at him she noticed the dust sticking to his lashes.

'You look tired. Did you enjoy the trip?'

'Rather. Gets more virginal the further one travels. It was picturesque, you'll love it. But, how did my little girl spend the day?'

Carol stiffened. Not only because of the guilt she was feeling but because she knew the tenacious demands of Farukh's most innocuous questions. She must be careful. His grip on her lost its warmth.

'Let's see now. What did I do?' Her face puckered thoughtfully, and slipping from his embrace she padded over to the looking-glass strung from a rusty nail. She took a brush from the sloping wooden shelf beneath it and pulled it through her hair. What if I tell him? Answer as casually as the question was put, she wondered. It was a temptation.

Behind her, Farukh moved, hanging up his coat, slipping off his shoes, and feigning ease.

'Let's see,' she said, wetting her lips, 'you went at about seven, seven-thirty? I slept quite late. I think I ate breakfast at eleven o'clock!' She made a face. 'I don't know what the cook will think of this memsahib who sleeps all day.'

'Then?'

124

'Then I had a bath, washed my hair. I hope I don't run out of shampoo. How in the world will I get more?'

'Mushtaq will have some brought up. Then?'

'Well, I went down to the gorge and painted for a while. Take a look,' she said, rummaging through a sheaf of papers and handing him a slightly curling sheet.

'That's pretty. You went down alone?'

'Who do you suppose went with me? There's hardly any company here!' She retrieved the sheet from him, groping for time to marshal the next sequence.

'Then we had lunch and, oh, you'll never guess what we did . . .'

'Who's we?'

'The Major, the medical officer and a few others . . . I don't know who.' Carol's tone was flat with annoyance.

'Sorry, I didn't mean to interrupt. Anyway, there's no cause to be annoyed.'

'I'm not annoyed,' she said drily.

Farukh flushed.

'Well, won't you tell me? You said something about my never being able to guess . . .'

'Oh yes,' said Carol, desperately salvaging her enthusiasm, 'I made it to the other side of the river! Can you believe it? Mushtaq went across in the afternoon and I asked to go with him. It was incredibly thrilling. Pickets all over the place guarding us. I'll never forget this terrible tribal who sprang up and almost at us out of nowhere. He was an animal. Filthy, with a nasty stare. He just stood there ogling until I couldn't stand it.' Carol shuddered involuntarily. 'I don't think we'd last a day in this place without the army.'

'It's not that bad,' smiled Farukh, 'though a woman has to be careful, I suppose.'

'I was terribly scared,' she said seriously. 'But it's fascinating too. I bet no American woman has been there!'

'So then?'

'It took about half an hour. Couldn't wander very far.

125

Then we had tea and I came back here, slept a little and read a lot. Almost finished my book. It's good. You should read it.'

Farukh's lean face was sly with suspicion. 'Is that all?'

'And what else do you think I've done? Oh yes,' she added dangerously, 'before my bath I sat upon that stinking pot full of your damned shit – the sweeper hadn't been to clean the mess – then I brushed my teeth, gargled . . .'

'Now why are you angry? I just asked a civil question. I always tell you everything I do. Or do you have something to hide?'

There we go again, thought Carol, the familiar bitterness boiling up within her. With an effort of will she remembered that today she could afford not to retaliate. She wanted to prevent the endless inevitable scene . . . She recalled the Major's caresses soothing her and his warm, hard embrace. Yes, she had avenged Farukh's grotesque jealousy – helped its nightmares come true!

Carol was suddenly shocked by her reaction. Was that all it amounted to? Was her romantic afternoon interlude with the Major only an ugly act of revenge?

'What are you doing to me? Oh God, what are you doing . . .?' she whispered, aghast, and Farukh, sensing he had pushed her too far, blanched and said, 'I'm sorry . . . I don't know what comes over me . . . I'm sorry . . .'

❖

The officers were already gathered in the Mess, awaiting the visitors. The sun had slipped behind the hills and Carol and Farukh, after snuffing out the candles in their room, walked hand in hand into the glare of the Petromax-lit sitting-room.

The officers rose politely, shook hands with Farukh and bowed, smiling warmly at Carol.

The couple were offered the recently vacated seats closest to the blazing log fire.

126

'How did you like our work at Pattan?' inquired the Major.

'Excellent bridge,' said Farukh. 'What impressed me most, though, was the road itself, the Karakoram Highway. A magnificent feat. I went up to where it ends. I can't imagine how you'll continue hacking it into those mountains.'

'Progress is measured in yards, not miles. It *is* tough.' For a moment Mushtaq's face shed its social affability. He showed an unexpected sadness. 'We've lost men – dynamite, avalanches, landslides, sudden crazy winds that lift men off the ledges . . .'

The room fell silent. They became aware of the evening wind rattling the windows, its hiss half submerged by the crash of the river. The wind would increase and howl and it would whistle through the night as if fierce demons had been let loose.

Carol ventured hesitantly. 'H . . . how can you tell where to cut the road? I mean . . .'

'That was all taken care of two thousand years ago,' smiled Mushtaq, his face lighting up. ' We are following the ancient Silk Route of traders from Central Asia. Their caravans carried jade, bolts of silk and tea – some perished and some made it to the Indus plains. The Silk Route follows the Indus gorge most of the way and then swerves east from Gilgit through Hunza to the Khunjrab Pass on the Chinese frontier. It continues to Yarkand, Kashgar and other fabled cities of Sinkiang!'

'How far is that from here?' asked Carol.

'About 350 miles. The road will wind through Kohistan for about 100 miles and then enter the Gilgit, Hunza and Baltistan agencies, where the Hindu Kush on the west, Karakorams on the north and north-east, and the Himalayas to the south interlock with the Pamirs, at the very "Roof of the World". It is spectacular! Especially where the snows of Nanga Parbat and Rakaposhi look down on the ancient path.'

127

'I wish I could see it all,' sighed Farukh.

'Well, the Northern Area covers over 27,000 miles. It forms our borders with Afghanistan, Iran, India and China. You'll be able to see a lot of it once the road's complete.'

'I heard at Pattan – the Chinese are working on the road from their end?' asked Farukh.

'Yes.'

'There'll be quite a celebration when the two teams meet.'

'You bet!' laughed Mushtaq.

Farukh leaned forward. 'I met some decent chaps at Pattan. Ran into a childhood friend in fact. Captain Ahmed. We used to be neighbours.'

'You met a friend? You didn't tell me,' smiled Carol. Her voice was acid.

'Didn't I? Oh, so sorry.'

Carol clenched her fists and blushed. 'It's all right. I was only joking.' She lowered her eyes fleetingly. The circle of men sat in an awkward silence. The Major cleared his throat.

'D'you know what?' Carol smiled, 'I've been brushing up on my vocabulary. Can't make as poor a showing at Scrabble as last night!'

They laughed, and the conversation eased. Suddenly, Carol heard her husband say: 'It was nice of you to show Carol the other side of the Indus. She can't stop talking about it.' He beamed around the gathering.

'Yes,' the Major said hastily, 'your wife is delightfully adventuresome.'

He gave Carol a quick, cold look. She might have warned him.

'What will it be? Whisky-and-water?' he asked Farukh.

'Please.'

Mushtaq busied himself at the table crowded with bottles and cheap, thick glasses. Carol, her face hidden from Farukh by the swing of her hair, tried to concentrate on what the doctor was saying.

Earlier that evening, feeling a belated twinge of guilt,

128

Mushtaq had decided to avoid her. Even so, pouring Farukh's drink, his glance slid in her direction.

He walked across the room.

'Thanks,' Farukh took the glass. 'Can't be much different across the river?' he inquired.

'The camp here makes a difference. I'll take you across sometime. It's weird, but one is really quite helpless there. We had to stay quite close to the bridge, but you I could take deeper into the area.'

'Any time you say, Mushtaq.' Farukh beamed contentedly.

'By the way,' Mushtaq continued, settling in the chair next to his, 'I meant to tell you. We have an interesting glacier about a six-hour trek from here. It's more than 14,000 feet above sea level. Worth visiting. Would you like to try it tomorrow? I'm afraid I'll be busy, but you can go.'

'Wonderful,' said Farukh. He caught Carol's eye. 'Like to come?'

'It might be too tiring for her,' interposed the Major smoothly. 'Besides, I wouldn't advise taking your wife that far away from civilization.'

She pulled a face. 'I miss all the fun!'

'But,' she laughed, turning to Farukh, 'you go, darling. I'll be happy here with my paint box and my books.'

She addressed Mushtaq. 'How about a drink for me?'

'I'm sorry. Any preferences?'

'Beer?' she asked.

'Oh, yes. Terribly sorry, I forgot. It arrived this evening. I don't know where the orderly's disappeared to. If you'll excuse me a moment, I'll fetch some.'

Mushtaq went into the pantry and pulled two bottles from an open crate. Through the door leading to the kitchen, he saw the tribal and the girl from the plains squatting on the kitchen floor before a pile of chappatis and a small enamel bowl holding a curry.

129

'Is there enough food, Barey Mian?' he inquired hospitably.

Qasim jumped up.

'Yes, Sir,' he salaamed. 'We are grateful. We thank you.'

'If you require anything else, tell the cook.'

Qasim touched his forehead and remained standing until Mushtaq returned to the sitting-room.

Mushtaq handed Carol a frothing glass. 'I forgot to mention, the truck that brought our beer brought a couple of civilians as well.'

'Where from?'

'Lahore, I believe.'

'Aren't they joining us?'

Mushtaq laughed. 'They are just a poor night-watchman and his daughter. He is taking her to his ancestral village to get her married. It is deep in the unadministered territory.'

He took a chair by Carol.

Farukh was engrossed in conversation with the engineer, who was detailing for him the technical difficulties encountered in the construction of the road. The unit doctor and the remaining officers were grouped around the table, pouring drinks, talking and laughing.

'What does she look like?'

'Who?'

'The girl you mentioned . . . the one who's to be married on the other side of the river?'

'You want to see them?'

'May I?'

Mushtaq motioned to the Mess orderly who had just come in. 'I want to speak to the civilian and his daughter. Tell them to come after they finish their dinner.'

'Yes, Sir,' the orderly said smartly.

Mushtaq turned to Carol, 'I must say I was quite surprised to see the girl. She is altogether Punjabi, while her father surely is from here.'

130

Chapter 15

The orderly ushered Qasim and Zaitoon into the room. Qasim stood hesitantly at the fringe of the party. Zaitoon, in her agony of shyness, her head covered by a huge shawl, cowered by his side. Blinded by the glare of the Petromax, awed by the tall men in western suits, and by the blurred presence of an 'Angraze' woman aglow with golden hair, she felt out of her depth.

'Come, Barey Mian, come here, both of you,' the Major beckoned paternally.

Qasim stepped awkwardly within the semi-circle of chairs around the fire, salaaming, and Zaitoon edged in close behind him. The officers, drawn by curiosity, drifted back to their chairs. Finding herself unbearably conspicuous in the centre of these sophisticated people, Zaitoon folded her knees and squatted abruptly before Carol. She settled to one side so that she could see only Carol, the Major and the fire.

'Sit down, Barey Mian,' the Major invited Qasim.

Qasim sat gingerly on his heels in the centre of the circle, facing the Major anxiously. He shifted the cartridge strap so that his pistol rested comfortably on his thigh.

'I have arranged for you to spend the night here. Tomorrow morning our transport will take you to Pattan.'

'Allah bless you,' said Qasim, his eyes full of gratitude.

'You cross the river at Pattan?'

'Yes, sir.'

'How far do you travel from there?'

'I have not been to my village for a long time, sir, but with the new road it shouldn't take more than a day.'

Nervously, with the hem of his shirt, Qasim wiped some chappati crumbs off his mouth. The red tassel of his trouser-cord dangled disconcertingly between the folds of his shalwar.

'What about our Dubair bridge. Can't you reach your village by crossing here?'

'Yes, sir. But it would be a long trek upstream. Now that you have a bridge at Pattan . . .'

'I see.'

Mushtaq conducted the interview in a bantering, condescending manner, He endeavoured to amuse his audience by baiting the old tribal, exploiting his simplicity and awe. It helped to pass the evening.

'Tell me, Barey Mian, why are you so anxious to get to your village? Is it a feud? How many old enemies are you going to bump off?'

Mushtaq was gratified by Qasim's fervent denials.

'Ah, the revered Chinaman does not wish to tell us the truth,' he teased good-naturedly. Qasim, rising to the bait, whirled angrily.

'Chinaman!' he protested. Removing the turban from his shaved head, he thrust his bearded face forward.

'Look at this,' he said, tapping his nose that dipped, hooked and sprang out between his flat cheeks and slanting eyes. 'Is this a Chinaman's nose? No! It leaps forth as a banner of my race! A legacy from Persian ancestors who came through those hills with Cyrus and Darais . . . or from the Yahudis even . . . some say the lost tribe of Israel settled here . . . or . . .'

'Ah, yes,' the Major said, 'the lost tribe of Israel! Cyrus and Darais! But what about Taimur the Lame? and Changez Khan? and Kublai Khan? and Subuktagen and the other Mongols who swarmed through these mountains to India?'

Qasim, lightly dismissing the Mongols, said, 'They came. And the Greeks came with Sikander!' He had been through this scene before when people called him a Chinaman. Each time he felt obliged to vindicate the honour of his ancestors.

'See here,' he pushed back a sleeve and waved a powerful, hirsute hand. The skin of his palm was like pale, cracked leather. 'These veins flow with Kohistani blood, brave mountain blood.'

Meanwhile, Zaitoon, crouching on her haunches, stared at Carol in wide-eyed admiration. The halo of golden, fire-lit hair, Carol's light bright skin and her strange tight trousers, fascinated her.

Carol glanced at Zaitoon indulgently and said, 'She's beautiful.'

Zaitoon, overawed and confused by the sudden attention, made Carol uneasy. There was a slight strain in her smile. She asked, 'Tumhara shadi honay ka hai? (Are you getting married?)'

The construction of the sentence and the stilted foreign accent kindled Zaitoon's smile. Then, she burrowed her head so low Mushtaq could barely see her nose.

Why must these women be so goddam coy, thought Carol.

'You ought to know better than ask such delicate questions, dear,' reprimanded Farukh primly. 'Our women, particularly the young girls, are modest, you know.'

Furious at the rebuke, Carol's face burned red. Tears smarting in her eyes made them sparkle:

'Really! One would imagine they achieved one of the highest birth rates in the world by immaculate conception!'

The room was suddenly still, hot with Carol's anger and Farukh's consternation.

'D . . . don't talk like that,' he spluttered.

Mushtaq laughed uneasily. 'It's all right. We're among friends. Beneath their shyness, these little girls can be delightfully earthy, you know.'

He turned to Carol. 'The girl is probably confused with so many strangers around. I should imagine she's nervous.'

133

Carol glanced at Zaitoon's bowed head, barely concealing her resentment, exasperated with these attitudes which were so alien to her. Attempting a smile that looked brittle and forced, she glanced away – and caught Qasim's ice-brown eyes measuring her with cold menace.

He had not understood a word, but he grasped the scorn in the woman's demeanour.

Carol's anger flared into blind rage. His stare held the same alien, ruthless capacity to humiliate that she had seen in the tribal's glances that morning. Turning to the Major, she rasped out, 'I'm sure he is not her father. They look too different. Ask him! Go on, ask him!'

Mushtaq, glad to side-track any impending quarrel between Carol and Farukh, leaned forward. 'I believe the girl is your daughter?'

'She is my daughter, sir.'

The Major's eyes slid over to the girl and back to Qasim.

'And, maybe, she isn't your daughter, Barey Mian? The Memsahib here thinks not.'

Qasim raised his head and glowered at the probing face. He thought of a similar question put to him by Nikka years ago at their first encounter – the earth had been cool and wet with the passing of the storm; he had been hot-headed then and closer to the proud standards of his youth. The intervening years had taught him the ignominy of his illiteracy, and an awe of educated men of position. These men held bewildering power over the likes of him and could upset his plans at a whim. He little understood their ways.

'My lord,' he spoke with an anguished stare, 'I got her when she was four or five years old. Ever since I have cared for her like my own and she has been a devoted daughter.'

'You got her? Where from?'

'We were on a train from Jullundur at the time of Partition. The train was ambushed. Her parents were killed. I had jumped off the train before the mob attacked. After the killing, when I ran along the tracks to Lahore, the child called to me,

134

thinking I was her father. I carried her to Lahore.'

Qasim spoke slowly, carefully, his drawn face and sad brown eyes full of candour.

Mushtaq knew he was telling the truth. A few paces from him the girl sat still, her chin resting on her knees.

'So be it, Barey Mian. I didn't mean to pry. Forgive me.'

The Major was sorry for having forced up a piece of information that perhaps had been kept from the girl. The tribal's talk touched him, and he was weary.

Qasim wondered if he ought to leave. He awaited a sign.

'Whom do you work for?'

The question came from behind him and Qasim swung his shoulders to see who had spoken. It was Farukh.

'Sir, I am night-watchman for Rehman & Sons. I mind their steelware godowns.'

The doctor, sitting opposite the fire on the far side, asked, 'Where do you stay in Lahore?' He was an angular, sober young man.

Qasim, still squatting in the centre of the room, pivoted on his heels.

'At Qila Gujjar Singh, Sir.'

Sorely wishing to establish some sort of an identity before the buffeting superiority of the strangers, he said, 'I live next to Nikka Pehelwan. We are like brothers.' He raised two stiff fingers to illustrate the closeness of their relationship. Pride surged through him and he sat up straighter. He would have given much for Nikka's reassuring presence now. The deep social chasm between them would have been bridged by the fearless set of Nikka's strong neck, his reckless smile, and his witty bravado.

The officers, indulging Qasim's pride in his friend, bombarded him with questions. Qasim, swivelling obligingly on his haunches, answered each one, sensing a certain jocular acceptance of himself.

Meanwhile, Carol noticed a movement in the girl's shoulders. Why, the child was crying! The discovery filled

135

her with remorse. Hadn't she known all along that the old tribal was not her father?

Zaitoon cried silently, unseen tears spilling on her knees. In her subconscious had lain a dim suspicion of the truth, a hint of pain closeted away and buried. All of it now lay brutally exhumed, and, tears soaking her shalwar, she kept thinking inanely, 'Just the same he is my father . . .'

On an impulse, Carol reached out to touch her. She stroked the coarse shawl covering her head. Startled and embarrassed, Zaitoon's crouched body stiffened.

Carol slipped out unobtrusively and went down the corridor to her room. She returned with a paper bag containing an embroidered chaddar, a slab of chocolate and some oranges. Quietly she resumed her seat.

'Take it,' she said gently to Zaitoon. The shadow cast by Carol's body shielded the girl from view. Zaitoon raised her head slowly and was full of gratitude for the woman who sat on the edge of her chair to screen her. In the instant their eyes met, the green and black of their irises fused in an age-old communion — an understanding they shared of their vulnerabilities as women. For an intuitive instant Carol felt herself submerged in the helpless drift of Zaitoon's life. Free will! she thought contemptuously, recalling heated discussions with her friends on campus. This girl had no more control over her destiny than a caged animal . . . perhaps, neither had she . . .

Zaitoon wiped her wet face and shyly slipped the gifts under her shawl. An orange rolled down her thighs and nestled against her belly. She blew her nose into her chaddar and wiped the residue with the back of her hand. Her face once again was composed. Except for her red eyes, there was nothing to disclose that she had been crying.

Carol sat back feeling drained of emotion.

'That was nice of you,' Mushtaq whispered.

She bit her lip and frowned ruefully. 'Hardly. I feel so ashamed.'

136

'It's not your fault. We didn't know she'd take it so hard. I imagine her mind must have erased the memory of her parents' slaughter . . . obliterated the horror . . . an act of pure self-defence on its part. It's a pity though. She looks quite wretched.'

Mushtaq reflected on Carol's behaviour. Farukh shouldn't have provoked her. There was no need for remarks like 'Our women are modest . . .' He was such a prig. But Farukh wasn't the only one to blame . . . they had all, at different times, flaunted attitudes that must appear hypocritical to her. Not considering her feelings, they had perhaps ridiculed the values she held dear. She must miss her own people, he thought. He'd hammer some sense into Farukh . . . All considered, she had come out rather well; with spontaneity and courage and warmth . . .

His glance slid to Zaitoon and the need for redress nagged him too. He bent towards her.

'Your father,' he whispered, 'is a remarkable man! He loves you dearly, doesn't he?'

Zaitoon nodded, not raising her eyes. Her gravity affected Mushtaq. 'You've been to school?' he asked.

'I studied up to the third class,' she said, looking up.

'Intelligent eyes!' observed the Major to Carol. He smiled at the girl and, smiling shyly, she looked down.

❖

Qasim was talking to the others, richly narrating Nikka's exploits until the pehelwan's blustery, brawling presence was tangible in the room. 'Ah, yes,' he said in reply to a question put by the doctor. 'Nikka did spend four months in gaol. That was almost six years ago. It didn't mean a thing though,' Qasim indicated the triviality of the charge by a flick of his wrist. 'Just a mild reprimand from the mighty one. You know the man I mean. It taught Nikka a lesson all right!'

137

During a lull in the conversation, the Major called to him, and Qasim, shuffling on his haunches, moved closer.

'Barey Mian, I congratulate you. You have a well brought-up daughter.'

'It's God's will, Major Sahib,' said Qasim, touching his turban. His heart drummed with pride.

'You've found her a husband?'

'Sir, she is grown up now and must be married soon.'

'Is the man from your village?'

'Yes, sir.'

'What terms have you negotiated?'

'He's well off for these parts, sir,' said Qasim, evading the question respectfully.

Mushtaq did not press the point.

'I see.'

Mushtaq had been in the tribal regions long enough to be well acquainted with the marriage formalities. A wife was a symbol of status, the embodiment of a man's honour and the focus of his role as provider. A valuable commodity indeed, and dearly bought. He glanced at the girl. Her head was bowed. He could see nothing but the line of Zaitoon's hair beneath her chaddar.

'Do you think she will be happy with the tribals?' he asked, trying to conceal his compassion. 'It's a hard life for your people.'

'We've had a hard enough life on the plains as well, sir.'

The tribal's reply echoed finality, and Major Mushtaq realised it would be futile to air his misgivings further. He called to the jawan who had been hovering in and out, and said, 'Ashiq, see that they are well cared for.'

He stood up. 'God be with you,' he said, dismissing Qasim and Zaitoon.

❖

Ashiq Hussain led the way to a dank, cluttered store-room.

138

He placed the lantern on an upturned crate and cleared enough space to lay two straw mats.

Like most conscripts, Ashiq was tall and sturdy. He was twenty-two and his family as yet had not got down to seeing him married. Of peasant stock, from the Mianwali District, his skin was burnt dark as the earth of the fields in twilight. His bright, black eyes were set wide apart in his handsome face.

Ashiq raised a quilt and Zaitoon catching hold of the other end helped him spread it on the mat. She studiously avoided his eyes.

He knelt on the bedding, smoothing it, reluctant to leave. Lighting a candle, he allowed the wax to drip and stuck the candle on the crate. There was nothing more to be done. Lifting the lantern, he said, 'I have put a box of matches by the candle, Barey Mian. I am only two rooms away. I sleep in the pantry. Let me know if you want anything.'

He glanced at Zaitoon, who was looking at him. She smiled, and said swiftly, almost under her breath, 'Thank you.'

Ashiq Hussain's heart missed a beat. He stumbled from the room.

❖❖

Zaitoon spread Carol's glamorous gift on the quilt. Two and a half yards of bright green nylon embroidered with flowers in gold thread. She traced the delicate work with her fingers and the smooth cloth beneath the gold felt wondrous. She draped the chaddar over her head and shoulders.

'How does it look, Abba?'

She knelt beside Qasim, who lay beneath his quilt watching her. Qasim, not used to such finery, felt the material gingerly.

'It's very beautiful. Where did you get it?'

'The memsahib gave it to me when you were talking to the others.'

'It's beautiful,' he repeated. Taken by the gold thread, he

139

traced the pattern delicately with his fingers. 'Did you thank her?' he asked.

'Yes,' she said. 'What a strange memsahib. She was wearing trousers!' Zaitoon giggled.

'Their ways are different, child.'

'Abba, she was drinking something with a strange smell. Her breath was awful. Was it wine?'

'Probably.'

'God forbid! Toba!' muttered Zaitoon, scandalised by the revelation. She touched both ears in quick succession to ward off the possibility of such a sacrilegious calamity happening to herself.

'But Abba, she sat alone among all those men, drinking wine . . .'

'Their ways are different from ours, child. Put out the candle and go to sleep now.'

Zaitoon folded her precious chaddar carefully, snuffed the candle, and slipped into her bed. It was cold. Much colder than it had ever been on the plains. She lay shivering until her body warmed the quilt.

After a while, repeating Qasim's words in the dark, she asked:

'Abba, her ways are different from ours?'

'Yes, child,' replied Qasim perfunctorily, already half asleep.

'As different as my ways will be from those of your people in the hills?'

'Hush, Zaitoon. What nonsense you talk.'

'But, Abba, I am not of the hills. I am not of your tribe. I am not even yours,' she said quietly.

Lying in a strange room, surrounded by strange objects and persons, suddenly faced by a future unknown and baffling, her voice sounded forlorn; as desolate as the arid, brooding mountains to which she had come.

A tenuous echo from the past surfaced to her conscious-

140

ness. Tonelessly she said, 'My father and my mother are dead.'

The words rocked eerily in Qasim's mind, conjuring up memories. He groped for her in the dark, accidentally brushing the tears she had concealed.

'Zaitoon,' he said, 'Zaitoon, why d'you say that? Am I not your father? Haven't I loved you dearly? I had three children, once. But now you're all I have in the world. Munni, please stop crying. Am I not dear to you?'

'Forgive me, Abba,' she sobbed, touching Qasim's gnarled hands to her cheeks. Kissing his fingers, she wept, and weeping she fell asleep.

Chapter 16

After dinner, while they sipped coffee around the dining-table, Mushtaq directed the arrangements for Farukh's next day's excursion to the glacier.

He then called for Ashiq. The jawan stood at attention, while the Major, resting his elbows on the table, picked his teeth thoughtfully.

'Tell the girl, if she ever requires assistance, to come straight to us. She may ask her husband to see me sometime. We could give him work. You know what I mean?'

'Yes, sir.'

Ashiq Hussain saluted and withdrew.

❖

Qasim listened to Zaitoon's regular breathing. He felt a phase in his life was at an end. It was strange that he should suddenly feel so old. There, in Lahore, amid good friends and unchanging surroundings, age had come upon him graciously, like the touch of petals. He had known he was growing older but now, lying among the strangers of this camp, he felt old. 'Honourable elder' they had called him, 'Barey Mian'! And tied up with the realisation was the certainty that this was the end of a phase. His life had been given meaning and direction by Zaitoon's presence: seasons had roared and surged in him like waves swept high by the powerful currents of Nikka's life. Now, their force spent, the waves retreated, leaving him a frothing edge of memories.

How long ago it was! He had been ripe with manhood

142

then and strong: his arms rock-hard with power. He felt his arms beneath the quilt. They retained their shape but there was now a softness in his flesh. His veins had pulsated with energy, and now, beneath a touch, yielded to the pressure.

How prickly and quick he had been, and how proud.

❖

At dawn, Ashiq saw Qasim slip past the pantry window on his way to the toilet. Throwing the quilt aside he sprang to his feet. Smoothing his clothes, and running his fingers through his hair, he stole along the corridor to the girl's room. He opened the door, and his hands trembled. He was breathless as though he had run a mile.

Zaitoon glanced up nervously from the bedding-roll she was tying with a coarse rope. The dank store-room was lit by only a candle.

'I just came to check if you and your father were awake. The truck leaves in an hour.' Ashiq Hussain cleared his throat awkwardly.

'We are almost ready,' said Zaitoon, embarrassed at finding herself alone with the man.

'Bibi, I have something to say to you. May I?' he pleaded timidly, squatting opposite her and talking across the roll of bedding.

The girl looked at him, embarrassed.

Hastily he added, 'I have a message from the Major Sahib. He wants me to tell you that if you have any trouble with those hill people you are to come straight back to our camp. You'd only have to walk across either bridge. We will protect you. He also said you may ask your betrothed to see the Major Sahib for work, if he wishes to, that is.'

Zaitoon wondered at the cryptic message. She smiled briefly and said, 'Please give my thanks to the Major Sahib.'

'Bibi, there's something else . . .'

The girl nodded imperceptibly – waiting.

Ashiq groped for the first word, trying desperately to regain his wits. Speeches rehearsed last night in the seclusion of the pantry now dissolved into idiotic snatches.

Zaitoon fidgeted. Fearing she might rush from the room, his heart gave a sickening leap.

At last he blurted out, 'You're a child. Even though your eyes have the beauty of a woman, they have not seen the world!

'Your father told the Major Sahib that you're not of the hills. What do you know of them? Ask me, I know how they live – all the murders, the bloody family feuds. You are like me. You will not be happy there. Please don't go. I will tell the Major Sahib that you don't wish to go. You have nothing to fear, I . . . I will care for you.'

'No,' cried Zaitoon, 'don't say anything to the Major. It is my father's wish. I must go with him!'

Ashiq had meant to argue persuasively but squatting before the cringing, resentful girl his resolve melted.

'Bibi, don't get angry,' he pleaded. 'I don't want to upset you. I don't mean any harm. . . . Do exactly as you wish. But remember, we're your friends. The Major Sahib will protect you.'

His compassionate, beguiling eyes conveyed more than he dared put into words. He stood up slowly, 'Khuda Hafiz, God be with you,' he said.

Walking out dismally he closed the door behind him.

Zaitoon sat still until Qasim returned.

❖

At eight o'clock the truck was ready to leave. They hauled their belongings into the back of it and Zaitoon cast about anxiously. Ashiq was nowhere to be seen.

'You ready, Barey Mian?' the driver shouted from his perch behind the wheel. Qasim climbed in beside him. Zaitoon sat next to Qasim by the window.

144

Roaring in first gear the truck was half way down the drive when they heard a desperate voice calling for them to stop. Ashiq rushed alongside the truck window, out of breath. 'Coming to Pattan with you,' he panted, 'Major Sahib's given me some work there.'

Seeing the three of them in front, he vaulted into the rear of the truck. In the square cabin window up front he watched the girl's profile.

The road was rough and unsurfaced. It had only a layer of shingle and was sometimes blocked by rocks and minor landslides, which the passengers cleared. Bits of it had crumbled off where the edges were not, as yet, properly supported. It would take them two or three hours to reach Pattan.

❖

Refreshed by a night's sleep and elated with the leisure of travel Zaitoon gazed in wonder at rock and earth. She was stunned by the flight of the sheer granite cliffs and the thundering tumult of the river. Heavy blue waters smashed against submerged rock and towered into pillars of geysering white, before being frothed into rapids. Unusual bluegreens swirled at the vortex of giant whirlpools.

More and more the Indus cast its spell over her, a formidable attraction beckoning her down. And, bouncing on her hard seat in the truck, the strangely luminous air burnished her vision: the colours around her deepened and intensified. They became three dimensional. Were she to reach out, she felt she could touch the darkness in the granite, hold the air in her hands and stain her fingers in the jewelled colours of the river. Trapped between the cliffs of the gorge, the leviathan waters looked like a seething, sapphire snake.

They were more than half way to Pattan when the driver eased the truck to the edge of the road and stopped. Flanked

145

by stretches of chalk-white sand, the river here formed a wide, emerald lagoon.

'Can I go down there?' breathed Zaitoon, and Ashiq and Qasim agreed to the descent.

Sprawled on a warm rock, Sakhi lowered the sheepskin cap to shade his eyes. He had followed the sound of the truck in its passage up the mountain road, its labouring whine distinct from the roar of the river.

'The Major's truck,' he thought contemptuously. Touching his flushed cheeks to the stone, he was shaken again by a paroxysm of mirth, recalling the Major's ludicrous antics and his abject humiliation in his love tryst with Carol. Last night, convulsed by fits of laughter, the three clansmen had enacted the scene before their kinsfolk. The villagers had slapped their thighs and howled with delight. Scandal touching the Major was an exhilarating treat. The story would enliven any future encounters with him and provide an endless source of jokes and gossip.

Sakhi didn't bother to sit up. He had seen enough trucks in the past year to satiate his initial curiosity. When the work in their area had first started, he and his brother had laboured on the road. Once the novelty had worn off they felt it was not worth their while to demean themselves doing manual labour for others. Sakhi felt he had come a long way since that day when, eyes wide, he had gingerly climbed into the seat in a jeep – and later put down a bucket of water for it to drink.

When the motor faded, Sakhi wondered if a tyre had punctured, and he lifted the top of his head above the rock, to look.

The three-tonner stood a hundred yards upstream at a bend in the road. A man in uniform had jumped from the rear to join a small group already standing at the front. Sakhi could not be sure if one of the travellers was a woman. He scrambled towards a rock almost directly opposite.

Slipping into position in a cleft, he could see plainly the

146

woman and the two men in their descent down the steep
face of the gorge.

❖

Gun in hand, the driver remained on guard by the truck.
Squatting by the rim of the road he dutifully scanned the
mountains on the opposite bank. Satisfied that they were
alone, he relaxed his vigil.

Sakhi watched the three figures scramble down the cliff.
He could tell by the grip of Qasim's tread, and by the knot of
his turban, that he was of his own race. The girl's dark
colour, apparent even at that distance, her timorous, unaccustomed, stumbling descent, her clothes, revealed that
she was from the plains. These two, he was sure now, were
the man and the girl his father was expecting.

His heart started to beat fast. He was immediately filled
with resentment at the young jawan's presence. Not only
was the old tribal accepting a ride from the hated soldiers,
but he was allowing the young jawan to walk with the girl –
his girl!

The sun was well up in the sky but as yet it did not reach
down into the gorge. Beneath the line of shadow, Sakhi
saw the soldier's arm go up to steady the girl. He couldn't
be sure whether the man touched her, but Sakhi's lips
distended viciously. He raised the muzzle of his gun and
adroitly began his furtive descent, his eyes reflecting the
mad brilliance of the river.

Leading the way, the Kohistani sought the easiest path for
the girl to follow. Again she slipped and this time the jawan's grip on her arm steadied her all the way down to the
sand embankment.

'This,' thought Sakhi with contemptuous rancour, 'so this
is the girl my clansman brings me from the plains!'

He cleared his throat and spat spitefully on the rocks. A
bright drift of laughter reached him from below. Hawk-

147

eyed, he followed each movement with growing feelings of humiliation and jealousy. Hatred and fury burned within him, yet he dared not descend any further.

❖

Once they reached the chalk-white sand, Zaitoon stepped away shyly from the jawan and, following Qasim, sat beside him on a rock. Qasim's eyes glowed with pride and his wan cheeks twitched in a jubilant dance.

'Munni, this is my land – do you wonder I love it so?' Tears threatened to start down his cheeks. 'We are here at last,' he sighed, revealing the agony he had suffered in years of separation.

'It is beautiful, Abba,' agreed Zaitoon, enraptured.

Before them, the lagoon spread so wide they could just make out the gleaming line of sand containing it at the other extreme.

'These waters look still from here, but the current is swift, see . . .' said Qasim, tossing a twig as far as he could. It raced away at an astonishing speed.

'Is it very deep? It's clear as glass yet I can't see the bottom.' And unexpectedly she asked, in a voice hushed by the mystical effect of the landscape around her, 'Abba, the man I am to marry . . . do you know him?'

This was the first time she had asked about him. She could have asked a hundred questions. What did he look like, how did he live, had Qasim ever seen him?

'I saw him a long time back, when he was a child. His father has assured me he is a good boy. He is a man of our tribe, bibi, and I can safely leave you in his care.'

'Leave me, father? Won't you stay with us?' Zaitoon pleaded.

Qasim smiled. 'Don't worry, Munni, I will stay a while, but your husband will take good care of you. You will like him. He is fine looking. Only a few years older than you.'

148

At once her heart was buoyant – and at the same time filled with misgiving. Would he like her? In a country where lightness of complexion was a mark of beauty, her own deep brown skin dismayed her. But the jawan liked her. His eyes left no doubt of it. She fell to dreaming. Surely her future husband would like her young face and her thick lashes. She felt alternately fearful and elated.

❖

Ashiq stood apart. Having realised their need for privacy he walked a short distance and sprawled on a bed of sand behind a crag. Abandoning himself to his fancies, he reflected on the girl. She had been shy and smiling. He had thought at the time that his grip on her hand had affected her, though now he wondered if he had not imagined it all. Holding up his palm, he searched the miracle her touch had wrought. Yes, he had felt his warmth pass to her and back between them. His eyes flickered idly on the dark cliffs across the river, and he caught – or he imagined he caught – a movement in an anchored tumble of rock half way up; it was a motion as shadowy as a veil of sand dispersed by wind.

Sensing, even from that distance, the direction of the jawan's scrutiny, Sakhi froze.

Ashiq stood up. His eyes instinctively sought Zaitoon. Quite near he saw her bending down to a ripple-washed rock. She pushed back her sleeve, plunged an arm into the water, and screamed.

Leaping over the stones, his heart pounding, Ashiq rushed to her side. 'What is it?' he asked, relieved to find her uninjured.

'I don't know,' she whispered, 'I – I was just frightened . . . The water was so cold, it burned me . . . like fire,' she stammered.

Ashiq Hussain smiled. Drawing a large, soiled piece of

149

cloth from his pocket, he began tenderly to wipe her wet hand. 'Wrap your shawl well around you,' he advised, helping her with the loose ends until she was totally covered.

Raising his head, he carefully scanned the cliff, and once again he caught the subtle movement.

'Come. Let's go,' he said, and Qasim, having detected the direction of the jawan's wary eyes, led the way quietly.

Chapter 17

Following a winding descent, the truck rolled into an un-
likely pocket of civilisation. Tractors, earth-movers and
cranes droned and roared on newly-levelled ground, raising
a vast cloud of dust. The jungle of mountains had yielded to
a more normal surface, a tiny oasis given over to the
twentieth century. They were in Pattan. Flowing through it,
narrowed by solid walls of granite only slightly above the
level of the water, the river at this point allowed the new
bridge to span it.

Qasim observed clusters of scruffy tribals working on the
road with pick-axes and shovels. He read the marks of his
ancestry in each arrogant face, noted the familiar sheepskin
waistcoats and shirts made from beaten wool. Uncured
leather wrapped around their legs, taking on the shape of
their calves, resembled knee-length boots.

Coated by khaki dust, the truck stopped before a brick
structure, a row of rooms opening on an elongated verandah. Here four officers sat studying a map. When Qasim
salaamed, one of them, returning his salutation, said, 'We've
been expecting you, Barey Mian. Some food is ready if you
would like to eat.'

Ashiq was instructed to see to the guests in the kitchen.

As before, the presence of the girl aroused interest. Soldiers, drivers, overseers and tribals gathered outside the
kitchen entrance and peeped in from a window at the back.

'What's there to see? Go on, get to your work!' shouted
the cook, bolting the kitchen door. The soldiers, satisfied
with the glimpse and somewhat abashed by the reprimand,

moved away, but the tribals hung around the wire-mesh window peering in as at animals in a cage.

Ashiq Hussain studied the faces with heightening anger. 'Get away, you bastards,' he growled, stamping towards the window. Insolent eyes stared back at him in immutable contempt.

Infuriated by their avid, leering countenances, Ashiq impulsively reached for a full bucket by the sink and threw the water at them. The pyramid of craning necks and faces wobbled for a moment, then, swearing and jeering, the wet faces resumed their positions.

'I will deal with these mangy dogs,' snarled Qasim, pushing Ashiq aside. He scowled at the inquisitive tribals, and at the wrath of a man of their own lineage, they blinked in astonishment.

'We're only looking at the woman who came with the jawan from the plains,' one of them said apologetically in tribal dialect.

'She has not come with the jawan. She is my daughter!' hissed Qasim. 'I'll wrench out your tongues, you carrion. I'll gouge the swinish eyes from your shameless faces . . .' His clawed fingers quivered. They dispersed rapidly, and he sat down, trembling quietly.

'You're going to leave this girl with them?' asked Ashiq. 'There'll be no one to protect her.'

'They didn't know she was of our race. Now they will protect her with their lives!'

'Hah! Kill her, more likely!'

'Hold your tongue!' Qasim retaliated furiously. 'And get away from the girl! Haven't you any decency, sitting so close to her?'

Ashiq stood up and strode out of the kitchen.

'Let's go,' said Qasim shortly.

Lifting their belongings from the truck, Qasim and Zaitoon placed them in a heap on the fine dust. Ashiq stood by, declining to help. Zaitoon gave him a sidelong smile and he

152

walked up, silently assisting her father in raising the tin trunk to his head. He strapped the bedding-roll to Qasim's broad back, and Zaitoon picked up the remaining bundles.

Ashiq, saluting the officers, walked down the wide, dusty pathway with them to the bridge. At the bridge-head Qasim turned to him. 'There is no need to come any further, my son.'

Ashiq caught the heavily-burdened man in a warm embrace. 'Forgive me if I said anything to displease you.'

'No, my son, it is I who ask your forgiveness. And convey our gratitude to the Major Sahib. My child and I are truly thankful. Allah be with you.'

'Allah be with you,' replied Ashiq.

Looking at Zaitoon with anguished eyes, he touched her arm and repeated, 'God be with you.'

Qasim and Zaitoon walked on to the dark tarmac strip straddling the river. Half way across the bridge, Zaitoon stopped to look over the railing at the central vigour of the waters. 'I cross this spot and my life changes,' she thought with sudden reluctance. But the step into her new life had been taken a month back and she was moving fatefully on its momentum. She glanced back at Ashiq standing still and straight by the bridge-head, and she felt a pang of loss.

Ashiq kept standing. He had seen the girl stop and half turn to look at him. It suddenly occurred to him that Zaitoon always seemed to have been poised for flight; even when she entered a room. It was a quiver of her supple body that started in the soles and high, finely drawn arches of her feet.

❖

The sun, already at a sharp angle, brushed them tepidly. Leaving the bridge they trudged up a sharp incline, and through a tunnelling fissure into the closed world of mountains.

153

Qasim, in an enveloping sense of familiarity, traversed the almost pathless wilderness with the assurance of a homing bird.

'A short distance and we'll be there,' he said to the weary girl.

The stark heights they were crossing vividly impressed on Zaitoon what might lie beyond. Brown mountains rose endlessly, followed far up and away by endless snow. Before them stretched centuries of an intractable wilderness, un-peopled and soundless. Zaitoon's limbs were aching and the uncanny stillness weighed down her slender body. She walked faster, and Qasim had to quicken his step.

Half an hour later, he stopped. 'Zaitoon, cover your head, someone is coming.'

Soon she too heard the crunch of footsteps.

All in white, a figure moved into view round a hill; large and white it loomed in the dusky stillness.

Salaam-alaikum, Misri Khan,' Qasim's voice boomed joyously in the quiet, and hastening their steps the two men met and embraced. Misri Khan was wearing an enormous flared robe over his puffed-out trousers. The elaborate twists of his white turban spoke eloquently of the pains he had taken for the occasion. Seeing him close, Zaitoon was amazed at the similarity between them. Misri Khan was younger and ruddier, but he had the same eyes, tipped at the corners, and the same sharp, hawk-like profile as Qasim. He appeared self-assured, hard and arrogant.

Stooping beside the visitor, he slipped the trunk on to his own head. 'News travels fast. I heard of your arrival a few hours back and was on my way to Pattan to fetch you.'

He laid his palm flat on Zaitoon's head to bless her.

While they walked, Misri Khan supplied Qasim with news of his kinsmen.

Rounding the shoulder of a hill, Qasim paused. Shading his eyes against the slanting rays of the sun, he gazed at the valley below.

154

'We have arrived!' He looked at the girl exultantly, his heart close to bursting.

They stood on what looked like the rim of a great bowl. The mountains once again stood a little apart and the base of several hills formed a gently undulating valley. Zaitoon studied the flat mud and stone huts sprinkled about the foot of the hills, and the cultivated strips of lush green crop that tiered upwards like a giant stairway. She could make out no single living form.

Once they stepped within the mud-rampart of the village, each house spewed out its ragged human content and the villagers came running. Three or four fierce dogs set to barking and were restrained. Zaitoon covered her head and the lower half of her face with her shawl. The children, their noses running, their cheeks a fierce scorched red, stared at Zaitoon out of large, light eyes. Their hair was matted with dust, streaked bronze by the sun, and their eyes were amber, green and blue.

A spry, stooped old woman clutched Zaitoon's arm with talon-like fingers. After greeting Qasim and being blessed by him, she led Zaitoon possessively from the crowd towards her hut. The men remained in a knot about Qasim, but the women and children, breaking away, followed the old woman and the girl.

❖

Hamida peered at her prospective daughter-in-law through puffy, undefined lids. She had been tall, but arthritis and hard labour had bent her, so that her head bobbed level with the girl's. When her glance focused on Zaitoon's inquisitive, apprehensive eyes, she gave an ingratiating chuckle and, anxious to make the stranger feel welcome, ran her claw-like fingers affectionately over Zaitoon's head. Zaitoon studied the sallow face with a concealed revulsion. Deep scars on Hamida's cheeks distended her toothless mouth in

155

a curious grin. Old at forty, she had suffered a malicious disease that had shrunk strips of her skin and stamped her face with a perennial grimace. Even when her sons had died and tears had run down her scarred cheeks, she had appeared to be smiling.

The chattering, curious women followed them into a hut, bombarding Zaitoon with questions she was barely able to understand. For a time, she sat huddled on the dirt floor in a corner of the hovel, mutely staring at the unkempt rough faces.

Presently a huge clay tray filled with flat maize bread was placed on the floor in the centre of the room. Breaking chunks of the rubbery bread, the women dipped them in a pan of water and fell to eating.

Much later, Qasim and Zaitoon were led to the jagged entrance of a cave. They crawled to enter, but once inside they could move around freely.

They spread their bedding on the floor and lay down for the night. It was bitterly cold and the exhausted girl snuggled close to her father for warmth. She fell asleep almost at once.

A few hours later, she awoke, unaccountably restless. She had a vague recollection of an unpleasant dream: she had been standing by the river, admiring its vivid colours, when a hand had come out of the ice-blue depths and dragged her in, pulling her down, down . . . Now her experiences of the previous day crowded confusedly into her mind. A new wakeful fear crystallised. With the shrewd instinct of the damned, she sensed the savagery of the people she had just met. She knew poverty and the harshness of their fight for survival made them the way they were, and her mind revolted at the certainty that to share their lives she would have to become like them.

The frightened girl began to cry, her muffled sobs absorbed by the ancient walls of the cave. Her father beside her slept undisturbed.

❖

The piercing wail of a jackal rent the night, and the village dogs started barking. Terrified, Zaitoon flung herself upon Qasim.

'What is it, child?' he asked. 'That's only a jackal. It won't harm you.'

The girl sobbed aloud. Qasim, not accustomed to hear her cry, was perturbed. 'What is the matter, Zaitoon?' he asked again.

'Abba, take me to the plains when you go. Please, don't leave me here. Take me with you.'

'Hush, Munni, be quiet,' he said, gently holding her close.

'Abba,' she sobbed, 'I don't want to marry. Look how poorly they live; how they eat! Dirty maize bread and water! My stomach hurts.'

Qasim tried to laugh. 'I ate the same bread, and I have no belly-ache.' Then he spoke seriously, stroking her head, 'My child, they are not as poor as they appear to you. It's only their way of life. You will get used to it soon. Then you will like your husband and my people. Why, we've only just come here.'

The girl clung to him desperately, digging her fingers into his shirt, her legs grasping him in a vice. He felt her body quiver against him.

'Abba,' she begged in a fierce whisper, 'take me back. I'll look after you always. How will you manage without me — and the food? If I must marry, marry me to someone from the plains. That jawan at the camp, Abba, I think he likes me. I will die rather than live here.'

Qasim was furious. He was shocked by her brazen choice of words and the boldness of her contempt for his people. A sudden dread that perhaps he had not directed the course of the girl's life correctly upset him and kindled his wrath. He

157

wrenched at her slender, clinging fingers and pushed her away.

'Hush, Zaitoon, that's no way to speak to your father. It is not seemly. A decent girl doesn't tell her father to whom he should marry her.'

'But father . . .'

'Now understand this . . .' Qasim's tone was icily incisive. 'I've given my word. Your marriage is to be a week from today. Tomorrow your betrothed goes to invite guests from the neighbouring villages. I've given my word. On it depends my honour. It is dearer to me than life. If you besmirch it, I will kill you with my bare hands.'

He sat up, heedless of the cold that needled his uncovered body. Zaitoon cringed at his unexpected fury. He groped for her and his hand closed round her throat.

'You make me break my word, girl, and you cover my name with dung! Do you understand that? Do you?'

She lay quite still, her eyes large with fright and comprehension.

'Yes,' she croaked, her will utterly defeated.

The pressure on her throat lessened. Qasim unlaced his fingers and let go.

But his nagging fear for the girl, his misgivings, would not be stilled. The feel of her soft, vulnerable neck persisted in his fingers. A moment later, torn by remorse, he kissed her. He stroked her head and whispered brokenly, 'I have given my word, child, my word . . .'

The girl reached for Qasim and in her dread clasped him comfortingly close to herself.

Chapter 18

Tawny hills vibrated to the sharp, quick beat of drums. A group of young men danced in a circle. Waving their arms, whirling at a dizzy pace, they leapt into the air. Occasionally, a joyous volley of gun-fire heightened the revels.

The marriage had been solemnised, the feast served, and amidst laughter and cheering the groom was led to the room where his bride awaited him.

A man atop the valley rim let out a fierce, wild cry and the sound echoed down the valley. Catching it the men flung it back, until the carefree ululation spread, reverberating among the mountains. The clean cold air was filled with a noise as natural to the wilderness as moaning winds. Then like a wind dying, the sound diminished, until quiet settled once more upon the valley.

They were alone now. Diaphanous and tinsel-dusted, her bridal ghoongat formed a tantalising veil over her face and form. The groom awkwardly, wordlessly, lifted the veil to see his bride's face. She must have been almost as curious, for her eyes, which he had expected to be demurely lowered, met his own in dizzying appraisal. Sakhi moved back a trifle, smiling self-consciously. And now the girl lowered her eyes. He appeared tall to her and incredibly strong. The hair beneath his turban and on his moustaches glistened gold, and in the shadowy lamplight his sun-gilded face gleamed, as did his vivid blue eyes. Her heart beat faster, and a warm glow suffused her body.

Sakhi surveyed his diffident bride with mounting excitement. Here was a woman all his own, he thought with proprietorial lust and pride, a woman with strangely thick

159

lashes and large black eyes that had flashed in one look her entire sensuality. But, even as he thought this, the corroding jealousy of the past few days suddenly surged up in him in a murderous fusion of hate and fever. He tore the ghoongat from her head and holding her arms in a cruel grip he panted inarticulate hatred into her face.

Zaitoon looked at him wildly, terrified as he dragged her up and roughly yanked her red satin shirt over her head. Her arms flew to cover her breasts. He tugged at the cord of her shalwar and the silk fell to her ankles. Before she could raise her trousers Sakhi flung her back. He crouched, lifting her legs free of the silk. Fiercely kicking out, Zaitoon leapt over the charpoy. She screamed. She backed towards the straw and mud-plastered wall, and screamed. Leaning against it, covering her chest and crotch with her hands, she screamed. Sakhi stood across the room, incapacitated by the shrill animal noise, and she screamed and screamed. 'Abba, save me,' she shrieked. Why didn't Qasim come? Or any of the others?

Sakhi stood still. She knew as long as she screamed she could hold him off. She stopped. Sakhi moved hesitantly and again she shrieked. He froze against the wall. He didn't move. After a while she grew quiet. He looked defeated and abashed.

Panting and trembling she glared at him. Sakhi slid down to his haunches and squatted. The slope of his shoulders, the way he removed his pagri from his head and placed his arms on his knees conveyed his utter capitulation. Even more in the way he turned his eyes from her mortified nudity, he tried to show his respect. In a moment he restored to her her dignity.

Her breathing quietened. She took in the white satin waistcoat, gold embroidered, embellishing his shirt. Gathered above his waist the shirt hung in deep folds to his calves; and beneath it the arrogant convolutions in his shalwar. The pomegranate blossom tucked behind his ear,

160

his teeth gleaming between stained lips, the dark smudge of antimony, bespoke an appealing vanity.

Sakhi looked up again. He had never seen a wholly naked woman before. He registered her astonishing female desirability, the strand of her hair undone, falling on skin lighter where the breasts swell, and the round, out-thrusting breasts. He admired her lean, strong thighs, and his eyes were drawn to the curling jet hair that peeped rebelliously through protective fingers. Sakhi lowered his face to his knees.

Zaitoon's fear slowly left her. She darted forward and picking up her clothes, quickly put them on. She perched on the charpoy. When Sakhi raised his head she grew fearful, and then calm. His features were drawn and nervous, subservient with desire and a desire to make amends. They looked at each other, Zaitoon hurt and questioning, Sakhi mutely contrite. Sakhi eased down further and sat on the dirt floor. He looked away but his eyes already had spoken of love.

The sap that had risen in her since puberty and tormented her with indefinable cravings for so long surged to a feverish pitch. Brought up in Muslim seclusion she had not understood the impulse that had caused her often to bury her face in Qasim's clothes hanging from a nail. Breathing in their maleness she had glowed with happiness, taking her impulse to be a sign of her deep affection. Knowing only Qasim and Nikka she had loved them with a mixture of filial devotion and vague unacknowledged sexual stirrings. She had had romantic fantasies in which tribal lovers, bold and tender, wafted her to remote mountain hide-outs and adored her for ever. She felt at the furious centre of her tumult a deep calm, a certainty that at last her needs would be fulfilled.

'Get into bed. It's cold,' Sakhi said.

Zaitoon snuggled beneath the quilt at the far side of the bed. Sakhi got up, and lay beside her. She went completely rigid.

161

When his leg gingerly touched hers she did not move. He ran his toe down her calf. Slowly he turned, the sag in the narrow charpoy moulding them together.

Sakhi's hand tenderly pressed her breast. Zaitoon craved the touch.

In dreams Zaitoon had accepted her lover's hands on her breasts not as a preliminary caress but as the final surrender to carnal intimacy. Brought up in a sexual vacuum she did not think of sex as good or bad – it merely did not exist. Neither Miriam, nor Qasim, nor any of the women she visited ever mentioned it. She floundered unenlightened in a morass of sexual yearning. Once, snuggled up to Miriam she had rocked her hips and Miriam had snapped, 'Stop it!' Zaitoon had been surprised, and hurt by the rebuke that put an end to her innocent pleasure. She had felt rejected.

Sakhi's fingers slid lower, probing the curling hair. For the first time she became aware of a wet, burning sensation, almost a painful inflammation, between her thighs. She had been discomfited by it before and had hugged her chest to ease her ache. Taboos, unconsciously absorbed, had prevented her from exploring lower and she had not really known any relief. His fingers were rough but it was a roughness she hankered after – she discovered now the natural centre of her love. Sakhi's breath was infinitely sweet in her ears and her own breath weaved carefully in and out, intent on listening to the new notes pulsing in her body. She was dimly aware of Sakhi removing her shalwar and her nakedness was suddenly the most natural thing in the world.

❖

Sakhi had touched too intimately. It hurt. In a prim reflex movement Zaitoon pushed away his hand. 'No!'

'Why not? It's my cunt!' he breathed, holding her crotch in a warm squeeze, and yes, Zaitoon thought, his fever was

162

her own. She wanted to dissolve into his blood and be flesh of his flesh.

Sakhi was above her. She lusted to graft herself to him, and not knowing even how to hold him to herself, lay stiff beneath him. Sakhi tried to penetrate her. Obstructed by her straight stiff legs, he sat back on his heels. His heart welled with tenderness and pride at his bride's obvious innocence.

'Like this,' he whispered, gently teaching her legs to separate.

Holding himself, his fingers groping, he pushed. She felt her own palpitating softness yield a bit, and then there was pain. It snapped her senses back to her surroundings. Her body, after all, had not been prepared for pain. His action was shockingly strange and her abandon in their preceding intimacies suddenly seemed to her indecent. 'What are you doing?' she gasped. 'Stop it!' Her body twisted and convulsed. Hardly feeling her hands pushing at his chest Sakhi pressed harder and Zaitoon screamed.

Zaitoon became aware of the extraordinary motion of his body. She squirmed, helpless beneath the animal retraction and thrust. Not knowing the intricacies of the male organ she did not know that an extension of Sakhi was inside her. She never felt it. She felt only the rhythm of a suction and press against her crotch and gradually, penetrating her pain and her screams, the rhythm beat within her too. With each impact she felt an astonishing sweetness radiate from her loins, a deep stirring within her that churned her senses and turned her blood to honey. Straining towards him, her nails digging into his back, she sobbed in anguished but releasing moans.

❖

At dawn, pillowing her head on her arms, Zaitoon scrutinised the man sleeping by her. Her eyes misted with love in tracing the sensual, clearly defined curves of a mouth

163

that was stern and firm-lipped even in repose, the slight hook on his narrow nose and the bronze, ear-length hair that lay tousled in thick disorder. She saw masculinity in each line and feature, in the width of his broad shoulders and wrists. The suggestion of something primitive, a trace of cruelty felt rather than seen, enhanced his appeal. Though he was asleep, her smile was shy and tremulous in alternating waves of tenderness and passion. She wanted to touch not his face but his feet, to rub her lashes on the soles of his feet and kiss them; to hold his legs to her bosom in an ecstasy of devotion.

Her adoring eyes slid from his thighs and chest to his face – and she suddenly realised that Sakhi was watching her. The arrogance and vanity of his temper was reflected in the cool appraisal that met her startled look.

Her heart jumped. Dazzled by the blue animation of his eyes, Zaitoon's pupils narrowed to fine points, as though she had looked on waters mirroring sunlight, the incandescent river of her dream.

Rising from the bed and keeping her face averted, she slipped from the room. Leaning against the mud wall of their hut, bathed in the cold light of the sun rising behind cloud-obscured summits, she took deep breaths to calm the confused excitement she felt. A few moments later Sakhi called to her and she went in. Her head was bowed in remembrance of the night before, and her lips trembled like moth's wings. Sakhi pulled her to him. Hiding her face on his chest, she felt filled with life.

❖

The morning meal, on the second day of their marriage, lay half-eaten on the charpoy. The clay platter contained sweetened yellow rice and spitted lamb left over from the wedding feast. Sakhi and Zaitoon sat in constrained silence. Zaitoon wished she had not spoken.

Sakhi's profile was grim with anger.

'So! The mighty Major wants to see me, does he? He might dole me out some work?'

Zaitoon, scared by his sudden malice, sat mute.

Sakhi was seething with jealousy . . . the jawan's grip on the girl's arm, her laughter and ease in his company – the persistent vision inflamed him.

'Why did you let him touch you?' he hissed, turning dangerously.

Zaitoon stared at him in blank amazement.

'I saw you,' he shouted. 'I saw the jawan hold your arm all the way down to the river.' Sakhi's face was contorted with fury.

Zaitoon, unable to fathom his accusation, felt stricken. She bowed her head, her lips quivering in subdued weeping.

'You laughed together as if you were lovers. I could hear you all the way across the river,' cried Sakhi, burying his face in his hands.

After a while he removed the platter to the floor and lay back on the charpoy, studying the girl who sat hunched by the edge of the bed.

'You think your Major's quite something, don't you? A few days back I surprised the bastard crawling on all fours, sniffing at an Angraze woman like a dog! We threw stones at them – laughed at them. Coming to our territory as if it belonged to them: to their bastard forefathers!' He spat contemptuously. 'And that filthy dog spoke to you, offered your husband work! Listen, I don't work for anyone – ever,' he blazed in wrath. 'If I see any of those swine again I'll kill them!'

Zaitoon sat frozen. The sound of people gathered outside filtered through the tense stillness of their room.

'I think your father is leaving. Don't you wish to bid him farewell?'

Something in his tone made Zaitoon search his face. It did not matter that he mocked her, but she resented his unmis-

165

takable contempt of Qasim. He looked down on her father for having consorted with the ludicrous Major. Nor should he have allowed the girl such lax proximity to the jawan.

❖

Qasim waited for Zaitoon. He had seen her only once since her marriage and she had been deeply reticent. He had blessed her and looked into her face with tender probing. It grieved him to leave her, but it had to be. Her marriage to Sakhi would consummate an old, fervent longing. Through their children she would be one with his blood! He planned to visit the village each year, and he had exacted a promise from Misri Khan that Zaitoon was to be brought to Lahore for the delivery of her first child. Miriam, he knew, would be reassured to hear of this and so would Nikka.

Qasim glanced anxiously at the hut allotted to the newly-weds. Forty odd, the inhabitants of the village were gathered near him. The women stood bunched at a little distance from the men. Having blessed the women and their children, he again joined the men.

The door of the hut swung open and Sakhi came out. Zaitoon followed close behind, her flushed face framed by the green chaddar presented by the Memsahib. The bunch of ragged women sniffled in anticipation of a scene reminiscent of their own marriage farewells as Zaitoon's forlorn figure approached her father. They noted with satisfaction that she was weeping.

Qasim had an unreasoning impulse to take her back with him on some pretext or other. Miriam after all might have been right. He should have listened to the child's violent plea the night they arrived. His departure imminent, he felt he had acted in undue haste. Too late, he tried to fight this wave of sentimentality and fear. It had been brought on by the parting, he reasoned; she was bound to be happy. 'Allah,' he

166

thought, 'if anything should happen to her I will not be able to bear it!' Filled with misgiving he went to her.

Zaitoon felt piteously vulnerable and slender in his arms. Now that the moment was near Qasim did not know what to say. 'Hush, Munni,' he murmured, holding her close to him. 'You will be coming to Lahore soon – to have your first-born. I'll visit you often, I promise. I'll bring Miriam and Nikka to see you . . .' Valiantly submerging his own grief he tried to soothe her.

Sakhi's mother stepped forward. Gently she pulled her son's wife away from Qasim and towards her.

Leaving her in Hamida's arms, Qasim, his back hunched like an old man's, walked up to the men waiting to accompany him to Pattan.

Zaitoon brushed her eyes and stood staring. Her total severance from her carefree past was personified by Qasim's imminent departure. The enormity of the change she faced struck her with brutal force. In an intuitive flash – sapphire eyes and ice-blue waters merged with the terror of her dream in the cave – it was an ominous presentiment. 'Father,' she screamed, 'Don't go. Don't go!'

Qasim glanced at her briefly and turned away again.

'Abba, I'm coming with you. Abba!' she cried, breaking the old woman's hold and running to Qasim. 'Wait for me!'

She reached him and, panting, wrapped her limbs round him in a frenzied hug. 'I'm coming with you. Take me, Abba,' she begged. A village dog barked excitedly about them.

❖❖

'Zaitoon,' Qasim whispered in despair, 'think of the people watching you. You're a married woman now . . . not a child. Your place is with your husband. He is a good man. Haven't you liked him?'

167

'I don't know, Abba ... I don't know him. Why must you leave so soon? Stay here or take me with you.'

Sakhi pushed his way through the men gathered round Qasim. He was mortified by his bride's tempestuous display before all his kinsfolk. His voice was level but his grubby fingers bit vengefully into her flesh when he told her,

'Come now, your father will visit us again soon.'

'Yes, of course I will,' said Qasim, a little too stridently, desperately trying to disguise his broken, suddenly old-sounding voice.

Chapter 19

That whole day the girl wept. Sakhi, miserably aware that his severity had contributed to her hysteria, tried to mollify her. He brought her bread and meat but she flung them away. He tried to talk to her with what gentleness he was capable of, but she only cried, 'I want to go back.' She would not even look at him. Hamida tried to soothe her but she cried, 'Don't touch me.' There was no appeasing her. Sakhi was distraught and humiliated. Zaitoon was distressed and frightened. Yet she felt an odd satisfaction, a timorous sense of triumph, in the clumsy efforts to placate her. She had gauged the savage subjugating will of the man she was married to. His uneasiness and his efforts to calm her were a desperate comfort.

The past week had been too much for her: her emotions had soared to unaccustomed heights of adulation, tenderness and passion; her dreams had rocketed to the stars. Then came the mercurial change that sent her crashing back into blind chasms.

Sakhi and Hamida at last left her alone, sitting on the floor in a corner of the squalid room, her head buried on her knees.

In the evening Sakhi returned to find her huddled in the same position. Crouching before her he caught her arms and, peering at her face, compelled her to look at him. Zaitoon's dark, red-rimmed eyes, blazing like a furnace, scorched him.

Routed by centuries of ruthless pride, submerged beneath the hard toil, buried in a way of life that could afford no sentiment, a spark of pity nevertheless fought through.

'But you liked me yesterday,' Sakhi said softly, 'didn't you?'

Zaitoon studied his face, his captivating eyes now pleading and remorseful. Closing her swollen lids, she buried her face in his lap.

Four days after his marriage Sakhi decided to resume his chores. Leading a gaunt, ravaged ox up a hill to a fallow strip of earth, his path lay along a sprouting of young rice. His brother, Yunus Khan, was working in the rice patch.

Dexterously loosening the crust at the base of the young shoots, Yunus Khan appeared too absorbed to notice the noisy passing of his brother. Sakhi frowned. Grabbing the ox by its tail he stopped the beast and stood looking defiantly at Yunus. Yunus Khan's mouth was a hard line. His large jaw worked like a trowel on a wad of tobacco. Crowded disproportionately above his lips were his pugnacious features and a sloping forehead; and his ears stuck out.

'Salaam-alaikum, brother.' Sakhi saluted, pointedly awaiting the customary response.

Crumbling the soil with long, knobby fingers, Yunus Khan idly patted it level. He wiped his face with the back of his sleeve and sat back in ponderous self-absorption.

Sakhi stood mute with anger. He struck the ox truculently to make it go and at last Yunus turned his slanting eyes his way.

'Waleykum-salaam,' he replied. 'How is your wife from the plains? You know, she requires a man to control her . . .' he murmured in thin-lipped scorn. His eyes, the same colour as Sakhi's, were conciliatory but the calculated pity lurking in them stung Sakhi. Viciously turning away, he aimed a stone at the animal climbing ahead.

All morning, cruelly wounded by his brother's taunt, Sakhi laboured furiously. He flushed with shame when he thought of his efforts to appease the recalcitrant girl. Undoubtedly the news of her abrasive temper and of his docile

170

efforts to mollify her had spread all over the village. What must they think of him, he wondered, his cheeks tightening as he descried the distant clutter of huts belonging to his kinsmen. His memory recalled the girl, bare-headed, brazenly running to cling to her father – exposing herself to the stares of all his clansmen. Most likely they doubted his manhood! 'I will show them,' he thought, lunging at his plough.

Quick to anger, in a land where pride and wrath are nurtured from boyhood, he burned with an insane ungovernable fury.

At noon his mother called to remind him to chop some wood. Sakhi did not reply. She called his name stridently, again and again, opening her toothless mouth in imperative command.

'Can't you see I'm working, you old hag!' he shouted finally, and she stopped calling.

❖

Having tended to their scattered strips of earth, his clansmen had dispersed. Most of them had gone from the village to labour on the road, meet friends, or just to wander by the river as it changed colour with the approaching dusk. The valley was mellow with the smoke of cooking fires. Women prepared meagre rations for the children and for their men returning with the dark.

Sakhi worked with obsessive vigour. He was stripped to the waist, and his lean, rock-hard body gleamed with sweat. Having ploughed the fallow patch twice over, he began to work on a steppe not yet quite hewn from the mountainside. Skirting massive boulders, he ploughed dry, hard clay. With strength born of anger he cleared the surface of incidental rocks, rolling them outwards to the boundaries. There was one jagged, half-submerged rock he was sure he could uproot. Applying leverage with the plough, he set the ox to

171

pull. It strained with all its might, skidding in the effort, but the rock did not shift. Sakhi pushed and prodded the ox cruelly with his staff. The exhausted beast tried again and again. Then it skidded to its stomach and refused to budge.

'Get up,' roared Sakhi, swearing as he struck a blow. The ox stretched its neck on the grit, resting obstinately. Sakhi shouted and fell on the animal, beating it with his heavy stick, which fell pitilessly on a sore on its spine. The beast grunted, lifting its neck in pain. Sakhi's eyes dilated, and a venomous satisfaction shuddered through him. He hit the ox again and again, until the flesh gaped open. The beast roared and writhed, desperately trying to stand and get away from its tormentor.

Hearing the noise, Sakhi's mother came out of her hut. She focused her weak sight on the steppe, and the effort stretched her chronic grin even more grotesquely.

Hamida's long legs carried her bent, stringy body swiftly to where her son was belabouring the beast. She caught at his flailing arms. 'Let it be, you will kill him,' she screeched. Sakhi pushed the old woman aside. Again she flung herself at him, wedging her body between the man and the ox. Sakhi glowered in insane fury. 'I'll teach you,' he hissed, 'I'll teach you meddling women. You think you can make a fool of me? Do you?'

Hamida cowered under the raised stick. The blow caught her shoulder. She scrambled like a crab down the sloping terrain. Sakhi skidded after her, wielding his staff. She tried to run, but a blow hit her legs and she fell forward. Zaitoon, who had followed Hamida, was appalled. She could hear women come running from varying directions behind her.

'For God's sake stop it,' she wailed. 'For God's sake, you'll kill her!' She could hear the shrill remonstrance of the women close behind. She tried to take hold of the swinging stick. It knocked painfully against her knuckles but she caught it and tried to wrench it away. Sakhi struck her on her thighs, on her head, shouting, 'You are my woman! I'll

172

teach you to obey me!' Zaitoon stumbled and sprawled face down.

Mercifully the screeching women were upon him. Sakhi turned and flung the staff up the mountain slope. He strode at a furious pace and disappeared behind some rocks. Zaitoon, trembling like a leaf, and moaning in pain, was helped to her feet by the women.

She spent the rest of the evening taking over Hamida's chores. The old woman lay rolled up in a threadbare blanket on the floor, ominously quiet.

❖

Hamida lay stiff beneath her blanket, dazed with shock. Her mind seemed to drift in and out of consciousness. Late at night it cleared and she felt she would die. But death, to one who had seen so much of it, did not greatly matter.

Early next morning, sensing the girl's presence, she whispered, 'Zaitoon, I think I will die soon.'

There was no self-pity in her feeble voice.

Zaitoon felt she ought to say something, but words failed her. She felt grief. Once again, she was to be abandoned. She started to cry, at the same time relieving her hopelessness and convincingly conveying the proper sentiment.

But Hamida did not die. Instead, two days after the brutal beating, she recovered enough to sit on a warm rock and sun her shrivelled body.

❖

Her work done, Zaitoon would sit by the resilient old woman, massaging her wasted arms and legs and shoulders. Hamida talked of her youth, of the price her vivacious beauty had fetched on marriage, and of the events that led to the blood feuds, and to the violent deaths of three of her sons who had been older than Sakhi and Yunus. She gossiped about long-dead ancestors, many of whom she had never seen, and anecdote by anecdote, she documented the restless history of her fierce clan.

Zaitoon, anxious to learn, absorbed every detail.

Her existence in those few days mirrored the grim drudgery of the mountain people. Subsisting on baked maize and water, supplemented occasionally by a little rice, she laboured all day, chaffing, kneading, washing, and tending the animals and the young green rice-shoots and the sprouting maize. She collected animal droppings and, patting them into neat discs with her hands, plastered them to the hut. Dried by the sun, they provided cooking fuel. Occasionally she directed the flow of irrigation waters, ingeniously channelled from the stream into the terraced patches of cultivation. Gradually, in her quest for firewood, Zaitoon became familiar with the terrain.

She also grew immune to the tyrannical, animal-trainer treatment meted out by Sakhi. In his presence she drifted into a stupor, until nothing really hurt her. He beat her on the slightest pretext. She no longer thought of marriage with any sense of romance. She now lived only to placate him, keeping her head averted unless it was to listen to a command. Then her eyes were anxious and obsequious like those of Hamida.

At night she acquiesced docilely. Sometimes though, when the lamplight gilded their isolation, she surrendered to him with an unreasoning passion. Sakhi wondered at this, but on the whole he was delighted. He looked his brother in the eye, and swaggered. At times he was kind, but these exceptions were followed by needless severity.

Zaitoon's instinct for self-preservation alone kept her going. At night she lay awake, her stupor lifting awhile as she indulged her fancies. She longed for Qasim's love, for Miriam's companionship, for the protective aura of Nikka's status. In the plains, she had not even been aware of these

174

securities. Now she longingly lived for her promised visit to Lahore...

Heavy with child, she sits by Miriam. Miriam weeps, caressing her tired limbs, enfolding her in her protective flesh. She flares at Qasim: The child is not to be sent back. She will not allow it! Qasim remonstrates and Miriam, pulling Zaitoon's shirt open, dramatically reveals the cruel welts and bruises. Zaitoon hangs her head in shame.

Surely Qasim will cry! He will stroke her hair and, holding her tenderly, declare a terrible vendetta against Sakhi.

Zaitoon knew it took nine months for a child to come. She was sure to have a child by then. But nine months is a long time for a miserable young girl. And two months into her marriage an incident convinced her she might not live that long.

Chapter 20

Carol meandered apathetically around the Mess, dividing her time between her paint box and paperbacks, waiting fervently for Farukh to dash off on excursions contrived by Mushtaq. Only then did she emerge from her inertia. She was infatuated with the Major, and she wondered if she had ever really loved Farukh.

A year after coming to Lahore it had slowly dawned on Carol that the repressed erotic climate was beginning to affect her. In the States, what she had thought was a unique attraction for Farukh had in fact been her fascination with the exotic, and later the attraction had disconcertingly extended itself to include his friends and relatives – and even acquaintances. She realised her casual American ways here, in a country where few women were seen unveiled, made her youth and striking looks an immediate challenge. She got more than her share of attention – more than any woman ought! She knew Farukh was right when he said: 'These goddamned men even fall in love with holes in trees! Don't let it flatter you.' But she *was* flattered. Being naturally responsive she could not remain unaffected.

God knows Carol had tried to modify her behaviour. She had conformed as well as anyone brought up to be free and easy with men could! – she thought, reflecting on the advances she had resisted, at first casually, then with increasing strain.

The men were not overtly sexual: rather she sensed their sexual tension. Their desire for her carried a natural tenderness that was reflected in their behaviour to all women. They

176

showed a surprisingly gentle consideration of her vulnerabilities, of the differences between the sexes that made her feel complete – and completed the men. The bronze, liquid-eyed men became increasingly disturbing . . . and the Major had slipped through her defences, shattering a heroic resistance of which only she was aware.

Each time Mushtaq stood before her Carol was swamped anew by desire. It was as if the struggle with Farukh's jealousy, combined with the bewildering forces let loose within her in Pakistan, had broken in a storm of feelings centred on Mushtaq. A glimpse of him, by chance in the morning along the Mess corridor, or out of her window, left her enfeebled and breathless.

Noticing her pallor and worried by her erratic behaviour, Farukh secretly surmised that at long last his wife was pregnant.

Early in the morning, not wishing to disturb Carol, he dressed quietly. Before leaving, he tiptoed round the bed to kiss her goodbye and, finding Carol's eyes wide open in unseeing reverie, inquired, 'What's the matter, darling? Anything wrong?'

Carol shook her head. 'No. Oh, I feel sleepy. Are you going?'

'You don't look well. I think it's the altitude.'

'At only five thousand feet above sea-level?' Her voice curled a contemptuous question-mark.

'That's high enough to upset anyone not used to the mountains. You look pale. I think we should return to Lahore.'

'Lahore . . . sure, it's up to you.' Carol kicked the quilt, and turned away irritably.

Having heard of the irascibility of expectant women Farukh held his temper. He sat docilely on the edge of her bed.

'Bye, darling. I'm going,' he whispered, nervously touching the bare arms that covered her face.

177

❖

Mushtaq returned from Pattan an hour after Farukh had left for Bisham, the hill reputedly garrisoned by Alexander the Great on his way to India.

He glanced at his wrist-watch. It would take Farukh four hours to cover that distance. That gave them ample time. Knocking lightly on Carol's door he went in.

Carol stood in the glow of the log fire. She was wearing a flimsy slip and was gratified by Mushtaq's startled look of possessive admiration. He went to her quickly.

Cupping her breasts with both hands, Mushtaq pressed against Carol impatiently. She lifted her mouth and Mushtaq kissed her. He seldom remembered this preliminary caress and Carol's insistence on it amused him. Kissing was to him a gesture of affection. He kissed his wife with the same quality of feeling he reserved for his children. From romantic scenes in foreign movies he surmised that kissing represented the act of love, indicating what in Pakistani films was conveyed by a pair of converging lotus flowers. He found kissing Carol mildly pleasurable, but chiefly because of the excitement it aroused in her.

'There's something I want to say to you,' she said seriously.

'Can't it wait?'

'Please . . .'

Carol stepped back and, curling her legs beneath her, she sat down on the stuffed sofa to one side of the fire. Mushtaq perched on its arm, hungrily ogling the rich, flame-licked hues of her body.

'What is it, sweetheart?'

Carol held his eyes: 'Marry me.'

Mushtaq blanched at the unexpected demand. A block of ice plopped into his stomach.

'I love you, darling,' she breathed. 'I can't bear to live

178

without you. You don't know how I feel,' and she pressed her breasts against his coat sleeve, lowering her head. 'God, I'd do anything for you. I would really – wear a burkha if you wanted me to.'

Growing up in the 1950s, Carol was inexorably conditioned to marriage. She had only one recourse with which to reconcile her feelings and her actions. She had found her true love. He must marry her.

'Oh, if you stopped loving me, I'd kill myself!'

Mushtaq stared. Carol, despite her egotism, must realise he was having a fling, merely killing time. She knew he had a wife and four children to whom he belonged irrevocably.

'What about Farukh?' he asked lamely.

'I don't love him, you know that! Even if you don't marry me, I shall leave him,' she declared. 'Oh, darling, please get me away from him or I'll die,' she sobbed.

Her tears aroused in Mushtaq a bewildering desire to discard everything and marry this woman; possess for ever her eager childless body. Inflamed by the sleek configuration of creases he could see through the filmy nylon, by the malleable curve of her breasts so rich to his touch, he knelt before her. Nuzzling his face between her thighs, he cried, 'Of course I will marry you, sweetheart, if that's what you want.'

They lay on the carpet near the fire. Carol was covering Mushtaq's face with rapturous, moist kisses. 'I love you,' she sighed.

❖

'Let's see to the fire,' he said.

Pushing her aside gently, he rose.

'You'll have to break the news to Farukh. Oh dear, I wonder how he'll take it,' Carol mused aloud.

A dour, self-pitying anger welled up in Mushtaq. He had been coerced. His capitulation to her proposal was born of his long separation from his family, his need for a woman in the loneliness of his remote posting. The quicker he set things straight, the better. All this talk of dying and demented passion! She would get over it in time.

'Talking of marriages,' he said, 'I was invited to a wedding feast. Remember the girl, the one with the old watchman from Lahore? Her father sent the invitation. I was to take as many guests as I liked.'

Carol sat up. 'I'd have loved to go. Why didn't you take me?' she cried excitedly.

'Certainly not, young lady!'

'I've often thought of the girl, you know. I felt I understood her . . . No . . . it's more as if she'd explained something to me. I'd like to know her better: how she grew up, what she did after she stopped going to school. How she laughs and talks with her friends. Her life is so different from mine, and yet I feel a *real* bond, an understanding on some deep level. She was so self-conscious with us, I wonder what she dreams about . . .'

But Carol, a child of the bright Californian sun and surf, could no more understand the beguiling twilight world of veils and women's quarters than Zaitoon could comprehend her independent life in America.

Reflecting on this Mushtaq said, 'It wouldn't be easy for you really to understand her. You'd find her life in the zenanna with the other women pitifully limited and claustrophobic – she'd probably find yours – if she could ever glimpse it – terrifyingly insecure and needlessly competitive.'

'Perhaps you're right. All the same I wish you'd taken me to the wedding.'

'You know I wouldn't take you across the river again. For all we know, those ruffians from the ledge would most likely have been there. You wouldn't have liked that.'

Carol frowned. 'You are getting abominably like Farukh; with your caution and sermons.'

180

'Yes, and soon you will loathe me as much.'

'Never, never!' protested Carol vehemently.

'Yes, you will,' he said, 'and then you'll find yourself a dashing brigadier.'

'Not if we were married.'

Mushtaq tapped her forehead playfully. 'Knock those silly ideas out of your head, will you? However much I'd like to you know I can't. Nor for that matter can you.'

'You could get a divorce.'

'No. It's not so easy.'

'It's easy for you Muslim men. All you have to do is tell your wife "talak" three times and wait three months. I know it.'

'You don't understand at all. In spite of what you hear about our being able to have four wives, we take marriage and divorce very seriously. It involves more than just emotions. It's a social responsibility . . . For one thing, at the very least, my wife's life would become unbearably confined, drab and unhappy. And we're cousins, you know. Our families would make my life – and yours – miserable. We'd be ostracised.'

He knelt above Carol and, holding her crestfallen face between his hands, shook it affectionately. 'Don't be silly, darling. You know I love you, but Farukh is my friend – and there are so many obligations – you have them too, you know. Come on, give me a smile?'

Carol's eyes were closed. Mushtaq kissed her. 'You'll realise it's better this way. Come on, smile.'

'Why not?' she said, 'but first . . .'

Her furious eyes blazed open. Swinging her hand deliberately, she slapped Mushtaq full in the face. She laughed when anger blotched his skin.

'All right, now *you* smile!' she said quietly.

Chapter 21

Zaitoon wandered far from the village one morning in her search for kindling. Her feet were now somewhat used to the uneven land and she set herself to climb a steep hill. While she caught her breath, her eyes scanned the barren place for brushwood.

One by one, hacked by ancient settlers, the fir trees that once stood here had been destroyed. Later, whole hills, purchased by wealthy merchants, were stripped. Logs floated down the Indus to the plains until no tree was left. Barely distinguishable from the slate rocks near Zaitoon, humped an ancient, withered, sawn-off trunk.

Abstractedly lifting her glance, Zaitoon noticed a faint, incongruous line stretched across a distant mountain as if someone with a brush-stroke had tried to mark the centre of the hill. Zaitoon's pulse quickened. It had to be the road on which she and Qasim had travelled. She could not see the river, but by tracing the sinking line of worn-away granite she sensed the passage of the river gorge. Desperately she wanted to see again the turbulent waters of the magnificent river. Looking about, and satisfied no one was watching her, she hurried down the hill.

It was rough going. She skirted the base of a towering peak through a maze of defiles and ridges. Finally she came upon a path that led to the river.

Soon she was able to make out the unmistakable roar of the waters.

The track went all the way down the gorge to the river-beach and into the soft white sand.

Prepared for the shock of icy cold, Zaitoon leaned to touch the water. Something seemed to float towards her

182

from the depths, a shadow about to break the surface. Reliving her bad dream, she imagined the blurred movement of a hand about to reach out . . .

A thick bundle of entwined flotsam churned up to be dragged under again almost at once. She looked about her and was stricken by a sense of her isolation.

Scampering frantically up the cliff face, Zaitoon climbed to a high ledge. A wide view here lifted the pall of loneliness. Right across the broad span of the river, level with her, was the road; a line of winding grey – cleaving to the gorge as though afraid of losing its way in the wilderness.

A heavily loaded truck rumbled into view, changed by distance to a mechanical toy. Zaitoon followed its passage, and the world resumed its rational perspective: the river once again was a gorgeous mass of water, widening at times into flat blue lagoons, and cascading into a froth where it was forced down a tortuous incline.

Zaitoon settled comfortably on the ledge. She had not felt carefree in a long while. A jeep passed, bumping and bobbing. Two men sat in front. Eagerly trying to decipher the khaki uniforms, she fancied Ashiq at the wheel and next to him the Major. Recalling the Major's concern for her and the tender eyes of the dark jawan, she wished she had waved to them. She knew she belonged with them.

A small pebble clattered down the vertical stone massif behind her. Striking a rock a few paces away, it leapt outward and she watched its jerky fall all the way to the sand. Glancing up to scan the impassive cliff, she saw no movement, heard no untoward sound, but just the same an uneasiness slowly gripped her heart.

Keeping to the shelter of the rocks, she quickly retraced her steps to the track. The sun was low and the trail cold with wind and dark. It wound like a tunnel between the hills.

Yunus Khan observed the girl's fearful retreat. He had witnessed her scramble up to the ledge, and the elation that

183

lit her face at seeing the jeep. Naturally quiet, with no apparent effort at stealth, he shadowed her with an easy tread. A few paces ahead he heard her slip and stumble. Waiting a moment, he caught her gasping breath.

Circling wide of Zaitoon's route, Yunus Khan idly made his way to the hamlet, arriving almost fifteen minutes ahead of her.

Sakhi that day had gone to a neighbouring village. They wanted a goat for a marriage feast and Sakhi, who had one to barter, drove a hard bargain. When he approached his village late in the evening, Yunus met him. They embraced and sat on a rock talking late into the freezing night.

Zaitoon was asleep when Sakhi snuggled roughly up to her under their common quilt. Disturbed, she muttered heavily.

'What did you say?' he asked.

'You're late.' Her tongue was thick with sleep.

'Yes,' Sakhi lay still for a while. 'You went to the river?'

Zaitoon's mind leapt awake. She paused a second before replying: 'U-hum . . .' She feigned a drowsy nonchalance.

'Don't go there again.'

His peremptory tone was charged with malice.

Zaitoon lay awake long after Sakhi had fallen asleep.

Early the next morning Sakhi left, shooing the bartered goat before him with a small stick.

Zaitoon rushed through her chores. Sakhi's cryptic injunction of the night before weighed down her spirits with the dull despondency of a half-remembered nightmare. She longed with all her heart to be by the river, to look upon the road that hushed her misery. Certain that Sakhi would not return until much later, she scurried circumspectly down the track. She slid between a clump of rocks, concealed from view by an overhang of the cliff. Reasonably confident of her privacy, she muttered a silent prayer.

Traffic on the road was desultory. A convoy of three trucks finally lumbered by, and thereafter nothing.

184

Zaitoon feasted her eyes on the river, on the dust so slow to settle back on the road. She had a momentary twinge of guilt, instantly drowned in the roar of the water. She tarried. Compromising with caution, she swore to start on her way back the moment another vehicle passed.

It was an hour before the jeep droned into view. The solitary figure at the wheel was barely perceptible. Zaitoon sat up. On an impulse she smiled and merrily waved her hands.

Even if the driver had scanned the view it is doubtful he would have seen the flutter of the slender brown arms in a jungle of granite.

A stone hit Zaitoon hard on her spine. She whirled, her eyes frantically searching the boulders. Another stone hit her head and bounced on, clattering down the rocks. She looked up in terror. To one side of the overhang, almost vertically above her, stood Sakhi. Impassive and intent, the sapphire fire of his eyes did not shift. In the strange Himalayan luminosity that intensifies angles and colours, he towered, inhuman. His gaze held the cool power of an avenging god.

Sakhi's hand flicked again, and the stone grazed her forehead. With her eyes riveted on him in bewilderment and terror, hurriedly Zaitoon scrambled for safety. He jumped, landing as lightly as a cat on a small flat rock. Another leap and he was level with her. Zaitoon tried to scramble backwards, blindly scraping her knuckles on the rock wall.

Skimming the boulders in vast strides, Sakhi seized her. He dragged her along the crag. 'You whore,' he hissed. His fury was so intense she thought he would kill her. He cleared his throat and spat full in her face. 'You dirty, black little bitch, waving at those pigs . . .' Gripping her with one hand he waved the other in a lewd caricature of the girl's brief gesture. 'Waving at that shit-eating swine. You wanted him to stop and fuck you, didn't you!'

Zaitoon stood in a cataleptic trance. Sakhi shook her like

185

a rattle, and at last she cried, 'Forgive me, forgive me, I won't do it again . . . Forgive me,' she kept repeating the words to quell his murderous rage.

Sakhi's face was bestial with anger. 'I will kill you, you lying slut!'

He slapped her hard, and swinging her pitilessly by the arm, as a child swings a doll, he flung her from him. A sharp flint cut into her breast, and in a wild lunge she blindly butted her head between the man's legs. In the brief scuffle, the cord of Sakhi's trousers came undone and the baggy gathers at the waist of his shalwar flopped to his ankles. Sakhi froze. Transfixed on the ledge, he blanched. What if someone had witnessed his ultimate humiliation?

Zaitoon knelt in misgiving and suspense. There was no viler insult a woman could inflict on a man.

Sakhi quickly secured the cord of his shalwar round his waist, glowering with thunderous hatred. Zaitoon flinched. He aimed a swift kick between her legs, and she fell back. Sakhi kicked her again and again and pain stabbed through her. She heard herself screaming.

At last he lifted her inert body across his shoulders and carried her home.

That night Zaitoon resolved to run away. Her sleepless eyes bright with shock, her body racked by pain, she knew that in flight lay her only hope of survival. She waited two days, giving herself a chance to heal.

The following morning when she set out with the empty water container, Hamida's weak voice trilled behind her. 'Zaitoon . . . Why are you taking the blanket? Here, you can have my chaddar.'

Zaitoon felt the bundle of maize bread she had collected press painfully against her fluttering stomach as she turned to face the old woman who was leaning against the decayed door-post.

'I don't feel well,' she called, 'and it's cold by the stream.'

Zaitoon and Hamida stood a moment facing each other.

The older woman felt an emptiness she could not identify.

'All right. But be back soon, my child,' she pleaded.

Zaitoon nodded. The dark blanket around her head bobbed reassuringly. Turning away, she walked slowly up the slope and over the valley rim.

At the stream Zaitoon scooped the clear liquid in her palms and drank until the icy water numbed the fear in the pit of her stomach. She filled the container and sat awhile by the happy little rock-strewn water-course.

Then, carefully she ventured into the unfamiliar hills.

Chapter 22

Sakhi slouched on the overhang. His ears were alert for the slightest sound and his deceptively somnolent eyes were ready to pick any movement at all in the familiar, convoluted landscape. Here he had caught Zaitoon waving at the army jeep.

Sakhi knew each crest and hidden gully for miles around.

An eagle forayed into the gorge and, sweeping up the cliff-face, perched just beneath him, pecking at some unrecognisable prey.

The man and the eagle caught the sound simultaneously. Closing his talons on the carrion, the bird stiffened. He pecked tentatively once more and decided to take to the air.

Sakhi wondered if the swoosh of wings would deter her, but then he heard a distinct crunch on the gravel. She wouldn't dare, he thought. With morbid elation, his lips set in a thin smile; he waited.

The footsteps down the track grew definite and Sakhi now saw the sheepskin cap of a man on his way to the river. He let go his breath and lay back.

Late in the afternoon he lazily threaded his way to the village.

His mother stood at a small distance from the mud rampart surrounding the settlement, as if waiting for him. Anxiety stiffened his spine.

The grimace on Hamida's face widened alarmingly when she spied him. She appeared frightened and her old clawing hands fluttered.

'What is it?' he rasped.

188

The old woman wiped her eyes. 'Zaitoon has gone,' she squeaked.

'Where?' he asked harshly.

'She went to the stream this morning,' Hamida pleaded. 'I wonder what's happened to the child.'

'Why didn't you tell me earlier?' he snarled, his face ashen.

'I've been waiting . . . I didn't know where you'd gone. I went looking all over.'

'Have you told the others?'

'No,' she reassured him gravely.

The old woman suddenly beat her breasts.

'Hai,' she moaned. 'Hai, what has happened to her? Go and look for her . . .' she added needlessly.

Sakhi was already on his way.

He ran. He leapt nimbly across the boulders traversing the undulating distance at a speed that quickened the breeze against him. His heart was a furnace of anger. 'My God. If she has run away . . .' The thought sickened him. No. Most likely, she had slipped and hurt herself. Possibly even now a mountain leopard was at her. He prayed it might be so. She couldn't have run away. She wouldn't dare . . .

At the brook Sakhi scanned the surrounding hills. There was no trace of her. Then he saw the container placed upright on a stone. It was full to the brim. In desperation he searched for pug-marks or any sign of struggle or accident in the soft sand by the bubbling water.

He swore aloud, and in impotent rage beat his fists on his forehead. 'I knew that bitch would run away.' He had known it, and he had taken no measures to prevent it. He had invited the disgrace that now affected his entire clan. 'I should have killed her by the river!' Sakhi lifted a large rock and heaved it angrily into the shallows. He sat on the gritty earth and dashed his fists against the gravel. Later he climbed to some height to search the landscape minutely.

His eyes smarting with shame, he finally lumbered home.

189

The dusky air was pungent with smoke from cooking fires.

A huddle of men met him at his door. Yunus Khan's glacial, lantern-jawed face swam forward. The expectant faces of his cousins and clansmen swayed and parted to yield his shame and sorrow a silent passage into the hut.

A moment later, Yunus slipped in and closed the door. Sakhi was strapping a bandolier round his chest. He picked up his ancient Lee-Enfield, its woodwork decorated with silver studs. 'I'm going after her,' he said, raising his eyes to meet his brother's in a haze of distraction.

One behind the other, they emerged, eyes ablaze in fanatic determination. The crowd of tribals dispersed in a hushed understanding, each to get his own gun and prepare for the hunt. Not a word was said. They identified with the man's disgrace, taking the burden on themselves. Collectively, they meant to salvage the honour of the clan. The runaway's only route lay across the river. Once across, she was lost to them for ever. How then would they hold up their heads? The threatening disgrace hung like an acrid smell around them. It would poison their existence unless they found the girl.

There was only one punishment for a runaway wife.

Wordlessly, the men organised their hunt and walked into the twilight-shrouded mountains.

❖

Hamida sat in the middle of the waiting women. She buried her involuntary smile on her knees, shading her eyes, and the women could not see her tears course down the deep grooves on her face.

Honour! she thought bitterly. Everything for honour – and another life lost! Her loved ones dead and now the girl she was beginning to hold so dear sacrificed. She knew the infallibility of the mountain huntsmen.

The old woman was overcome by the memory of her three

190

dead sons: the weight of each child in her body for nine months, the excruciating pain, drudgery, sweat: and scant years later, the heartbreak when, one by one, each of her sons was carried home on a crude stretcher swinging from the men's shoulders, their faces grim with the weight of the corpse under an impoverished shroud. In each grief, a nameless dread: how many more lives would the dead one claim? The set faces of the men, their eyes burning with hate and a lust for revenge, their old make-shift guns for ever loved and polished, the leather slings decorated with coloured bands and tassels, cherished even more for the men they killed.

Men and honour. And now the girl . . .

Visions floated confusedly in her mind. She, who had been so proud and valiant and wholeheartedly subservient to the ruthless code of her forebears, now loathed it with all her heart. Surely God would punish her for this. She knew now she would die.

Her grey, henna-streaked head shook as with palsy, and the women stroking her hair murmured, 'There, there, don't fret. They'll be back soon with that bitch's corpse, your son's honour vindicated!'

Chapter 23

As the search-parties were leaving the village Zaitoon was discovering a path through the chaos of boulders, and had scrambled to the end of a narrow cleft. It opened on to a gritty rectangular plateau, and crawling from the dim passage, she sprawled face down on the earth. Gasping with exhaustion, eyes closed, she lay dead to the world.

A little later, she sat up to find her thighs still shaking.

This was the first time she had paused to rest since leaving the stream in the morning. Her every thought bent on flight, she had driven her body relentlessly through the mountains, intuitively following the river downstream.

On trembling knees, she surveyed the sterile landscape. Not a trace of life: not even the droppings of a mountaingoat. No sound but that of the cold breeze swooshing up from the deep shadows of the cleft and from concealed channels and gullies. Trailing her blanket, she wobbled towards a cluster of boulders.

Only after settling among them, sheltered from the evening wind and secure from view, did she allow her thoughts to surface. They crowded in on her in a clamouring disorder.

Twilight was fading. A dismal shade smudged the greypink sky rent by sharp mountain peaks.

Frightened by the shadows, Zaitoon snuggled into the darkness of her blanket. Its flimsy protection shut out the night. It joggled disconcertingly when Zaitoon tore at the bread. Her hunger appeased, she shut her eyes and lay inert. Inexplicably, the wind had ceased. The immense quiet of the empty world brooded around her and she grew tense, straining for any sound. The stillness poured its disquiet into her rigid body. She grew vastly afraid. She imagined strange creatures stalking the nocturnal wilderness. Snarling beasts tore at her – inhuman things crept up to touch her; the air within her blanket was lacerated by screams! And throughout, like a malign disease spreading, was the consciousness of Sakhi's insane wrath, his murderous cruelty.

Inching her fingers to the edge of her blanket, she peered out.

It was a velvety, moonless night. Enormous icy stars pierced her face with darts of cold. She looked stealthily at the rocks. Their insubstantial shadows harboured grotesque images. Eyes wide with terror, Zaitoon sprang up. She touched the hard reassuring contours of one of the stones. There was no movement but the knock of her heart.

Trembling, she sat down again, burrowing into her blanket.

Her eyes shut, Zaitoon began to pray. Concentrating on the cryptic Arabic incantations, she extracted from them a faith that once had transformed her childhood nightmares into peaceful dreams. Her voice rose to a whisper. Interspersing the mystic syllables with Punjabi, she begged, 'Allah help me, help me. Don't let me be afraid ... Allah protect me from the animals ...'

An inconsequential speck, lost in the endless chasms and heights of the Karakoram range, the girl gradually soothed herself with the comforting cadences. In a whisper, prayer and appeal poured from her mouth, and images advanced – of Miriam, of Nikka sitting on the sagging string-bed before his shop, and of Qasim. For a split second she saw Ashiq's handsome brown face and adoring eyes. She tried to hold the image, screwing her eyes shut beneath the blanket, but the features refused to form distinctly. All at once they fused with the image of Sakhi in the golden handsomeness of the day of their marriage, with the flaming pomegranate blossom behind his ear and his eyes lined with antimony; his hair falling copper from the centre-parting; and the lamplight

193

gleaming gold on his strong arms. She sensed the possessed, intoxicating brilliance of his eyes . . .

'But you liked me last night,' he says, and his contrite, bewildered look makes her reach out to stroke his cheeks . . .

Suddenly she longed to see him. With all her heart she wanted Sakhi to find her. His face, ravaged by concern, broken with remorse, floated before her – gently he wooed her . . .

And his soft caressing words lulled her to sleep.

❖

The sun climbed the mountain slope, thawed the rocks and touched back to life the numbed body of the sleeping girl.

Zaitoon blinked at the glare. She peered over the boulders at the sweep of scrubless, flinty earth and at the walls of cliffs surrounding it. To her right the plateau ended in a thin, sun-edged line that plunged abruptly into a precipice. There was no trace of habitation. Gusty little draughts from hidden crevices swept the crust and died among the boulders. For a while Zaitoon sat still, marshalling her sleep-stunned faculties. Her muscles felt stiff. Then, drawing the blanket round her shoulders, she scampered across the stretch of exposed land and burrowed down a narrow gap between two turreting cliffs.

All morning, tracing her direction from the sun, Zaitoon picked the most difficult route. She knew the easier passages would be the first to be searched by the tribals.

At noon, threading through a maze of winding gullies, Zaitoon climbed down into a dark, subterranean world of cold shadows. Like vermin in search of dim crevices, Zaitoon felt safe only in the dark. The air was dank along the narrow corridor and the stones beneath her feet were slippery. Far above, a slice of pale sky silhouetted the torn edges of the ravine.

Late in the afternoon she came across a drip of water

194

gathering into a shallow, basket-sized pool in the rocks. Gratefully scooping it in her hands, she slaked her thirst. She was ravenous. She ate some bread, chewing carefully to prolong its savour, and desisted from eating more. What if she did not find the bridge tomorrow? The thought put her in a cold sweat.

She knew she had made good progress that day. Buoyed up by the conviction that she would find the bridge soon, she had used her body callously. Disregarding the strain that tore her muscles and the stones that cut into her flesh, she had disassociated herself from the frame. Her body was to serve only one purpose: to convey her to the bridge at Dubair.

A moist breeze now fanned her skin and the girl began to shiver. She clasped her hands to her throat and sat down by the shallow pool. What if she had moved too far inland? Where was she? She was a fledgling far from its nest, lost in this drain deep in the earth, with icy winds whistling around her.

Overcome by a sudden wave of panic, she began to scramble across boulders like a crab. Barefoot, she tried to climb an almost vertical bluff and slithered down, scraping her skin. In pain, she cowered against the stone wall. Eyes seemed to peer from the shadows, yellow and fiendish, and fearsome shapes . . .

All at once she screamed, her voice keening at a hysterical pitch, and the echo of her scream congealed her panic into an immediate need for action.

Holding her breath, she scuttled swiftly along the stony bed of the chasm. A desperate instinct guided her, and, an hour later, she crawled over the crumbling edge of the ravine on to a sun-baked plateau.

The sun hung low in the sky between snow-softened summits. It nuzzled up to the girl as she lay face down, gasping for breath and trembling, and its warm magic calmed her. Pushing back her hair she stood up and looked

195

around. She trudged to a rocky niche and there, protected from the wind, settled down to her second night in the immense loneliness of the stony waste.

❖

All the next day, and the next, Zaitoon climbed into the mountains. The air grew rarer, and she breathed it in quick, exhausted gasps. High on the slopes dirty white glaciers nosed their way into the valley. She drank at the streams that trickled from them, and hot with exertion, splashed her face.

As the sun set it drained away the heat and the wind turned icy. Zaitoon was deathly cold. Huddled in the lee of an overhang she shivered. Her teeth chattered, until a cold, numbing sensation drugged her to sleep.

It took Zaitoon a while to be fully awake the next day. Had she not been so young and strong, she might have died of the cold. She could tell it was noon. The sun rode high and the rocks, once again radiating its heat, had revived her frozen body.

The girl sat up, vexed that she had slept through half the day. She ate a chappati, dipping it in the stream to soften the hard dry bread, and counted the remaining discs of maize. Only five! She had eaten two chappatis a day. She must eat even less. She stood up, surveying the bleak hills. Already she was out of breath. Recalling the numbing cold of the night before she decided to climb down to a lower altitude. Skirting the desolate hills she gradually descended. By evening she could tell from the warmer feel of the air and her eased breathing that she was considerably lower.

❖

Zaitoon gasped in dismay. She had struggled up a steep slope confident she would glimpse the river from there. The high ridge she had conquered swooped down and up again in a solid brown mass. All around was a maelstrom of mountains. They billowed out like frozen waves. The sun hung low now and at the farthest point snow-topped heights merged into clouds.

Zaitoon knew that somewhere in the serpentine vaults of the ravine and in the glacier-riven valleys she had lost her direction, and that the river gorge could be hidden anywhere in the myriad furrows between the mountains.

Darkness fell, and with it came fear. Mountains closed in on her like a pack of wolves.

Zaitoon shook her head in disbelief. 'These are not the same mountains,' she thought in horror of the hills she had loved at sight – whose magic and splendour lived in Qasim's reminiscences. Now she was appalled at the country's sudden menace. She realised that Qasim's presence, and even the presence of Sakhi and the tribesmen had concealed from her a truth; that the land she stood on was her enemy: a hostile inscrutable maze.

In trepidation, she scurried towards an eruption of rock. For the fifth night she curled up beneath her blanket.

Chapter 24

Leaning back on a ledge, Sakhi stretched his arms up and straightened his cramped legs. He felt bruised by the incessant weight of the gun across his thighs, and dusting the ground with his turban, he carefully placed the weapon by his side.

Gradually his body resumed its former posture: neck strained forward, shoulders and back slumped against the rock.

From here he could survey the bridge and all the accesses leading to it. He stared fixedly at the shiny asphalt surface of the bridge reflecting the sun, and his eyes throbbed painfully.

The moment he heard a sound, his muscles jumped alert and the ache in his body vanished. Silently he picked up the gun.

A soft footfall and then the scrape of leather on rock.

Sakhi slouched back, and a little later, when the tread he had recognised grew distinct, he called,

'Here, brother.'

The footsteps changed direction and Yunus Khan hauled his scraggy limbs over the edge.

'No sign of her yet?' he asked.

Sakhi shook his head. 'No, but she's bound to try the bridge sooner or later.'

He had said this to himself again and again, fending off the fear that she might have taken another route.

Beyond the bridge, in the distance, a cloud of dust travelled along the ground marking the passage of an invisible vehicle heading towards Pattan.

Yunus Khan blew into the muzzle of his gun and cocked one eye to peer into it.

'Munawar and his son also have joined the search,' he said, referring to an uncle who lived two villages downstream. 'They're all out combing the mountains. Someone is bound to stumble on the corpse sooner or later. She can't be alive, it's four days now.'

'Four days!' Sakhi dredged his lungs with a snort and spat out the brownish phlegm he stored like the venom of a scorpion. 'Four days and no sign of her! Well, she has not crossed here.'

He studied the crashing, impassable expanse of the river boiling under the bridge. 'What if she's crossed at Dubair?' he asked, voicing the apprehension that had been gnawing at him since morning.

'Hah!' Yunus Khan's guttural laugh was contemptuous. 'You think she'd find her way through the mountains? All the way to Dubair? Even if she knew it as we do, her miserable body would give out. She cannot go half way without our hearing of it.'

Sakhi whirled on his brother angrily. 'You think she has wings? If the men have searched the mountains as you say, then she is alive! I tell you she's alive, or the jackals and vultures would have led them to her.'

His face suddenly turned ugly with suspicion. 'Are you lying, brother?' he hissed. 'Has she already crossed the bridge to Dubair? Are you trying to spare my feelings? You're deceiving me! You have betrayed my trust!' he cried, scrambling to his feet. '*You* say the clansmen are searching the mountains: No! they've all been comfortably asleep while she slipped past. You've not cared for my honour, brother, you have not cared!'

Both men were standing. Yunus Khan's face was ashen. He seized the ragged front of Sakhi's jacket and threw him sprawling back on a boulder. Sakhi hit it with a thud, bracing his legs to keep him upright.

Yunus Khan towered over him. Standing deliberately on Sakhi's feet to prevent him from moving, he pinioned his brother's arms against the rock. His elongated face descended to within an inch of Sakhi's.

'You fool! Your honour? Why didn't you think of it when you allowed the bitch to run away? You knew she'd run. Are you a buggered up eunuch? You should have slit her throat right then!'

Their faces almost touching, Sakhi saw his own fatigue reflected. New lines marked his brother's eyes, etched by the dust and exhaustion of the last few days.

Sakhi's vision misted. Deep in those cold, vituperative eyes nailing him to the rock was a spark of tenderness, of a bond forged over the years.

With a last punishing shove, Yunus Khan stepped back. Torn by a sense of shame and failure Sakhi slid to the ledge floor. Burying his face in the dusty folds of his jacket, he broke into furious weeping.

Yunus Khan fondled his brother's hair. He pressed his blubbering, distorted face to his chest. It was not strange that Sakhi cried, for men here wept as copiously as women. In this land where subtle expressions of grief were misconstrued, men, dominant in all spheres, were jealous of their supremacy in sorrow. They lamented loudest.

Sakhi's racking sobs subsided and Yunus Khan, having wiped his brother's wet face with the loose end of his turban, leapt wearily from the ledge.

❖

An hour later Sakhi sat up to watch his father walk across the bridge. So, he gloated, his misgivings were not absurd after all. Yunus Khan had seen fit to send Misri Khan on a foray.

❖

200

Immaculate in white garments, his embroidered red velvet jacket flamboyant in the sun, Misri Khan walked confidently. At the bridge-head, he saluted a drowsy guard and headed for the billows of dust rising from Pattan.

Misri Khan sat down with a group of Gujjar nomads whom he would not have deigned to notice in normal circumstances. He exchanged pleasantries and engaged them in animated small talk. Had they known anything at all about the girl, it would have come out in the course of his circumspect manoeuvring of the conversation. They had no news.

He sauntered among the gangs of tribals labouring on the road, and satisfied that they knew nothing either, ambled towards the officers' quarters.

Two uniformed men sprawled on chairs on either side of a rickety table on the verandah. Misri Khan climbed the steps.

'Salaam-alaikum,' he called, with his customary arrogance. The younger officer, who by now was fed up with the demands of arrogant patriarchs in imposing turbans and waistcoats, returned the greeting curtly.

'What is it?' he asked, drumming the wooden armrests of his chair.

'Son, I have to go to Dubair on an urgent matter. I wondered, can I get a ride?'

The officer studied the tribal with the air of a man empowered to withhold a favour, and then he capitulated with a dismissive wave of his hand.

'Oh, hop into any jeep. They keep coming and going.'

Crushed by such curtness, Misri Khan salaamed with affronted dignity. He had hoped to draw the young man into talk. Turning his broad back on them he strode to the open depot cluttered with machinery.

A truck reversed, pointing its nose to the road, and Misri Khan ran up to the driver. 'Can you take me to Dubair? I have the officer's permission.'

'Sure, get in,' the driver leaned across the front seat and obligingly held the door.

201

Kohistanis trudged wearily along the road in straggling groups, bent almost double with heavy loads of salt and maize in goat-skins and sacks tied on their backs.

Looking at them the driver said, 'You're lucky to get a ride.'

Misri Khan grunted and nodded, 'I've ridden before.'

They had been bouncing along on the shingles for an hour when Misri Khan artfully broached the subject of his mission.

'I believe your camp was visited by a young girl from the plains?'

'Ah, yes . . .' said the driver. He changed gears for a steep ascent.

Misri Khan had expected the man to elaborate. He glanced at him stealthily. Obviously, his attention had been distracted in negotiating the steep, unsurfaced curves.

'About the girl. I . . .'

'What of her?' the driver cut in, and again Misri glanced at him in surprise.

'I – I heard she came with an old tribal.'

'You probably know more about her than I. After all she was being taken to your territory.'

Misri Khan felt sweat dampen his forehead. The way the man spoke could mean he knew something. Perhaps the girl was already in Dubair, telling stories and spreading their humiliation.

Misri Khan feared the worst.

The jawan by his side drove with sullen concentration. Misri Khan dared not ask any more – his agitation was such that he might blurt out something best left unsaid. In any case, he would know the truth at Dubair.

They drove in silence. When they were only twenty minutes from their destination, the driver relented. Trying to break the ice, he inquired, 'What takes you to Dubair?'

Misri Khan looked sharply at the polite, inquiring eyes. He breathed easier. The question was in good faith.

202

'I have some relatives nearabouts. Got to see them on business.' Then, unable to contain what was paramount in his thoughts, he asked, 'The girl must have been here about eight or nine weeks back? Have you heard of her since?'

Ashiq Hussain's grip on the wheel tightened. 'No . . . Have you?' He studied the old man with a sudden hostile interest.

Disconcerted by the scrutiny, Misri Khan shook his head and looked out of the window at the jade-blue river.

'What's it about? Why does an old man like you ask so many questions about a young girl?'

Misri Khan trembled in silent anger. The man was a fool. He did not know of the knife he had inside his waistcoat. It would take but a second to slit his throat! The undirected machine, of course, would crash down the gorge.

Ashiq judiciously refrained from provoking the old man any further.

❖

At Dubair, Misri Khan stomped straight to the Officers' Mess and demanded to see the Major. His excitement and the dire conclusions his galloping imagination invoked, left no scope for tactical manoeuvrings.

Starting from the kitchen orderly and still refusing to state his business clearly, he was pushed up the scale of military rank. Each officer, intimidated by the bristling, importunate tribal, sent him on.

They knew the symptoms of tribal bloodshed and judging adroitly the measure of Misri Khan's murderous wrath, politely ushered him into the Major's room.

Major Mushtaq looked up from a graph, indicating to Misri Khan a chair across the desk. The tribal tested its stability with a suspicious shake, and climbing on to the seat, squatted to face the Major.

'I wish to talk to you alone, Major Sahib,' he said, and Mushtaq motioned to the orderly.

203

The moment the door clicked, Misri Khan demanded: 'Where is she?'

The old man's presumption had raced ahead at such a pace that by now he was convinced that the whole camp, the Major included, were part of a conspiracy to hoodwink him and whisk the girl to the plains.

Mushtaq wished he hadn't asked the orderly to leave. The word 'she' gave the interview an unexpected gravity. He wondered frantically who 'she' was, fearing that any wrong move on his part might incite the tribal to draw his knife. The Major knew that his authority and power carried no weight before an accusation of this nature.

'Who?' he asked carefully.

'The girl. The girl my cousin from the plains brought for my son.'

He expects me to know where the girl is that his cousin brought for his son! And I don't even know the bastard! Mushtaq mused cynically.

He studied his finger nails, and then he raised his eyes to meet the Kohistani's with as much candour as he could summon.

'A tribal brought a girl from the plains. He said she was his daughter. I think it was a month or so back. Is that the girl you mean? The Kohistani passed through here. If I recollect correctly, he meant to marry her off in your territory.'

Misri Khan swallowed. He tried to judge the Major's honesty. This much was, of course, the truth. Moreover, Mushtaq appeared sympathetic.

'She married my son', he said gruffly. 'She has run away. I was led to believe she might be here.'

'Not that I know of – and she can't be here without my hearing of it at once.'

'You'll know what to do if, perchance, she turns up in Dubair?'

'Of course.'

'My honour is in your hands, Sir.' Misri Khan was respectful for the first time since the interview began. 'I'll be grateful if you will inform me at once if you have any news of her. She's my son's wife. My duty will be done once she is found. After that he can handle his own responsibility.'

'Rest assured. I understand these matters,' Mushtaq promised. 'Now I will arrange for transport to convey you back to Pattan.' Mushtaq tapped the call-bell on his table.

He made a mental note to instruct whoever was on duty at the bridge to keep a lookout and bring the girl to him as quickly and as quietly as possible. If she made it across the river, he could easily slip her off to Lahore without anyone being the wiser.

On his way out Misri Khan stopped to observe the Angraze woman sitting on the verandah with another man. When she looked at him he lowered his eyes. So this was the Major's woman! The one his son had talked about. Turning to walk away, the old man grinned until the gaps at the back of his mouth showed. Ah, but the Major was a good man . . . he deserved the woman – such a woman with hair that recalled ripe, sun-touched maize and eyes the colour of pale green Kabuli grapes.

❖

Late that evening, back in Pattan, Sakhi saw his father tramp through the dust and step on to the bridge. He leapt from the ledge and rushed to meet him.

Misri Khan looked up wearily at the figure blocking his path. Recognising Sakhi, he took a quick step forward and placed his hand on his son's shoulder. 'It's all right. She's still with us, son. She hasn't crossed the river.'

'But she still lives!'

'Maybe . . . how can one tell?' The old man's heart ached at his son's misery. 'You need sleep,' he said gently. 'Go. I'll keep watch.'

205

'No, this requires young eyes.'

'Right now you are older than I am. Go on, you'll need your strength tomorrow.'

Sakhi glared at the old man. Then, lowering his eyes, he turned down the track towards his village.

Chapter 25

It looked like a rock: a solitary stone rising from the frozen ground – and then it moved! In the grey light of dawn, its outlines inflated perceptibly, there was a slight stir and, as if breathing out, the stone resumed its former shape.

At a distance of twenty yards, Zaitoon, touching the cliff behind her, cringed back in fear. Her nerves were raw. The slightest movement, the softest sound, the rattle of a loosened pebble, squeezed the breath from her lungs.

The stone had moved! Zaitoon stood still, praying for light. Rooted to the brown wasteland, the moving stone stuck out like a milepost, like the black slabs dug along roadsides, but without the white numbering.

The air grew brighter and again the rock stirred. A thin bare neck rose awkwardly from massive shoulders and the creature opened a wing.

It was a vulture. It roosted clumsily like one half of a bird. A dishevelled span of wing flopped quivering to one side. A breeze fluffed it and a few of its feathers, exhibiting their coarse quills, stood up in an ugly display.

The girl rubbed her arms to smooth the goose-pimples that had erupted all over her. A fetid whiff set her teeth on edge. This was the vilest, the most obscene thing she had ever looked upon. In its drowsy, slovenly state, the bird appeared to be diseased, its matted wing abominably maimed. The sight filled her with revulsion; it condensed in her a horror of all things ugly and filthy and predatory. Hating the bird, she sensed in a flash her own repulsive condition. She had scarcely eaten for days and had finally run out of her carefully portioned supply of bread the day before. A part of her perceived with painful clarity the vulturine length of her scrawny neck, her gaunt protruding shoulders, and the ragged blanket shrouding her hunched body as the feathers shrouded the bird's. The grotesque image filled her with self-loathing, and venting her hopeless fury, she screeched, 'Get up. Get up. You filthy, polluted devil!'

The bird craned its denuded neck, its red eyes fixed on the girl. Zaitoon picked up a stone and threw it at the soft, oozing thing. The vulture scrambled awkwardly to its feet. Its brutish eight-foot wing-span awry, it staggered towards her demonically like a monster.

'You want to eat me? You want to eat me?' cried Zaitoon. 'I'm alive . . . look, I'm alive!'

With dust swirling under its enormous wings the vulture rushed headlong towards her and in a thundering flurry was airborne over the cliff.

Hands spreadeagled, holding aloft the wings of her blanket, Zaitoon looked like a bird about to fly yet permanently grounded. Having swooped down, the vulture banked past the cliff. Soon she saw the sleek silhouette of wings spiralling in the white sky and slowly she crumpled to the earth.

Hills and more hills. Countless swollen mounds of tan earth studded with rock. Boulders as big as houses up-ended at improbable angles on weird slopes. Sheer sides coated with granite. Smaller stones gathered in hollows like water in pools. Arid and bleak.

Zaitoon saw a gigantic, sawn-off tree trunk. Only a few paces from it she realised it was a circular rock, the hue and grain of wood. Nature conspired to deceive her. She felt light-headed with fever and, moving, she submerged her tormented protests beneath a spate of dreams, drifting in a congenial mist of companions and conversation. Often, skipping ahead of her oppressed body, she chided it as if it were someone else. 'Oh, stop moaning,' she told her stumbl-

208

ing legs in exasperation. 'Come on. Move.' And when she came upon a shallow streamlet she scolded her stomach. 'Don't growl. Every time you feel thirsty, Allah provides!'

She would rest an arm jauntily on one hip, then thrust it forward in an expressive sweep, and her mouth moved ceaselessly, now smiling and coy, now angry and reproachful. In a recurring daydream she kept coming unexpectedly upon Sakhi...

She spies him high on the crest of a ridge ahead of her. Climbing a rock, she moves into the range of his vision. His face glows with incredulous joy. Staggering across the ridge he runs and holds her close. 'Oh, my God, I was afraid something had happened to you ... You don't know how scared I was.' Lifting her weightless body in his golden arms, he carries her to his village. 'Were you lost?' he asks.

'No,' she says with forgivable reproach, 'I ran away.'

'Oh! Then I must kill you. You know I must.'

Tears streaming down his face, he fumbles with the knife blade.

'No. No!' Zaitoon's cry echoes amid the boulders and her hands fly protectively to her throat.

⁂

Late in the afternoon, Zaitoon arrived at a stretch of flat ground, still walled by the mountains but ending in a straight fall. She went along the precipice, her eyes seeking a path to take her down and on to the next hill.

Guiding her descent were giant terraced layers of several ridges, and while she debated her route, a man appeared from between the rocks and stood on a ledge far below her.

Careful not to dislodge the pebbles, Zaitoon crawled to the edge of the overhang, and terror paralysed her. On a narrow outcrop between her and the man crouched a snow leopard, its small sleek head and lightly spotted body aimed straight at the hunter.

209

The man started climbing and the animal, coiled to spring, slithered backwards and glanced up. Zaitoon felt an electric panic from the animal transfer to her. She was sure the leopard, in one easy leap, could reach her level. Her arm groped blindly and finding a stone, she held it ready. She wanted to scream, but lay immobile and mute on her stomach.

Securing the gun strap and gripping the stony rock-face, the man scrambled over the cutting brim. He was face to face with the leopard which was backed against the cliff. Inching his hand to his shoulder, he slowly lowered the gun. Before he could fire, the cat, in a sudden flash, streaked through the blue air with the vividness of lightning.

The mountain silence exploded in a discordant series of inhuman howls and echoes. Stones and dust flew into the air, and when the leopard lifted its gory head Zaitoon clamped her mouth shut with her hand. But she could not control the puling moans that gurgled to her throat.

A shot ripped the air. There was an insane roar. Sliding forward, Zaitoon once again peered down and saw that the cat had been wounded. Curling in on itself it mewed and growled, snapping viciously. Another bullet sent it leaping into the air before it fell and lay clawing the cliff. It kept tearing earth and rock, and then it lay still.

A tribal, whom Zaitoon only now noticed, stood up. Moving cautiously, he threw a stone at the cat. Then he approached the mangled body of his companion whom the leopard had killed. Turning the body over, he looked at the face. From the rim of his ledge, cupping his hands to the mouth he shouted a message. There was an answering call from someone Zaitoon could not see. The man sat down to wait by the body.

A short while later a distant clamour rose. The wailing and screeching grew closer, and the mourning party arrived – men rushing ahead, women and children scampering in their wake.

210

Two younger men climbed to the ledge. Wrapping the body of the mangled hunter in a blanket, they carried it to the family. The wailing increased. A sturdy middle-aged man with a broad, clean-shaven face broke away and, keening fiercely, climbed to the ledge. He fell to cursing the dead leopard, whacking its thick fur with immense blows. Then he crouched and with bloody fingers gouged out its eyes. He spat on the leopard's face and pounded the gory mess with a stone. He castrated the animal. The men who had followed him stood by respectfully. Finally, separating him from the carcass and supporting him between them, they led him down.

A fly, abnormally bloated, circled her, and Zaitoon rolled away from the stale puddle of greenish bile she had cast up. The mountains now were silent. The bereaved had left with the remains of their clansman, taking the carcass of the leopard as well.

Gathering the blanket to her, Zaitoon found a way down to the path the mourners had taken. Her terror of wild beasts drove her to seek the even more fearful nearness of man. Picking the easiest descent, she came round a hill and had her first glimpse of vegetation. An isolated fence of tall pine edged the spine of a hill opposite, the slope of which bristled with thorny scrub and scraggy olive trees.

She moved closer, and the trees took on definition. The sun shot twilight darts, and the young pines, holding their arms poised like dancers, turned the trapped air golden. Zaitoon stepped among the cool, scented trees. The ground beneath her bruised feet was springy with pine needles mellowed by dew and soft as feathers. A little breeze moved, mingling the scent of grass and pine. The spicy, bitter-sweet scent brought the sensual bite of pepper-hot *pakoras* to her palate. Spasmodically the air was charged with a delectable warmth sifting through the cold. It felt like the air in the bazaar streets of Anarkali on a cool evening, when the aromatic heat from *pakora* frying-pans, from open braziers

211

barbecuing kebabs, alternated with the chill from cavernous hardware and metal shops. She realised with an elated start that she must have moved a long way downstream. In this enchanted world of golden shade and caressing scents, her privation and fear of the past eight days appeared bearable; yet on this same day she had met with the vulture and the leopard.

Zaitoon heard a distant bellow, and glimpsed a far-away settlement in a wide, green, cattle-dotted valley, divided by a faintly-etched stream. The hollow horizontal logs channelling the water for cultivation resembled the irrigation system of Sakhi's village. The hill across rose in fresh green terraces, and into the slope small rooms had been dug, of stone and mud and wood.

Slowly she moved through the darkening trees, touching them. She chewed pine needles and bits of stalk and grass that pushed through the carpet of needles. Her body responded gratefully to the caress of nature and she lay down in the softness, feeling the decayed vegetation cool her burning skin.

At night sounds of lament kept reaching up into the stillness, and she felt she knew the inhabitants of that village.

❖

Zaitoon awoke before dawn. The settlement below, except for the faint rustle of the stream gurgling through it, slept quietly. The wind had died but a dull roar persisted in her ears. Zaitoon shook her head. She was damp with sweat, and though her fever had subsided, she blamed it for the humming in her head. Or was it caused by hunger? She plugged her ears. When she removed her fingers, the muffled roar was still there.

She sat up blinking in the dark. Holding her breath she listened intently. Again she plugged her ears, and the hum returned when she removed her hands. Turning her head she

212

tried to follow the sound. Through a grey film tinting the air, touching the dew-drenched tree trunks, she groped her way, but it was as yet too dark. She sat a while waiting for dawn.

In a sudden surge of hope Zaitoon thought it must be the river she heard. Her mind became sharp and decisive. She knew she must leave the dangerous vicinity of the village before it stirred. Keeping the river in view, she would be able to steer her path to the bridge. 'Careful now, careful,' she cautioned herself, trying to contain her impatience, afraid of the slightest miscalculation or risk.

The hum increased while she moved. Her heart racing with anticipation, she at last scrambled over slabs of dark, rough granite, where the glimmer of dawn lit a sky-blue stretch of wet satin trembling against white banks. Her face crumpled in gratitude. She wanted to sink into the soft white sand and dip her face in the water.

She rushed down, not caring how, and flung herself on the beach. Rolling over and over, she reached the brink of the river. She drank the water and splashed herself until she felt numb with cold. There she lay, growing warm in the dry sand. Unexpectedly, something touched her – tickling the bare sole of her foot. Her spine arched back convulsively and she retracted her legs.

In a line beyond her feet, his arm stretched out, a man lay face down, his thick, yellowish fingers curling where her feet had just displaced the sand. She could not see his face, only a matted blur of brownish hair and the ragged length of his body. At right angles to him, supporting his head on his hand, sprawled another tribal. He had a hard, exceptionally pointed chin, and a hooked nose that almost dipped into his mouth. His hooded eyes moved down her body.

Zaitoon knew that a moment ago she had been alone. It was as if the men had risen from some foul depths in the sand.

An arm lunged at her ankles, and she recoiled. Close to her threatened the narrow, rapacious face of her tormentor

213

and the cracked, grimy nails that quivered like talons. Zaitoon sidled backwards. The man casually turned on his side. She hugged her shoulders trying to conceal her trembling.

Cold, speculative eyes measured her wet body. They took in the outline of her ribs, the panting swell of her damp shirt, and the mud in her hair and on her small, terrified face.

Zaitoon knew the madness of the still eyes. She stood up hesitantly and started to walk away.

'O, ay, where are you off to?'

She hurried her pace.

'Wide-eyed little gazelle, we love you. Won't you favour us?'

The crude, smug voice was close, and she whirled to face him. The man had touched her. The other, still sprawled on the sand, looked on coolly.

'Come, let me thaw your cold little heart.'

Zaitoon's desperate eyes held his in horrified reproof. He moved, and despite her terror Zaitoon thought he seemed to be enjoying the chase, like a villager cornering a flustered hen. She ran.

Next, she breathed the stench of his clothes, the sickening, bovine smell of his unwashed body. He overpowered her. She was down.

'You can't escape us, my dove.' The man's husky breath sank into her ears. She flailed at him. He caught her wrists, and it seemed her arms would snap. 'How thin I've grown,' she thought. She saw the other man get up slowly and walk towards them.

Chapter 26

The dank, thick-walled room, with its single pigeon-hole skylight, was quiet. Misri Khan lay on a stringy mat alongside a wall. He stroked his beard and from time to time he sighed aloud, muttering a winded string of words: 'Allaahhh, help us . . .'

Sakhi sat cross-legged, cramming his mouth with baked maize and drinking voracious gulps of water from an earthen bowl. He held out his hand. Lifting a *roti* from the fire-pit Hamida handed him the bread.

She crouched and, touching her cheek to the floor, blew into the fire. She sucked the air in with wide-mouthed 'Aaahs' and blew until the wood blazed and crackled. Breaking a rubbery chunk from a trayful of maize dough, she slapped it between her deft fingers until it took the shape of a huge pancake; then she tossed the *roti* on the fire. She glanced nervously at Sakhi. His eyes were red with sleeplessness. The change in him touched her: there was a grim maturity in the contours of his face, and in the deliberate movement of his limbs. She wanted to stroke his hair, fuss over him, and counsel and console him, but she dared not. Everything about her irritated him: her withered, crooked body, her thin, cracked voice; and especially her timid, defensive insistence on mothering him. A few days back she had ventured, 'Son, you must leave some things to Allah . . . you can't be everywhere all the time . . . If you don't eat and sleep properly you'll sicken.'

'You'll sicken,' he mimicked brutally, 'and who'll hunt your bitch of a daughter-in-law while I sleep . . . you?'

'The entire tribe's with you — you know she can't get

away . . .' Hamida seldom provoked the menfolk but that day she felt she must have her say. 'You shouldn't have beaten her like that, son. You knew she was different . . . you frightened her. She'd have come round to our ways in time . . .'

Sakhi had glowered murderously. He would have struck her but Misri Khan restrained him. The men had not spoken to her since. She gossiped with sympathetic clanswomen, but once the men returned, she contented herself with the grunts and moans accompanying her chores. Now she had no more sympathy for the girl. She only prayed for the end of the hunt and for her mournful household to return to normal.

The hunt was organised in shifts. Clansmen scoured the hills near-by and went deep into the mountains, searching meticulously. There was no sign of the girl. The village was tense and the women talked of nothing else. Magic and witchcraft coloured their speculations. She was from the plains. Who could tell what knowledge such women possessed? What dark forces befriended the girl? Anyway, this would teach the menfolk a lesson.

Young girls, barely in their teens, gave Sakhi covetous, sympathetic looks. He could have married any one of them.

❖

The room was grey with smoke and the open doorway framing the bright air gave it a supernatural brilliance. Hamida hobbled out, an arm on her aching hip. She returned, groaning beneath a burden of firewood. Sakhi turned to scowl at her, and she subsided quietly at Misri Khan's feet.

The room darkened with Yunus blocking the door-frame. Adjusting his sight he sauntered in and squatted across the fire from Sakhi.

'What's up?' Sakhi demanded.

216

'Finish your meal.'

Removing a half chewed morsel from his mouth, Sakhi placed it resolutely on the remaining scrap of *roti*.

'I've finished,' he said quietly, challenging his brother to say what was on his mind.

'Munawar Khan is here. He thinks two men from Cheerkhil saw the girl this morning.'

'Where?'

'At Cheerkhil.'

Sakhi sprang to his feet. 'So. She is alive! She did find her way through the mountains!' His strained voice cracked with bitterness.

They stared at each other. Yunus Khan was still squatting. 'You'd better be off,' he said quietly to Sakhi.

Snatching his gun and cartridge belt from the floor, Sakhi started.

'Wait!'

Sakhi turned impatiently.

'Change your shirt,' said Misri Khan.

'She might be at the bridge already . . .'

'It will take you too long on foot. We'll ride from Pattan. I'm coming with you.'

Misri Khan was already stripped. Hamida fluttered, unwinding his bedding-roll and the old man snatched his clothes from the bundle even before it fell open. Sakhi tore the filthy shirt from his body, and Hamida held out a new slate-grey militia shirt.

❖

Flanked by his two sons, Misri Khan strode across the bridge to Pattan.

Chapter 27

Carol's anger at the Major had dissolved. She was honest enough to admit to herself that her demand had been absurd. Marriage would have created grotesque complications for them both. And, strangely enough, she discovered she did not loathe Farukh any more.

Carol made a decision she had not even known she was debating. She would not go back to the States. What, after all, did she have to go back to? Another store? More school – or something equally dreary? Her family would welcome her for a month or two; but then she would have to make a life for herself. Pam or someone like her would make room for her in the same barely furnished third floor walk-up, or another like it. And then she would begin all over again – doing things she had found so meaningless before. She would hate to go back to standing behind a cosmetics counter!

Besides she had too much pride to admit failure – particularly after her defiant insistence on marrying Farukh. Her life in Pakistan was rich: it was exciting, and even glamorous. She had taken it too much for granted, and the crisis in her relationship with Farukh made her realise just how much she would miss it all. She had, after all, put some effort into her marriage. She had adjusted to the climate, the country, the differences in culture and the people – and had come to love them. It would be a shame to throw it all away.

One of the pleasant surprises of her marriage to Farukh was her very special status. As an American married to a Pakistani she was allowed much more freedom than a Pakistani wife. She could say things and get away with behaviour and dress that would have been shocking in a Pakistani – and even in an American. Cut loose from the constraints of her own culture, she did not feel restricted by the new. She had become used to moving, thinking and speaking with an increasing sense of freedom. Her inherent impulsiveness had burgeoned correspondingly . . . She had not understood the strange contradictions and forces in her new life – and often they tore her apart – but she felt she had come a long way to understanding . . . She was up against Farukh's jealousy of course. She suddenly thought his spate of words and posturings were not as restricting as they appeared. She knew she could handle him with a few adjustments in her thinking and behaviour.

Yes, she must make it up to Farukh. She might even stop taking the birth control pills she'd used so faithfully and secretively, an almost subconscious result of her reservations about this country and her marriage. Once they had children, his jealousy might subside . . . maybe, that's what she needed, children. They would anchor her . . . control the dangerous restlessness within her . . .

Carol's behaviour towards the Major had become more formal after their quarrel.

❖

Sakhi and Misri Khan hovered impatiently in front of the Mess Hall. They had been in Dubair an hour. Yunus Khan had been posted by them to watch the bridge. The Major, Sakhi and Misri Khan were told, was out inspecting the road. He was expected back at any moment.

On their arrival at Dubair they had rushed straight to the bridge. The guard on duty had brusquely assured them that he had not seen a single woman all day. They had searched the chaotic rubble of rock and hills across the river, and now they were looking for the Major.

219

Sakhi and Misri Khan ran in the dusty trail of the jeep when it rattled over the drive. It stopped at the side entrance to the Mess. Mushtaq was at the wheel.

They accosted him before he could climb down, crowding him in a clamour of salaams and questions. Mushtaq sat back.

'You're here again, are you?' he said wearily. 'Haven't you found the girl yet?'

Misri Khan pushed forward aggressively. 'No, sir. But we have news...'

Mushtaq glanced at the youth standing arrogantly by the older man. Taken aback by Sakhi's contempt he steadily returned his baleful stare.

Misri Khan touched the Major's chin impatiently with his rough forefinger to turn Mushtaq's attention back towards himself.

'He's my son, sir, the girl's husband. As I was saying, we have news, sir. She has been seen a few miles from here this morning...'

'Good afternoon, Major.'

The men turned their heads at the interruption. Carol stood framed in a window behind them.

'Good afternoon,' Mushtaq smiled and waved. 'Where's Farukh?'

Misri Khan and Sakhi stepped aside.

'Taking a bath,' she said coldly with a toss of her hair, refusing to meet the Major's eye.

She noticed the splendour of Misri Khan's array of ammunition. 'Aren't you going to introduce them?' Her glance slid to meet Sakhi's insolent appraisal. She blushed.

'He's the girl's husband,' Mushtaq said shortly.

'They're both gorgeous.'

Mushtaq was furious. 'Get in and close the window,' he commanded icily. 'I'll join you and Farukh in a little while.'

Carol shut the window wondering why Mushtaq was angry. Instantly Misri Khan resumed crowding Mushtaq

220

with importunate demands for action, assistance, and assurance.

'Just what do you want?' Mushtaq exploded. 'I've told you again and again the men on duty will report to me. They know the situation.'

'But we don't trust them,' Misri Khan insisted.

'Then stand guard yourselves.'

'Of course!' Sakhi spat contemptuously.

Mushtaq fixed his eyes sternly on Misri Khan. He stepped menacingly close, pointedly ignoring Sakhi. 'Look, I want no butchering here. No butchering . . . understand?'

'It's up to her husband . . .'

Mushtaq grasped him firmly by the shirt front. Misri Khan was a bit shorter.

'Old man, there will be no killing in my territory.'

'No, sir,' Misri Khan capitulated craftily. 'My son only wishes to claim his wife and take her back to our village.'

'I don't care a damn what he wishes or what he does so long as there's no killing here.' He let go of the shirt. 'God be with you,' he saluted curtly and marched inside.

❖

Carol watched the men from behind the curtain. A soft half-smile lit her face. She remembered Sakhi's challenging, arrogant eyes stab at the Major and defiantly revert to her. Her fantasy — set off by his startling handsomeness, his intense animalism, and her fascination with tribal lore and romantic savagery — took wing. Suppose she had been in place of that girl, she dreamed . . .

. . . He would think her so special . . . For his sake she would win over all the men and women and children of his village. In the remote reaches of his magnificent mountains, she would enlighten a clan of handsome savages and cavemen. She would be their wise, beloved goddess ministering Aspro and diarrhoea pills. She would learn how to give

221

injections. She'd collect boxes of antibiotics, and work sophisticated miracles. She'd flit about scrubbing, tidying up, and by her own example imbue the tribe with cleanliness. She would champion their causes and focus the benign glare of American academia upon these beautiful people, so pitifully concealed from the world by a fold in the earth. For a delightful moment she saw herself a gracious, tender-hearted, brave, blonde Margaret Mead, biographied and fictionalised into immortality . . .

Farukh stepped out from the bathroom, a towel around his lean waist.

'The Major back yet?' he asked.

'Yes,' said Carol indifferently.

❖

After lunch Farukh retired for a nap and Mushtaq joined Carol on the lawn.

The moment they settled in their chairs, he confronted her: 'You're unbelievable – acting up to that murderous scoundrel!'

'Oh? You mean the girl's husband? He's unbelievable too,' retorted Carol, stung to the quick by the sudden attack.

'You know how their minds work. He'll spread it all over, I'm keeping a tart! It's tough enough controlling these bastards without your making me appear ridiculous.'

'What are you talking about? I didn't do anything. I didn't say anything . . . I just asked you to introduce them.'

'You really are something, aren't you? Don't you know by now that women don't ask for introductions to such men?'

'You wouldn't happen to be jealous, now would you?'

'Jealous, my arse!'

'He's about the handsomest creature I've ever set eyes on,' Carol mocked him defiantly. 'His wife's one lucky girl!'

Mushtaq looked at her intently. 'Oh, surely you've heard

the news? The girl's run away. The whole bloody clan's out hunting her. I only hope her luck holds!'

'Hunting her? What will they do when they find her?'

'Beat her up. Probably kill her . . . She's hiding in the mountains – she could be trying to reach us. She's been on the run nine days. Imagine! Nine days in that tractless waste! I can't believe she's alive . . . they say she is!'

'How do they know?'

'A couple of bastards from Cheerkhil raped her. News spreads. She's not very far.'

'Oh God!'

Carol had a sudden sinking realisation of the girl's plight. She remembered the curious communion between them; and her large, sensitive eyes. She now felt they had revealed more than just the hopeless drift of her life; they had communicated faith and a dauntless courage. Through an awesome act of will the girl had chosen to deflect the direction of her life. Carol felt a compulsion to help her, even at risk to herself.

'Can't you do something?' she demanded.

'Very little. Unless she manages to get across. The husband won't dare kill her in the camp. Don't worry, she'll probably be okay. If not, too bad. It happens all the time.'

'What do you mean, "happens all the time"?'

'Oh, women get killed for one reason or other . . . imagined insults, family honour, infidelity . . .'

'Imagined infidelity?'

'Mostly.'

'What's the matter with the men here? Why are they so insanely jealous?'

'Jealousy, my dear, is not a monopoly – it's pretty universal.'

'Chopping off women's noses because of suspected infidelity isn't universal!'

'That's in the Punjab. Here they kill the girl. They'd kill her there too . . .'

Carol looked away. 'Do you think Farukh would kill me?'

'Who knows? I might, if you were my wife.'

She looked at him sharply. He was leaning forward, his eyes twinkling.

Suddenly a great deal became clear to her. 'So that's all I mean to you,' she said. 'That's really what's behind all the gallant and protective behaviour I've loved so much here, isn't it? I felt very special, and all the time I didn't matter to you any more than that girl does as an individual to those tribals, not any more than a bitch in heat. You make me sick. *All* of you.'

She stood up and walked slowly to the Mess door. Watching her, Mushtaq found her gait no longer provocative but crushed, subdued, and oddly touching.

Chapter 28

Carol's restless movements woke Farukh. Sleepily, he put his arm out to her. She started to jerk away but felt, suddenly, that she needed him. 'Come for a walk?' she asked.

Overflowing the ridge, shafts of evening sunlight set the river ablaze. They had walked a long way down to a sharp bend in the river. Carol's hair swung shining as she cavorted over the boulders and the pale sand. The walk had lifted her spirits. She leapt over a narrow vein of water and stood on a rock half submerged in the river. The awesome power of the water leaping to form glassy shafts and walls, boiling and foaming dangerously past, elated her. Scanning the scene with eager, shifting eyes, she tried to stamp its grandeur on her memory.

A sooty shadow in a pool of water distracted her and she turned round. A darkness swayed on the ripples, and, completing its rotation beneath the surface, the face bobbed up – a young, tribal woman's face.

Carol made a strangled sound and fell to her knees. In one leap Farukh was beside her. He saw the pallid water-logged face. 'God! Someone's cut the head clean off!'

With a motion that appeared serenely willed, the face turned away and, resting a bloodless cheek on the water for a second, hid beneath. A tangled, inky mass of hair swirled to the surface and floated on the lapping current.

Carol knelt horrified in the blue haze rising from the river. She knelt frozen in a trance that urged her to leap into the air on a scream and flee the mountains.

'Probably asked for it,' said Farukh.

With a cry she brushed against his shoulder and, jumping over the rocks, clawed her way up the gorge.

❖

It was a freezing night. The three tribals squatted close, talking softly. Sakhi stood up and, holding the quilted robe tight against the wind, he crossed the road to the bridge.

The guard on duty blocked his path, his bayonet glinting in the moonlight. 'No one's allowed here at night. Get back.'

Sakhi's lips moved back in a vicious snarl. Misri Khan had joined him. Noticing the bayonet he put a restraining hand on his son.

'Let these dogs be. Come on.'

He forced Sakhi back.

Snuggling in their blankets, Misri Khan and Yunus settled for the long night's vigil.

Sakhi kept ambling past the bridge-head, scrutinising the shadowy span from different angles. The guard on duty kept an eye on him.

❖

Carol meanwhile lay in her room, staring into the dark. '. . . asked for it,' isn't that what Farukh had said? Women the world over, through the ages, asked to be murdered, raped, exploited, enslaved, to get importunately impregnated, beaten-up, bullied and disinherited. It was an immutable law of nature. What had the tribal girl done to deserve such grotesque retribution? Had she fallen in love with the wrong man? Or was she simply the victim of a vendetta? Her brother might have killed his wife, and his wife's kin slaughtered her . . . there could be any number of reasons . . .

Whoever said people the world over are the same, was wrong. The more she travelled, the more she realised only the differences.

226

She knew Pakistani women with British accents. They wore jeans from the US and tops from Paris. Their children were at Eton or Harvard. She had related to them straightaway: and suddenly their amiable eyes flashed a mysterious quality that drew her into an incomprehensible world of sadness and opulence, of ancient wisdom and sensuality and cruelty . . .

She recalled Alia, one of her first friends in Pakistan. They said she was a princess. She lived in a splendid modern structure surrounded by the antiquity of priceless possessions – a charming laughing girl with a wide sensual face. Her enormous eyes had haunted Carol ever since they met. In friendship unveiled, layer by layer stripped of their guard, she had glimpsed in the recesses of those eyes the horror of generations of cloistered womanhood. And the pitiless arrogance of absolute power: a memory of ancient tyrannies, both male and female, and fulfilled desires. It was like peering into the secret vaults of a particular lineage or tumbling through a kaleidoscope of images created by the history of a race. A branch of Eve had parted some way in time from hers. There seemed a definite connection in Carol's mind between all this and the incomprehensible brutality of the tribals.

Minister to these savages! She squirmed in bed and half sobbed with self-contempt remembering her fantasy. She could no more survive among them than amidst a pride of lions. Even if she survived the privation, the filth and vermin and swarm of germs carrying alien diseases, her independent attitudes would get her killed! So much for her naive co-ed fantasy! She could study them, observe every detail of their life, maybe even understand them, but become one of them, never! She wasn't programmed to fit. She'd need an inherited memory of ancient rites, taboos and responses: inherited immunities: a different set of genes . . .

When they were travelling to Dubair she and Farukh had stopped in Saidu Sharif for tea. A knot of dancing, laughing

227

children had circled an almost limbless beggar. Every time he succeeded in sitting upright the children playfully knocked him over. The men in the bazaar picked their teeth and laughed indulgently. She had noticed this cruel habit of jeering at deformities before, and sick to her stomach wanted to scream at the men to stop the children.

'They'll wonder why you are fussing,' Farukh had said, laughing himself, 'They won't see your point of view at all, dear — every nation has its own outlet for cruelty.'

Perhaps he was right. In preventing natural outlets for cruelty the developed countries had turned hypocritical and the repressed heat had exploded in nuclear mushrooms. They did not laugh at deformities: they manufactured them.

Sleep would not come. She was seeing everything from a different perspective. Questions that had lurked in the back of her mind were suddenly answered. She felt her own conflicts nearing a resolution.

No wonder women here formed such intense friendships — to protect themselves where physical might outweighs the subtler strengths of womanhood ... At least in Pakistan they were not circumcised! Small mercy! A pathetic, defiant gesture here and there invited the inevitable thunderclap! Scour the mountains! Hunt the girl! That girl had unlocked a mystery, affording a telepathic peephole through which Carol had had a glimpse of her condition and the fateful condition of girls like her.

But the girl had run away! Thank God it had not been Zaitoon's head they had seen floating in the river.

Carol cried out, awakening Farukh.

'Can't you sleep?' He sat up, drawing her to him when he noticed she was weeping. He knew how much the incident at the river had upset her. It had upset him too.

Carol got out of bed to fetch a Kleenex.

'That verse by Iqbal ... what does he mean by "khudi"?' she asked.

'Khudi ... It's your willpower. No, more than just will-

228

power or ego. It's the strength of nature – a force, perhaps of God, within one.'

'Could you translate the verse? I feel I could understand it now.'

Farukh began to recite quietly, and the cadence of the poem sweetened the air:

> *Khudi ko kar buland itna,*
> Heighten your 'khudi' to such majesty,
> *ke har takdeer say pahaylay*
> that before every turn of fate
> *Khuda banday say khud poochay,*
> God himself asks man –
> *'Buta teri raza kya hai?'*
> 'Tell me, what do *you* wish?'

'It's like a prayer,' said Carol.

'It is.'

'You know, the girl who ran away? I think she forced her destiny; exercised her "khudi". I'm sure she'll make it . . .'

'Perhaps.'

'Christ! If she comes through I'll do something for her, I really will.'

There was responsibility in her voice and a new determination, and Farukh sensed the change in her.

'And . . . Farukh?'

'Yes?'

'I think I'm finally beginning to realise something . . . Your civilization is too ancient . . . too different . . . and it has ways that can hurt me . . . really hurt me . . . I'm going home.'

'Lahore?'

'San Jose.'

'Oh, you can't be serious! We'll talk about it tomorrow,' said Farukh indulgently. 'Things will look different . . . Now try to get to sleep.'

Chapter 29

The men had kept her hostage for two hours. When Zaitoon regained consciousness, her body screamed with pain. She wept, putting her trembling legs through the shalwar. Her brown skin gaped through new rents in the cloth. She had not seen her legs in days and gazed in revulsion at the twitching, fleshless shanks. A red spot spread on the cloth between her thighs. She folded her legs quickly and covered the stain with the front of her shirt. Printed with faded lavender flowers, it was torn down the front and at the shoulders. She closed her lids and her fingers flew up to push the hair from her face. Instead of falling back it stood round her head in a stiff tangle.

She viewed her condition dispassionately. Only three months ago in Lahore, she remembered, she had looked out on days crisp with winter, the evening air perfumed by grass, and she had walked under enormous, rustling trees – towering eucalyptus, banyans that stretched their branches to form shady verandahs, wooden benches encircling the gnarled trunks. Gargantuan mango trees that filled the sky. That early November now seemed like a bygone age, her youth viewed from afar.

Nikka and Miriam had taken her to Lawrence Gardens. Miriam had tossed back the flap of her burkha, uncovering her face. They each held a small, cone-shaped packet of roasted, salted grams, or lentils, which they poured out on their palms and stuffed into their mouths.

Her packet was half empty when a mad female creature, darting at them from nowhere, snatched it from her hand. Zaitoon gasped. The woman ran on in front, triumphantly

waving the packet over her head. Unexpectedly she turned
and rushed at them. Nikka protectively stepped between her
and his cowering womenfolk, deflecting her course.

'Hisst, hisst . . .' he threatened her, as if shooing a cat.

The crazy creature had smiled all the time, the carefree, mischievous smile of a ten-year-old. She could have
been anything from twenty to forty. Her ragged shirt hung
open at the neck and the flapping sides revealed the paler
swell at the top of her breasts.

She collapsed, grovelling at Nikka's feet and held up the
packet for him to take. Nikka drew back, and she looked up
at him handsomely, her even teeth flashing a full, insolent
smile. Eons of uncombed dust gave her black hair a hue
lighter than that of her sunburnt skin. The hair stood round
her face in a stiff wiggly tangle.

For a moment, Zaitoon saw herself rushing wild and
wanton over the mountains. She now knew the woman had
been raped. Abandoned and helpless, she had been living on
the charity of her rapists . . . and on theft.

In an anguished frenzy, Zaitoon pounded the sand. She
cupped her breasts, and pain in a red haze exploded inside
her.

A little later, she crawled between some rocks. The pain
from her breasts raged through her body. On the fringe of
consciousness, her mind wandered in delirium . . .

'How fat you are, how fat,' she teased, pummelling
Miriam's breasts. 'They're like a fat-tailed sheep's, we'll
have them when we celebrate Eid! Ummm . . . they must be
tasty . . .' She dug her face into the thin voile covering the
softness and nibbled playfully.

Fending off the probing little face, Miriam laughed.

'Toba, toba! Have you no shame? Talking such rubbish!
Some day you will be fat like me.' Holding Zaitoon's face
she kissed her . . .

And Zaitoon remembered the morning when she discovered the slight taut swell in her flesh — her promised

231

womanhood. Suddenly shy, she had glanced around, making sure of her privacy in the dingy bathing cubicle. The canister beneath the tap was filled to the brim, and the overflow, directed by the slope of the cement floor, poured through a bright hole at the base of the wall. Zaitoon knelt on the cool, gritty cement and peered through the hole. Beyond the gaping brightness was the back of another building. She was walled in by mountains of brick held precariously by gobs of caked mud. Water drained two storeys down the open cement channels into a gutter along the base. No one could see her. She crooked her slight neck and looked at herself. Her eyes and fingers probed the enchanting novelty. The softness was delicious to the touch of her childish, inquisitive fingers . . . this way and that . . . pummelling and distorting. A wondrous, possessive pride welled up in her. All along, she had accepted Miriam's pendulous bosoms as symbolic of her sex, and the incipient manifestation of breasts of her own filled her with ecstasy. She now longed each day for the privacy of her bath . . .

She floated through halcyon scenes of her past. They had a charming immediacy. Reminiscences melted into hallucination, and the delirium receded. Every now and then she would re-enter the present enough to know : 'I must find the bridge – I must get out of here . . .'

She crawled farther and farther from the beach, creeping up through fissures and stony crevices. For a time she snuggled beneath a slaty overhang, like a wounded animal, to lick her bruises.

❖

Zaitoon awakened late in the evening. Her pain had eased and her mind was alert again. The comforting roar of the river throbbed in her ears, and once more her instinct for life came to the surface.

Twilight shaded the hills. Restless winds in the rock

232

signalled nightfall and, dusting the sand from her clothes, she started along her path.

Zaitoon followed the tortuous course of the river by its sound. Now and again she glimpsed the inky void of waters far below.

Of a sudden, a blank stretch was straddled by a shadowy thickness. It was the bridge!

Far across gleamed the flicker of a light. Lost when she tried to focus her vision, it again winked unexpectedly when her eyes shifted.

She scurried over the rocks like a skeletal wraith. The bridge took on definition. It loomed nearer in the faint moonlight. Zaitoon was careful now, crouching in the shadows.

She climbed down a shallow well of boulders, and stepping on a stone, peered over. Beneath her, about twenty yards to her left the concrete started.

Her heart sang. She shrugged the burdensome blanket from her shoulders. She had no use for it. All she still needed to drag along was the numb weight of her pain.

Stealthily Zaitoon moved down to the base of the granite that had been her shelter. A few feet from her stretched the sand, a naked gleaming white, and then the bridge, flanked by smoky, V-shaped girders. The ghostly silhouette of the Chinese lions reared up at dim intervals. It was perfectly still. The breeze had died. An eerie light streaked the asphalt, and only the deafening rush and crash of the waters hinted at the river's invisible tumult.

Zaitoon examined the churning stillness. All her senses were alert.

She stood ready for a spurt, when she saw the movement. Momentarily something cut across the dim haze of the girders at the far end, the ghostly, barely discernible shadow of a man. She waited breathlessly, and the spectral form dissolved. Zaitoon climbed back over the stones.

Squatting on the floor of her well, she thought carefully.

233

She was too close to allow for the slightest error. Her impulse to run to whoever was on the bridge alternated with an instinctive desire to wait for light, and be sure to whom she was going. She was suddenly cold. She scrimmaged among the stones at her feet, and finding the blanket, covered herself. An unreasoning fear swept over her. Even now, with the glimmer of a light from Dubair winking at her, she might not make it.

❖

Her brain whirls. In her mind's eye she sees herself climbing down at last, huddling amidst the stones, and finally, scuttling swiftly across the sand, vanishing into the shadow of the girders.

She is nearly half way down the bridge when some instinct makes her grip the railing. The steel feels like ice. She stands still, and there is a slight vibration, as of someone moving as stealthily as she herself. She whips around, scanning the shadows, and the vibration ceases, but she knows she is not alone. There it is again, the slightest tremor, and now she knows it comes from ahead of her. She glances back for a way to retreat and then again strains ahead, probing the narrow shadows cast by the concrete pillars and lions. Except for them, the bridge lies bathed in moonlight. Not a pebble mars its smooth surface.

And then her blood congeals. A soft blackness has obscured the pattern in the railing. Terror freezes her, kneeling, to the asphalt. A form, tenuous as grey smoke, floats forward and involuntarily she moans. For an instant the smoky movement stops. Then it starts towards her, a pale, rolling blur – a man sneaking towards her on hands and knees. He sees her, shrunk and crumpled on the ground. She feels the throb of his rush and hides her face between her knees. When the groping fingers touch her, her nerves jerk in a single, convulsive paroxysm and she springs upright. The

234

man stoops level with her and his breath stings her face.

She looks at the pitiless curve of his lips, the unforgiving hurt in his eyes, and comprehends his heart. Now she is calm. So, I am to die after all, she thinks. Sakhi knows she will not scream. She is aware of his grief, and of the relentless pride and sense of honour that drives him. It is not an act of personal vengeance; he is dispensing justice – the conscience and weight of his race are behind him.

She feels him move and her destiny is compressed into seconds. She hurtles in a short-cut through all the wonders and wisdom of a life unlived. Instantly old, her tenure spent, she is ripe to die.

She feels so tired. Sakhi's hand bites into her fleshless shoulder. Allah, let it be swift. I can't bear any more.

She sees the blade flash, and in her terror she leans against Sakhi. The support of his hard body is almost tender. The steel is glacial on her throat . . .

❖

An icy perspiration drenched the rock Zaitoon was leaning on. She knew she had been standing here all along, pressed against the rock, but she also knew that what she had experienced was not a dream. Then what was it? A premonition? She was suddenly aware she had been given an unexpected insight. She was certain, that in these very moments she had lived through one version of her destiny and that somehow she had escaped it, though at a price. She would remain stamped with its horror. One did not cheat fate. If she had followed her natural inclination to run across the inviting stretch of sand to the bridge, her destiny would have taken the exact shape of what she had imagined. She was certain now that Sakhi was near-by, waiting to kill her.

She fell back into the dark hollow between the stones, with only a scrap of starlit sky above her. She closed her eyes.

Chapter 30

It was a cold, overcast morning. Earlier a fierce wind had gathered low masses of clouds, and now it rammed in sudden gusts against the windows of the Mess. The badly fitted woodwork creaked and somewhere a door banged shut.

Mushtaq asked the orderly to switch on the lights. At breakfast he was usually in a high good humour. Besides, the fiercer aspects of the elements exhilarated him. The rains would settle the dust and put a stop to the 'flu and fever which was currently incapacitating his jawans.

The orderly slid a scalding, butter-soaked *paratha* on to his side-plate. Breaking a chunk with his fingers, Mushtaq folded it round the curried brains and gulped the dripping morsel with satisfaction. In Carol's presence he never ate with his fingers.

He drained a glass of buttermilk, wiped his moustache and folded one end of the table napkin round his forefinger. He dexterously cleaned out some meat stuck between his molars. Carol and Farukh were sleeping late – perhaps on account of its being the last day of their stay. They were lucky the weather had held so long. In another ten days or so, when the weather cleared, Mushtaq's family would visit.

The incessant murmur of voices outside suddenly grew to a shrill pitched wrangle, and Mushtaq looked up.

'It's all right, Sir,' the orderly assured him. 'We have the usual crowd at the door.'

Mushtaq found it expedient to attend personally each morning to the requests or grouses brought by the tribals.

Quickly fastening the brass buttons down his military over-coat, he stepped outside.

The tribals pressed forward, and out of the corner of his eye, Mushtaq saw Misri Khan and Yunus. Scowling, they stood a little apart.

Having settled a dispute concerning compensation to be paid to the brother of an injured man, Mushtaq sighed with satisfaction, and the tribals drifted away. At that very moment Misri Khan and Yunus swooped on the Major like birds of prey.

'Yes?' Mushtaq raised an eyebrow.

'They won't allow us across the bridge. Suddenly they've decided we're not to cross at all. The guard pointed his gun with the little sword at us – at *me* . . .' Misri Khan brushed tears of anger from his eyes. He blew his nose noisily into the hem of his shirt. 'I, who am as old as his father! The pipsqueak dared insult me! Look . . .' he thrust his hennaed beard at Mushtaq, 'my venerable years won't abide this insult!'

Mushtaq shrewdly guessed the reason for the impasse.

The guards had been instructed not to allow loitering or too frequent passage to tribals. One never knew what they might do, especially if one of them got hold of a stick of dynamite. Any imagined injustice set them off. In Misri Khan's case, the girl's peril was known to the guards and they chose to be strict on her behalf.

'I'm sorry you have been put to this trouble, Barey Mian. Don't worry, I'll see to it right away.'

'You'll not only see to it, you will come with us!' Imperi-ously, Misri Khan pulled at the Major's arm.

Mushtaq was piqued, but he was too used to peremptory tribal ways to be angry. The wind bit his face and the prospect of a brisk walk beneath the racing clouds ex-hilarated him. Eager also for a first-hand look, he strode out with the tribals.

Near the bridge, Misri Khan and Yunus pulled ahead of

him. They strutted forward, cockily trying to shame the guards with their vindictive, haughty glances.

Sakhi, squatting patiently by the bridge-head, got up slowly. Nothing in his manner betrayed his night-long vigil. He stood erect and strong. Only the red veins in the whites of his eyes told Mushtaq that he must have been staring into the dark all night.

The sentries glowered balefully at the tribals. At the Major's approach they drew themselves up straight. Their eyes stared obediently ahead.

'Why didn't you allow them to cross last night? Didn't you get my orders?'

The sentries continued to stand at attention, looking straight ahead. They knew they were not required to answer. Then Mushtaq turned to the tribals and signalled to them to pass.

Misri Khan snickered aloud. He spat near the feet of one of the guards and, accompanied by his sons, stalked on to the bridge.

Mushtaq followed casually, curious as to where they would go. Once they were across, swiftly, without a word, the men separated, and were swallowed by their different trails.

Mushtaq ambled over the sandy beach to the rocks straight ahead. He sat down almost exactly where Zaitoon had descended the previous night. He looked at the sky. Flashes of lightning tore a distant mass of clouds followed by the faint, prolonged rumble of thunder. The awakening breeze swooshed and whined through many crevices.

Mushtaq wondered if he had heard something else, and then his blood ran cold. He heard it again, a faint, croaking voice calling, 'Major Sahib? Major Sahib?'

He turned imperceptibly and his glance climbed the crazy stairway of boulders. At a small distance he caught a glimpse of thin black fingers moving against the granite and a fuzzy, bobbing mass of hair.

238

Everything within him was alert.

'Hush, lie low,' he hissed, grateful to the fury of the winds and the noise of the river.

He turned to face the bridge, deliberately casual.

The three tribals had vanished but they might be anywhere: as near as the next rock or the next bend.

Mushtaq retraced his steps idly to the sand. Zaitoon's location was fixed in his mind. He started on a circuitous route that would take him up to her. His climb appeared to have no special purpose.

Once between the boulders, he scanned a projecting semicircle of rocks. He guessed from their shape that this inverted cradle hid the girl. He wondered that the men had not found her already. Perhaps the place of concealment was too obvious, too near the bridge for them to consider.

A weirdly modulated cry froze his movements – and he waited for the answering ululation. Both voices came from afar. Their distance reassured him, but he knew he must hurry.

Keeping his head low, he circled half way round the granite wall and slid through a crack to the huddled, skeletal creature. For a moment he wondered if it was the same girl.

She opened her mouth, and a croak broke from her dry throat. 'Hush,' he said softly, 'You're safe. Don't make a noise. I'll take you to safety . . .'

The girl, in an attempt to cover her nakedness, began to smooth and pull at her torn clothes. Mushtaq felt a surge of pity.

Careful not to show his head above the rim of granite, he spread first the girl's blanket on the ground, and then, removing his khaki great-coat, spread that on the blanket.

'You'll be all right. Don't worry,' he whispered. He pulled the girl down to the coat and helped her arms into the sleeves. He lifted her, huddled in a natal curl in the blanket. He could balance the bundle with one hand. Pear-like in shape, it weighed not much more than his five-year-old

239

daughter. He bent down and gently shifted the bundle to his back.

One of the soldiers saw Mushtaq with his burden emerge from the shadows of the rock. Bent against the strong wind he trotted towards him. 'Let me take that, Sir,' he offered.

'No,' Mushtaq snapped, and the man fell in step alongside him. The Major caught his eye and whispered something that the wind dispersed. The jawan inclined his head deferentially, looking puzzled. When the Major repeated the words, he caught them distinctly: 'I have the girl. Have the tribesmen returned?'

The guard shook his head, 'No, Sir.'

'Good. Call those jawans.'

The soldier signalled and three men loitering on the road started towards them at the double. Ashiq knew the Major was in the habit of collecting odd chunks of rock and wood and as he ran with the others he wondered what had caught his Commanding Officer's fancy this time.

They stood at attention a few yards down the bridge.

'Make way, walk behind me,' the Major ordered. He inclined his head at the guard by his side and the man fell back with the others.

'It's the girl,' the guard whispered, indicating the bundle.

Instinctively, Ashiq looked over his shoulder. His step faltered when he noticed Sakhi on the sand with his back to the bridge. 'It's the husband. You go ahead, I'll stall him,' he said. He turned casually and walked up to Sakhi.

'A-salaam-alaikum, friend; any news?'

Sakhi shook his head. He raised his preoccupied scowl to the jawan's beaming visage. Ashiq hastily looked off to the mountains. Sakhi followed his glance. He scanned the cliffs. They stood sharp and clear against the thunderous clouds. His eyes for a moment rested nervously on the group of men walking down the bridge.

Quickly Ashiq asked, 'What about the others?'

'Huh?'

240

'Your father and your brother . . . are they back? It will begin to pour.'

'They'll be here soon enough,' Sakhi's tone was curt. He started walking, and Ashiq had to lengthen his stride to keep up with him.

Maintaining a casual pace, the Major's group was half way down the bridge. Ashiq noticed a jawan slip ahead of the formation.

'What is the Major carrying?' Sakhi's voice was uncertain and tight.

'Allah knows! He has strange hobbies. He collects things: stones and chunks of wood . . .'

'Stones? In a blanket? A homespun tribal blanket?'

'What was that? I saw something move over there!' Ashiq grabbed Sakhi's arm and pointed desperately at the dark hills behind them.

Sakhi jerked his hand free savagely.

'Don't you dare touch me, you dog,' he snarled. Not even deigning to glance in the direction of Ashiq's outstretched hand, his suspicious, dangerous eyes reverted to the bundle bumping on the Major's back.

◆◆

Ten or twelve jawans were gathered at the bridge-head.

Mushtaq stepped on to the road and not far behind him Sakhi called, 'Major Sahib!'

A split second later the girl made a movement, but having sensed it in advance, Mushtaq disguised it by turning abruptly to face Sakhi.

'What have you got there . . . on your back?' Boorishly caricaturing Mushtaq, Sakhi humped his spine.

'Old roots . . . and herbs.'

An escaping strand of hair plastered Mushtaq's sweating forehead. Otherwise his face was as expressionless as his tone.

241

The soldiers, expecting trouble, crowded close. Sakhi made room for himself with a powerful thrust of his shoulders.

'Where did you get that blanket?' he hissed.

Partly improvising on the spur of the moment, partly following a trend of thought that had already anticipated the confrontation, Mushtaq put his strategy to the test. He knew he was going to put Sakhi under immense pressure. The outcome would depend on the youth's pride, on his intelligence and his reserves of self-control.

'Is it yours? I found it by the girl's body. She's in bad shape; you'd better bury her. I needed something to hold the roots, so I took the blanket. I will return it. I'm sorry to bring you this sad news.'

Blood drained from Sakhi's face, and then collected in two spots of colour that blazed on his cheeks. Mushtaq felt his awesome menace.

'Here, leave this at the Mess. Take a jeep, and be quick about it. Bring the blanket back.'

Ashiq stooped, touching his shoulder to the Major. He carefully transferred the bundle, marvelling at its lightness.

'No!' spluttered Sakhi. He lunged wildly but a wall of khaki uniforms blocked him.

Sakhi's eyes narrowed to luminous blue threads and in one swift action, his hand touched the sharp steel beneath his waistcoat.

Clenching his right fist, Mushtaq hit him. Sakhi doubled over in pain.

Slowly he raised his head, staring with murderous intent at the Major. His eyes shifted to the blanket receding through the gaps in the uniforms.

The Major, his voice an angry roar, shouted at his men. 'Get away, you shameless bastards. The youth has news of his wife's death and you stand around gaping!'

They understood him perfectly and withdrew to a convenient distance.

242

Sakhi straightened up, his face twisted by hate. Mushtaq sensed his terrible anguish; the burden was too large for the man.

'Listen,' he said. Bending the full force of his will over Sakhi, he said, 'Your wife is dead. Understand me? You have no option. You have to take my word for it. She is dead.' Seeing the flash of terror in Sakhi's face he said, 'The jawans know she is dead. I swear no one will say otherwise . . . If they make a liar of me they will be blasted like those rocks. I give you my word. Your honour will not be sullied. This is no man's business but yours.'

Sakhi's lips were drawn back from his teeth. His breath came shallow and quick. As understanding dawned, he turned ashen, trembling with the strain of the furious battle within him. A question formed in his eyes.

'Straight up there,' Mushtaq glanced briefly across the bridge, 'there is a kind of well in the rocks . . . right over there.'

Sakhi rushed off. Leaping up the boulders he looked into the stone-strewn bowl. Immediately he knew a great many things. His quick, hunter's eyes saw where the girl had leaned, and where she had fallen and bled. He knew the route she had come by, how emaciated she had become and where the blanket was spread.

Sakhi slid into the hollow and, kicking over a stone, picked up a piece of cloth. It held the faded print of mauve flowers. His fingers brushed the surface and he stood up with a fluffy knot of threads shed from the blanket.

Burying his head in his arms, crumpling to the stones, he wept. For the first time he faced a humiliation he could not avenge: a sorrow he dared not share.

❖

While Sakhi was in the rocky hide-out, Misri Khan and Yunus emerged from their trails and crossed the bridge.

They at once guessed from the expressions on the soldiers' faces that something had happened. A moment later they saw Sakhi coming towards them.

Stern with inquiry, Misri Khan and Yunus watched him. He walked past and silently they fell in step. When they were out of earshot of the jawans the men on either side of Sakhi stopped and Misri Khan touched his shoulder.

Sakhi stood still for only the time it took him to say 'She is dead,' and he walked ahead. But Yunus Khan blocked his path. 'How?' he demanded. 'Where's the body?'

Ignoring him, Sakhi swung furiously to face his father.

'She is dead. It is enough that I say so! I've buried her.' His voice was husky and deliberate and he trembled with uncontrollable wrath. He opened his fist and they looked at the cloth with faded mauve flowers and at the fluff of threads quivering in his palm. And then turning upon Yunus he snarled, 'Ask your filthy questions of the Major. He found the body.'

Misri Khan's face broke into a slow grin. The Major had witnessed the body. His son's claim was corroborated. The girl was dead! Misri Khan's massive shoulders straightened. He thrust his chest forward and his head rose high. It was as if a breeze had cleared the poisonous air suffocating them and had wafted an intolerable burden from their shoulders. He was a trifle bewildered by his son's misery and reticence but then he thought, 'I have forgotten what it is to grieve; I am too old.' He laid a hand on Sakhi's shoulder.

The Major, watching from afar, noticed Misri Khan's back straighten. He saw the triumphant swagger in Yunus Khan's gait and Sakhi's relaxed lope as they resumed their journey. Wiping his brow, he smiled. His promise to the youth would hold.

❖

Ashiq Hussain walked up with the tattered blanket.

244

'You took a long time getting back,' said Mushtaq.
'I think the girl's gone mad, Sir.'
'What girl?' Mushtaq asked stonily. 'I thought I instructed you to deposit the roots at the Mess.'
Ashiq was baffled for only a moment. 'Yes, Sir!' he
saluted and held out the blanket.
'There is no use for it any more. Burn it.'
Mushtaq recalled the girl's thin fingers pulling torn strips
of cloth over her bare skin. She would be all right, he mused.
In a few hours he would quietly stow her away in the vehicle
taking Farukh and Carol to Lahore. Let Carol take care of
her! She could hide her in the States! Or perhaps Ashiq could
propose marriage after a decent interval – she would be as
securely hidden in his village. Of course, the old Kohistani
who had brought her here must never know she was alive...
a pity... he had appeared to love her. Still, he was to blame
for imposing his will on something that was bound to end in
disaster...
'Isn't a jeep going to Pattan this afternoon?' he asked
abruptly.
'Yes, Sir.'
'I think it could leave earlier. Say, in about fifteen minutes? Those tribesmen are weary, they could do with a ride.'
He indicated the three tribesmen far up the road, and as he
spoke they followed the road round a bend in the hill and
disappeared.